The Spring of '68

By
Chris Cawood

Book Number: _145_ /3000

[signature]

Author Autograph

Other Books By Chris Cawood

Carp
(1997)

1998: The Year of the Beast
(1996)

How to Live to 100 (and enjoy it!)
(1996)

Tennessee's Coal Creek War
(1995)

Legacy of the Swamp Rat
(1994)

This book is the third of Chris Cawood's general fiction with a Southern setting. A selected number of each edition are numbered and autographed. If your book is numbered and autographed and you would like to reserve the next book with the same number, you may do so by calling the publisher at: **1-800-946-1967**

The Spring of '68

(A Novel)

By Chris Cawood

Magnolia Hill Press
Kingston, Tennessee

This is a work of fiction.

Cover design by Chris Cawood and Hartgraphics of Knoxville, Tennessee.

Printed in the United States.

Library of Congress Number: 98-65064

ISBN 0-9642231-5-5

5 4 3 2 1

Dedication

This book is dedicated to the Class of 1965 and all of us who experienced The Spring of '68.

Acknowledgment

Those who have read any of my previous works will find *The Spring of '68* to be differently written.

I want to acknowledge the help of my dear editor, Gaynell Seale, in working with me on this project and her skillful guidance in helping me to accomplish what I wanted to do.

As she has in all my previous projects, Gaynell led me with the skillful hands of a surgeon in excising here and there a word and giving suggestions to make this more readable.

1

I am William Cody Rogers. That is not just my name. It's who I am. I'm in the fall of my life—if you count life by seasons as I do. I figure to live to a hundred. I've just turned fifty-one. Longevity is a family trait. All four of my grandparents made it past ninety-five. My parents didn't, but they died in an accident.

My mind and body are numb. I sit here in front of flowers whose perfume I find stifling. The tent provides a bit of shade from the August morning's sun, but it doesn't take away the heat. Soon the flowers will be wilted and just a memory.

The casket is a beautiful polished wood—maple, I believe. My son and daughter helped me choose it. I care little for such things, but then, I suppose there are few who see any joy in death and its accoutrements.

My summer love's remains are inside, ready to be returned to the earth. The preacher is speaking, but I don't hear the words. The last three days have turned me into a blob of putty with no bones or visible means of physical support. My summer love—my wife of twenty-six years—is not in that box. I know. She has flown away.

THREE NIGHTS AGO WE had our last hours together. I regret it was at the hospital. She wanted to go home, but all the medical people said there was a chance she could overcome this crisis, as she had so many others, if she received the wonderful care that modern science can provide.

It was at the hospital, past midnight, when she left me. I had sat with her around the clock as I had for the last ten days. She and I knew our separation was near. I had turned the lights off and stuffed a towel along the base of the door to shut out the noise and light from the hallway. We were alone with the hum and whir of the machines that kept her alive.

I pulled the curtain back from the window. That wing of the hospital was in the older section that actually had windows that opened a bit. Her room was on the second floor and there was a tree near the window. Her only joy for the past weeks had been to watch cardinals who had made their home in that tree. By day, I placed some seed on the ledge and we would observe them eat.

That night, though, there was no bird that we could see. The moon was full and looked like the golden crust of a pie that my wife used to make.

"Can you see the moon?" I asked. "It's full. Just like when we met. Remember?"

I thought I saw a faint smile. It might have been just wishful thinking.

"Moon? Can you get me to where I can see it, Cody?"

"I don't see why not."

I scooted her bed around, but she was too weak to raise her head above the window sill.

"Hold me up?" she whispered. "I want to see it one last time."

I untangled some of the tubes and lifted her into my arms. I knew this would be frowned upon by the nurses. I didn't really care at that point. She was so light. There was hardly anything left after seven months with the swiftly moving cancer. Her hair was long but thin against the light of the moon.

I could lift her easily, not because of my strength, but because of her frailty. I remembered a bird's carcass I once had picked up from the ground. There were feathers and bones but nothing inside. Katy's body was nearly the same. She was like a cocoon that had just lost its butterfly or was about to. I was afraid one or more of her bones would crumble when I held her. But that was what she wanted and that was what I did. She would have done the same for me.

"Do you see the moon now, Katy?"

"Yes. It's beautiful." She put a hand out and touched the window pane as though she thought she could reach the face of the moon.

A wind arose and the leaves of the tree played back and forth across the pale moon. I could hear crickets and frogs along the little stream that ran beside the hospital.

"Do you see them?" she asked.

"See what?"

"The angels are flying around from the back of the moon. There're hundreds. Thousands." She stared toward the moon. "Do you hear them singing?" She looked at me.

"Angels? No, I don't. But I'm sure they're there. All I see are the leaves."

"Angels, Dear. They're coming for me. Oh, listen to their beautiful music."

I heard the song of crickets and frogs. She heard the voices of angels.

The preacher nods at me and says something. How devoted I was or similar words that he thinks might make a difference. He tries. He's a Christian.

I was a Christian and a lawyer until all this happened. Some say that two such beings cannot inhabit the same body. Now I question my religion and don't believe I'll return to my profession. This has been too much. Why would God take such a good and sweet woman and leave me alone?

Katy never questioned it. She was a woman of faith, full of grace. She tried to make it easier for me and the children. "I'm ready to go," she had said many times. "God's still working on you," she added and smiled. I could only think of forty or fifty years of loneliness and desperation that faced me. I would much rather we both lived to seventy-five together than for me to live to a hundred without her.

Toward the end when she became too weak to hold her Bible, she had me to read aloud to her. The Psalms,

Jesus speaking the sermon on the mount, Paul's words about fighting the good fight, and the promises of God's grace always being with us.

I sit here now with a small New Testament in one coat pocket and a paperback edition of Thoreau's *Walden* in the other.

Over the past ten days, I have read each from cover to cover. I thought the words that my wife so dearly loved and the words of an American philosopher would help me make sense of this. I have yet to work it out.

The preacher finishes, comes near, and takes my hand. He leans down and whispers. "May the Lord be with you and comfort you. Katy is at peace, free from pain, and in a better place."

My daughter and son stand. They walk to the casket and each pulls a rose from the blanket that straddles it. My daughter looks at me, turns back, and plucks one for me also. People come up to me. They nod, speak some words, and take my hand. It's all a blur.

When I stand, I go toward the casket, lean over, and kiss the wood that covers her face. I raise my head and notice the moisture that has fallen from my eyes to the polished wood. I didn't know I was crying. I thought all tears had dried up.

But it's when I sit in the car and the driver starts to pull away that the loneliness grips me with two hands at the gut and heart. I am afraid and I start to tremble.

2

G od, man, and Earth. I am determined to make some sense of each. It's a month after my wife's death and I still grope for answers. Yes, we had many good years together, as her church friends have told me. I should be thankful for those. But I wanted more.

"You have two beautiful children," another one told me. I do. A daughter and a son. Both grown, both out of college, both married, both employed as teachers—and both gone. My daughter, Sallie, teaches in Clarksville, and my son, Johnny, teaches and coaches in Johnson City. Both are about equi-distance from my home in Kingston, thirty miles west of Knoxville, Tennessee.

I can count back nine generations of Rogers in Tennessee. We were here before there was a State of Tennessee, before the State of Franklin, before the Cherokees ceded the lands west of the Clinch and Powell rivers to whites. I love this land where I was planted just as those Cherokees must have loved it. Why else the trail of tears?

One of my Rogers great-uncles was a congressman. He built a fine home, Speedwell, named after the town of our ancestors. The house has since been removed to Knoxville and is a tourist attraction. I was always taught to be proud of my heritage, not to bring disrespect or ignominy on the name of Rogers.

Katy loved the beauty of the hills, creeks, valleys, and lakes as much or more than I did. I had a favorite season—spring—with its beauty of regeneration and resurrection. Green. Everywhere you looked, it was green. They were hues of the same basic color—but different, as though an artist was mixing the shades on his palette to bring up the perfect green. Here he cast off the green of tulip poplars, there the green of new-budded maples, and there the darker shade of kudzu.

Katy loved the change as spring melted to summer, summer softened to fall, fall fell prey to winter, and winter died with a gasp of snow flurries over a bed of jonquils. She saw beauty in it all. She often said it was God's hand painting every leaf of every tree. I told her I thought He had better things to do. No, that was the best thing, she had said.

We lived beside a lake—part of the series formed from the Tennessee River when the Authority piled up concrete to halt its flow and widen its surface. In a boat during the still of evening in the fall, we would look on as though the surface of the lake was a mirror that recreated the thousands of trees with their leaves of red, orange, and yellow when the chlorophyll gave up and let the other chemicals show their colors. It was a mosaic of stained glass as beautiful as could be found in any church but in softer shades.

The Rogers were valley people. They were not hillbillies, as some refer to all those of Appalachian descent. There were hill people and there were valley people in the early settlement of the state, and the Rogers were always valley people—ever near the riverbank with the ability to float downstream a few miles when overpopulation threatened.

There was nothing particularly wrong with the hill people. They were just more isolated, tending to be more clannish than the valley people. No hill person was ever elected to Congress. They cared nothing about such things and you couldn't have wished it upon them.

My grandfather's father inherited some mountain land through his wife's side of the family. Two hundred acres of forest and streams and birds and animals. Some of it was so steep that sunrise didn't come until noon. He did nothing with it. Left it as virgin forest with trees hundreds of years old. Then the wood barons came in and cut without permission. My great-grandfather was in the valley and knew nothing of it until it was too late. The hill people knew, but they're not ones to meddle.

When the coal speculators came in the 1880s and 1890s with their three-piece suits and suspenders, he wouldn't give in to their entreaties to purchase the mineral rights for a few cents per acre. Their argument sounded good—"We'll just buy the mineral rights for the coal and such underground. You can still use the surface and won't even know we're there." His land was raped by the timber barons, so he didn't believe the coal people. He thought there was something sacred about trying to keep a sanctuary of land where there were streams and trees that man had not spoiled.

While others sold their rights and regretted it when the strip miners later bought the mineral rights and made the mountains look like sombreros in the evening sun, his son had two hundred acres that were growing new and larger trees.

Forty-one years ago when I was ten, my grandfather, my father, and I erected the beginnings of a cabin on the edge of the property near a dirt mountain road that was too narrow for two cars to pass. At ten, of course, I wasn't much help. But my grandfather acted as though I was—as if the cabin could not have been completed without my work.

It was not that we Rogers were suddenly going to become hill people instead of valley people. It was to be a rest in the wilderness, a retreat, a place we could go to and not be bothered by the modern appliances that were, even then, intruding into our lives. The cabin was then just walls, floor, and roof.

Later, when my grandfather passed on, my father turned the cabin over to me. Before he did that though, we added a few new walls, a porch front and back, and made a place for a bathroom—but with no fixtures.

Our two hundred acres bordered what later became the Big South Fork River and Recreation area. We first deeded the park a hundred acres and then another fifty. We kept fifty for our own use now and may deed it to Big South Fork later. Our family camped there while the children were growing up. They swung on vines, waded in streams, watched for squirrels, and listened to panther stories in front of the fireplace while wood burned and sent columns of sparks up the chimney.

I haven't been there in over two years. But that's where I'm headed. Last week, I signed the deed to my house. I've sold my boat, three of four vehicles, my condo in Florida, my stock in Wal-Mart, all the furnishings that the children didn't want, except for a very few that I'll need at the cabin.

During the months of Katy's illness, I found that my possessions were actually more burdensome than helpful. I discovered I was spending time looking after these belongings when I should have been with her. I belonged to my belongings. I was a slave to things and stuff. They were like anchors around my legs pulling me down and engulfing me with cares. I wasn't one hundred percent there for Katy at first, and I regret it.

So now, I have sold all. I sold my law practice out to my partners. They want to keep me on the payroll, let me come in once a month and look over some papers or such, so they can keep my name on the letterhead as *of counsel*. It all seems so useless now. What have I accomplished in twenty-five years of law practice? When it comes down to it, ninety-eight percent of lawsuits are about money or grudges. And I helped perpetuate it! God forgive me. Give me a useful life.

When I totaled up all my monetary wealth after the liquidation, I was not a millionaire. But I was more than a half millionaire. As in other things, it seemed that I was but a bit more than half of what the world considered successful. I wasn't all the way there, but at one time it was within my grasp.

Six hundred and fifty thousand dollars, plus the cabin and fifty acres of trees and streams. I was wealthy. Why had I continued to work for money anyway? This was more than any man deserved.

After paying all of Katy's remaining medical bills, I gave my son and daughter two hundred thousand dollars each and told them to use, save, or invest it wisely. It was their inheritance from Katy and me. They shouldn't expect any more at my death. I plan to use up the remainder.

They are good children and I knew I didn't have to

admonish them to use it wisely, but I did anyway—it's a parent's duty. They recoiled at the thought of having that much money. But I knew that they could use it better now in their formative family years than they could if I lived to a hundred and then passed it on to them. They would then be in their seventies.

With another eighty thousand, I set up trust funds for four grandchildren that I hoped to have although none was on the horizon. My accountant arranged it to where the money would be there for grandchild Number One and Two of my son and daughter for college expenses or to be given to them outright at age thirty. If there were no grandchildren, the money would pass to my son and daughter at my death. I didn't tell them about this as I thought they might think me pushy to encourage them to propagate.

Having shed my earthly burdens of wealth, I am ready to retreat to the mountain and learn the lessons of life. I will not become a hill person because my heritage is of the valley people. But I'm going to take the example of Thoreau and see how simply I can live. I put a hundred and fifty thousand into a bond account that will pay eight percent. Twelve thousand per year—a thousand dollars a month to live on. That should be enough for any reasonable person.

They're standing at the door now while I load my last boxes into the ten-foot long open metal trailer that is hooked to my old Jeep.

"This is crazy, Dad," Johnny says. "You should keep your money and live comfortably the rest of your life. You deserve it."

Sallie nods, tears at the corners of her eyes.

"I'm not going to become a hermit. I'll see you as much as I do now. I'm not forming a cult for my followers to traipse up the mountain. I won't be sitting on the front porch in a flowing white robe. I just need some time."

"Why don't you rent a condo in Gatlinburg or Pigeon Forge? They're in the mountains," Sallie asks.

"Please. I'd die a slower and more painful death than your mother. I couldn't piss off the front porch without hitting a hundred tourists in Bermuda shorts and obscene T-shirts. Now they're busing in loads of gamblers to Cherokee. The Smokies are saturated. Our cabin and the Big South Fork are the last vestiges of wilderness left around here."

A car pulls into the driveway. A woman exits, retrieves a dish from the back seat, and walks toward us.

"Another one," I say under my breath.

"Cody, I made you a peach cobbler," she says and hands me the still-warm bowl. "You're not moving, are you?"

"Just going away for a little bit. I need some rest."

"Where're you going, Hon?"

"Gatlinburg or Pigeon Forge."

"Really? I love Pigeon Forge. I could shop those outlet malls forever."

I nod and smile.

"Maybe I'll run into you up there."

"Maybe," I say.

"You know my number. If you need anything else, you call. You hear?"

"Thanks," I say and watch her walk back toward her car. She's wearing a dress two sizes too tight and a half foot too short for a person her age.

"Who was that?" my son asks.

"One of the widow-and-divorcée brigade from church. I can't get any rest for them coming over. There seems to be a competition for my soul . . . and body, if you can believe that. They all want more than to give me a cobbler."

"The nerve of them," my daughter says.

"Exactly. Another reason I'm going to the cabin."

"You told her that you're going to Pigeon Forge or Gatlinburg. You lied?" my daughter asks.

"God's grace covers a multitude of sins."

They're not convinced I'm doing what's best, but my children bow to my desire.

Tomorrow is the first day of autumn. I'm in the fall of my life. My love of summer is dead. Of God, man, and Earth, I will look for answers first about Earth at my cabin.

3

This is the day of the fall equinox. The hours of day and night are supposed to be approximately equal. It marks the beginning of autumn. From now until spring, dark hours will be longer than daylight.

This pretty well suits my mood. I'm generally in the dark. When I was eighteen, I knew that by the time I reached twenty-one I would know all the answers. Then when I reached twenty-one, the questions seemed a bit more difficult, but I knew I would solve them by the time I reached thirty. At thirty, I didn't even think about the questions, let alone contemplate the answers. Now at fifty-one, I have forgotten what the questions were. So, I will make up my own as soon as I settle in.

As I bump along the rutted pavement of the narrow road, I look back in the rearview mirror to where my little trailer with all my precious possessions is following. We are winding through the switchbacks and climbing almost unnoticeably the edge of the Cumberlands.

I came by way of Interstate 40 to Crossville and then north on U. S. 127 to Jamestown. The highway is famous for its summer festival of having the largest yard sale in the United States—stretching all along 127 through Kentucky and Tennessee. Jamestown is the county seat of Fentress and I know some lawyers there. I stopped at the post office and arranged for a box for my mail. There's no delivery where the cabin is. There're no people that far out.

I'll be receiving my monthly check from my bond investment and a book or two from the Mystery Book Club. Who knows, I might get some other mail—a winning sweepstakes announcement or a credit card application. There's a plaque on a building in Jamestown commemorating the fact that Mark Twain was conceived there. It strikes me as a bit strange and stretching a point.

Not far down the road is where Alvin York grew up and later returned as Sergeant York—the most famous enlisted man of World War I.

When I left Jamestown and Highway 127, I turned onto a state road that wound generally east by northeast. After ten or so miles, I took a paved county road that I am on now. County roads are generally paved better and more often nearer the county seat and the center of population. As they near the borders of other counties and away from the power structure of the county, they become pocked and rutted. I must be nearing Scott County because this stretch hasn't seen much maintenance since Sergeant York captured that bunch of Germans.

This is the good road compared to the one that will take me up the mountain and to the cabin. I see it ahead on the left. It appears to be a driveway to nowhere. A little gravel was once sprinkled here when the county road commissioner's brother owned the quarry. Now though, it depends upon the trucks that carry coal and wood out of the hills to scatter what rock it gets.

On a map, the Big South Fork looks like a saddle or squashed frog laid across the spine of Kentucky and Tennessee. More of the 120,000 acres are in Tennessee. It was authorized by Congress in 1974, pieced together by the Army Corps of Engineers, and finally dedicated by the National Park Service in 1991. The area combines wilderness at the core that stretches along the river and its gorge and then multi-use in the surrounding table of the plateau. There are no Gatlinburgs, Pigeon Forges, or T-Shirt shops. It is mountains, rock shelters, trails, and a couple of fast-moving rivers trying to find their way out.

Sunsets and sunrises in this range of mountains are better than those on picture postcards. When I was younger and more energetic, I climbed to a bare rock face on the rim of a nearby mountain to watch. In the morning, when mist lifted up the slopes on light breezes, the sun would make its appearance like the end of a blacksmith's hot iron burning through gauze. The sunsets were best when long, high cirrus clouds reflected the lessening rays from above and the rows of ridges below faded from bright green to dark blue with the sun perched in the middle.

My cabin is within rifle shot of not only Fentress and Scott counties but also Morgan. My land is supposedly in Fentress County, for that is where I pay my land taxes. But over the years, I have thought that Morgan or Scott could as easily have claimed it if they had gone to the expense of a proper survey. It is, in any regard, far enough from the county seat of all three counties to have fallen under the decree of benign neglect, for which I am thankful.

There is a coolness in the air as the altitude increases and the atmosphere thins a bit. Although it is the first day of autumn, the leaves have not yet begun any fading of their greenness, but the slant of the sun tells me it will not be long. Tree limbs from both sides of the now almost-dirt road extend over the middle as though they're trying to shake hands, giving me more lush shade than sunlight.

Another ten minutes and I slow, knowing the cabin is here somewhere near. The last mountain house was two miles back and there's not another one for another five miles. The cabin is isolated in the truest sense of the word. Two years allow for a great deal of growth of bushes and vines. I stare to my left down the mountain. My short driveway may have been swallowed up by the fast growth of spring and summer.

Then ahead of me no more than fifty yards, a figure runs up from the left, slinks across the road and up the bank on the right before disappearing into the forest. There are deer in the area, but it didn't look like one. It moved with the grace of a large panther, but slower, as though it hesitated when it saw my Jeep and then scooted on up the ridge.

The wildlife people have recently transplanted some black bears from the Smokies to the South Fork region, but it was a skinny bear if that was what it was. Black or shadowy, bigger than a dog but smaller than a bear.

Finally, there is the driveway. I slow, then stop, set the hand brake, and get out. The roof of the cabin is visible just fifty yards from the road. The drive appears passable, so I step back in and turn the Jeep and trailer off the road and down toward my new home for I don't know how long.

AMONG MY BOXES IN the trailer, I have brought a big chest of tools, for I expect that the cabin will be in great disrepair. I have allowed myself the sum of five thousand dollars, if I need it, to bring the structure up to liveable. But as I walk around it, the old sides, porches, and roof appear to be in decent shape. There's just one broken window and two or three torn screens. Vines and bushes need trimming around the entire circumference, but there is a foot path to the front and back porch that is still passable.

We never locked the doors, expecting that if somebody wanted in there was no lock that could keep them out. We just left a note at two or three places inside asking them to respect it as a cabin that we used from time to time, but that they could use it if necessary. Most of the time it worked okay. We had never left anything but basic wood chairs and benches inside. It was a camper's cabin, not a condo with all the conveniences of Nashville or Knoxville. It was shelter but little more than that.

I step around the perimeter gingerly. There are snakes here—copperheads and some timber rattlers are the poisonous ones. I know that they are supposed to be distinguishable by the shapes of their heads and other markings. It's just that I have never reconciled myself to getting close enough to make that distinction. And as I have become slightly nearsighted over the past ten years, this is not the time to start. They shall have no fear of me. I will give them whatever territory they desire.

I'm told that snakes mainly do not want to be startled or stepped upon. My tread is well placed and light. Being cold-blooded animals, snakes spend a great deal of their time sunning themselves to restore their full body temperature and flow of blood. They tend to nest near large rocks where they can crawl out in the morning and take the sun's rays without going very far.

One of the scariest stories I've heard was about a pioneer couple who chose to build their cabin around a great rock that they would use for the fireplace hearth and anchor of their home. After the cabin was completed in the dead of winter, the couple celebrated by building a huge fire in the new fireplace that sat upon the great stone. After they retired to their bed later in the night, a family of copperheads, feeling the warmth of their rock roof heighten to summer temperatures, took leave of their hibernation and began to crawl about the cabin. The young woman, rising for a drink of water, stepped on one and fell onto the floor among a dozen or so of the snakes who could find no way out of the new enclosure. In the dark, she didn't know what she had fallen into and yelled that the boards of the floor were biting her. Her husband heard her screams and came to her aid but fell victim to the snakes himself. They both were bitten repeatedly. She died a painful death. The man survived. He returned to the cabin a month later after he had healed some. He burned it to the ground and walked away from the mountain forever.

My grandfather told me the story when I was ten and we were building this very cabin. He told me that people still walked to that place which was known locally as Copperhead Rock. We pulled the great stone for this hearth a hundred yards down the mountain and checked it thoroughly for any hidden varmints before anchoring it and raising the stone chimney around it. My grandfather, from whom I received the *Cody* part of my name, was an artisan with hammer and saw as a carpenter and with the trowel, chisel, and level as a stone and brick mason. He took me up to somewhere near the top of the chimney and let me etch my name into the cement joint of two large rocks.

"Your name is carved in stone and will stand as long as this chimney," he told me and smiled.

I walk up the steps to the front porch, open the screen door, go through to the main door, and lift the latch. The door opens without a squeak. Bare wood walls and floor stare at me. It is about as I imagined. The metal roof had served its purpose. The cabin was built tight. There were no leaks. My grandfather would have been proud. He had told me the sheet-metal roof would last a hundred years with the proper maintenance. We had nailed it to the wood beams with lead-headed nails. The lead closed around the tops of the nails and the holes they made to form a seal where water could not penetrate. I brought a bucket of the nails with me if any repairs were necessary.

To my left is the kitchen area, such as it is, with a sink and cabinets. Beside it is the door to the room that my father and I made into a bathroom. I later added a basin, commode, and shower stall. I stand in the living room or main room. Two bedrooms separated by a hall with closets on both sides compose the remainder of the cabin. The hall leads to the back porch.

Minimalists would be proud of the simplicity. Real estate agents would describe it as *rustic*. The number of things that aren't here is longer than the list of conveniences that are. There is no phone. No cable T. V. No satellite T. V. Just no T.V. No electricity. No hot water. Really no running water in the normal sense of the word.

I walk to where two wooden chairs are in the living room. I remember them, but don't remember them being in this position. At the kitchen sink, I notice there is a drip of water from the pipe where the spring water is supposed to come in when it is turned on. It's just plain white plastic pipe. The turnoff is outside. Water is gravity fed from a spring that emerges from rock two hundred or so feet from the cabin and ten to fifteen feet higher in elevation. My running water is cold spring water that comes to me by its own force. My grandfather said that God created gravity before man invented pumps.

One of my first jobs, and I'm making a list now, will be to check the pipe and valve out back. I brought two hundred feet of new pipe with me in the trailer, believing there could very well be some breaks in the system caused by animal hoofs, sliding rocks, or some hunter or hiker stepping on it before he knew what it was. I brought a roll of screen, locks for the doors, and a propane gas tank and tubing for the one convenience that was left in the cabin—a gas range.

My plans are to use one bedroom for what it was designed—sleeping—and use the other for a study where I will build bookshelves. I do have a collection of books and *National Geographic*. My collection of the yellow magazines that a lot of people throw away or dispose of at yard sales covers a period of seventy-five years, and I am on my way to a full collection of over a hundred years. I also brought a thirty volume set of the Tennessee Code in hardbound green.

I push the door back into the bedroom nearest the kitchen and notice a faint odor. It smells of burnt paraffin—candle wax—or such. The room is a bit dark even at noon, but within seconds my eyes adjust and I see a ring of dark splotches standing out on the floor. A scratch of my fingernail against each proves what I thought. Four, five, or six people have sat around a circle and burned candles long into some not too distant night or nights. On the walls are colored stars and symbols which would make a policeman friend of mine immediately shout, "Satanism, Satanism!"

It could be. It's hard to believe that my cabin has been used as a church of the devil. Although I have some things to discuss with God about taking my Katy, I am not ready to desert to the enemy. If the devil wants me, he is going to have to take me kicking and screaming. My house shall not be a place of worship for him. They won't be back. A lock will help me be sure. But a forty-five revolver and a twelve-gauge shotgun will guarantee it. I add this room to my list to clean thoroughly.

The other bedroom has no sign of the occult, but in a corner is an old blanket and a pillow. I walk over and move them about with my foot. Nothing else. Then I see on the floor near the wall numbers written out in almost a childlike script from one to ten. Maybe the number of days he camped here. Why not like in the prison movies though—just making a straight line and striking a line across four marks to indicate five? Oh, well, I have a lock for the back door too.

AFTER LUNCH, I TAKE to work and spend the remainder of the day in readying the cabin and its surroundings for my first night. An hour of work with a sickle and pruning shears clears the growth from around it to a respectable ten feet.

A walk to the source of my cool spring water shows me three minor breaks in the piping which I repair quickly. My confidence is growing that I can actually survive here on my own.

I climb to the roof with a bucket of tar-like compound to reseal around the chimney and bring along a hammer and pocket full of nails to check the sheetmetal. When I reach the chimney, I look at the cement joints of the rock until I find my name that was put there when the stones were laid. I rub my thumb along the name and all the memories of my grandfather, my father, and me begin to flood back. I wipe the back of my hand across my face and kneel to the job I came here to do. There'll be plenty of time for reflection.

After the chimney is sealed around where it joins the roof, I retreat to the ground and retrieve a rope, an old cloth, and a medium-sized stone. I wrap the cloth around the stone and then tie the rope around the cloth and rock. When I reclimb the ladder and reach the chimney, I drop the cloth-wrapped rock down the chimney, rubbing it against the side walls. I repeat this several times to clean it, after a fashion.

With enough outside work completed to take me through the first night, I unload the remainder of what I brought with me—the only items of furniture being a bed, my favorite recliner, an old desk, and a chair. I set up the bed with a little difficulty. It is rather awkward for one person. It's not the same bed that Katy and I shared. I couldn't bear that. I gave that to Sallie.

Normally, when we came to the cabin to camp, we only brought cots and sleeping bags, but my new bed fits well in the room I've chosen. The mattress and box springs are new and have a fresh smell to them.

The recliner I place in front of the wood-burning stove in the living room. I have already checked the stove pipe from the back of the stove to the chimney and it seems in good shape. I take a piece of newspaper, light it, place it in the stove, and walk outside to observe the smoke coming from the chimney. It is drawing well and there appear to be no obstructions.

The stove is important. It will be my only source of heat when cold weather comes—and it won't be long. Within a week, I expect that a fire in the stove will feel good on the cool evenings and in the early morning chill of autumn.

I carry my boxes of books and personal belongings into the bedroom where the old blanket and pillow were and stack them on the floor. As soon as I finish the shelves in a week or so, I will unload them and place them in order.

The heaviest job is to maneuver the twenty-five-gallon loaded propane tank from the trailer to beneath the kitchen window. I roll it on its bottom edge while it leans into my upper body. It would be easier if I was going downhill instead of up the slight incline. When I finally get it into place and level, I slink over to the front steps and rest while catching my breath.

I look up to the road. No car or truck has passed in the six hours I've been here. Overhead the sky begins to take on a softer blue while the sun rests over a distant ridge a half hour from setting. I return to my job of fitting the tubing from the tank to the stove in the kitchen. I have to get this done before dark if I'm to have hot coffee in the morning. Just as the sun sets, the pilot light sparks to a blue point of flame. The burners and oven puff into blue halos when I turn them on. All is well. I believe I will make me a pot of coffee, take a cup of it to the front porch, and watch twilight come to the Cumberlands.

I carry along my dog-eared copy of Thoreau's *Walden* and sit on the wooden bench near the door of the front porch. Of the furniture that I will purchase, a rocking chair will be among the first items.

I behold the mountains and forest around me, sip my rich coffee, and read of Thoreau's retreat and some of the items he took with him nearly a hundred and fifty years ago.

> *". . . a few implements, a knife, an axe, a spade, a wheelbarrow, etc., and for the studious, lamplight, stationery, and access to a few books, rank next to necessaries, and can be obtained at a trifling cost."*

I have most of those. Plus I have a Jeep and a propane stove. I have more than Thoreau had in his cabin, but I'm not willing to do with less.

> *"To be a philosopher is not merely to have subtle thoughts, nor even to found a school, but so to love wisdom as to live according to its dictates, a life of simplicity, independence, magnanimity and trust. It is to solve some of the problems of life, not only theoretically, but practically."*

I close the little book and think. Darkness is now closing around me. Tomorrow I will consider God's word. I will find wisdom, I will live simply, and I will solve my problems. I am William Cody Rogers, and I will have God tell me why Katy was taken.

I HAVE PLACED TWO kerosene lamps in each room, but I notice when I put a match to them their light is meager compared to the vast darkness of the mountains.

At ten, I close the doors to the cabin as well as I can. Tomorrow I will put on the locks. Tonight I will sleep with my pistol on one side of my bed and my shotgun on the other. When I snuff the lamps in my bedroom and pull the blanket up to my chin, the change in my sleeping arrangements appears stark. At my house in Kingston, the light of the night was the harsh copper glow of streetlights. Here it is a bit of starlight just barely decipherable. At that house the sounds of the night were kids and cars. Here it is the chorus of thousands of crickets, cicadas, and frogs tuning up . . . ever tuning up.

My mind is so active that it seems like hours before I drift off.

A SCRATCHING ON THE floor next to my bed brings my eyes wide open. I press my watch and see the lighted dial says 3 a.m. The scratching continues. I ease my right hand to my pistol and my left to the flashlight under the pillow.

When I turn, shine the light, and point the pistol, a large opossum on the floor flops over onto her side and plays dead or is actually scared to death. I put the pistol down but keep the light trained on her eyes. This is a messy job, but somebody has to do it.

I pick the culprit up by her hairless tail, hoping all along that she will not awake from her self-induced coma and scratch me. She looks like a large albino rat, but I'm familiar with opossums—or possums as they are called locally. I walk toward the back door, down the steps, and five paces into the woods where I deposit her gently onto her side.

Back inside, I look beneath the sink and see that there is a large opening around the drain pipe. I grab some steel wool and stuff it into the hole until it's sealed.

Back in bed, I think about Thoreau and *Walden*. He never mentioned what you do about opossums.

4

The next morning, the stove is put to another test of heating water for my coffee. The metal percolator is one I picked up at a junk shop some time ago. Few of these are used anymore what with the electric conveniences. The coffee, filter, and water were prepared before I went to bed. All I have to do is turn on the burner. I am not a morning person. I am useless until three cups of coffee are mixing with my slow-moving blood. The burner sputters to life, and I adjust the flame to a medium high.

When I awoke this morning, I looked out and thought it was raining. My window was open and the screen wire was the only thing separating me from a clear view of the forest. It was dripping deep green with a dew so heavy spider webs were dotted with droplets.

I sit on the front porch and await the beat of the perking coffee. The only other sound is the dropping of water from soaked leaves onto the metal roof. It is a soothing rhythm that could easily rock me back to sleep. I stand and look up toward the road and then down the hill toward where my land joins the Big South Fork. I can't see it, but somewhere not far from where my field of vision ends the park service has brought a path almost to the edge of my land. I've been on it myself before. It's rarely walked since the more scenic river gorges are farther away. Only dedicated hikers would venture this far. I sit back down.

When the coffee has perked long enough, I push myself up, go to the kitchen, wash my face with the cold water that has accumulated in the pan in the sink, and then turn to the stove. I pour the first cup of coffee, look at it to see if it's dark enough, and sip it to check its flavor. That done, I remove the percolator basket and turn the burner down to low.

I walk back out to the front porch. There beside the door, but on the inside of the porch, is a small wooden bowl. I hadn't noticed it on my first outing a few minutes ago, but that just goes to show that I wasn't fully awake. It's sitting in plain view. I walk over and move it with my foot. Then, sure that it's not a booby trap, I pick it up and carry it with me to my bench.

The wood is about four inches deep and appears to be a slice of a log of about eight inches diameter that has been carved out. It's not the perfect work of a master woodcarver, but it's not bad. I run my thumb along the grooves of the grain of the wood. I wish I could make something half as nice. Admiring the texture of the wood, I almost don't notice the contents of the bowl—six walnuts and six early persimmons.

I pick up a persimmon and hold it up to a streak of sunlight now angling through the screen. The marbled purple and orange look tempting. I squeeze it slightly. It's ripe enough to eat. I bite into it hoping it won't draw my mouth. The sweetness echoes the softness of the morning. I remember my dad always joking that he was up in a persimmon tree having breakfast when he heard the news that Franklin Roosevelt was elected President. The story was supposed to illustrate how poor the family was. I didn't believe it, but it didn't keep him from repeating it. Then, I wonder if the bowl was there when the opossum made her visit in the early hours of the morning. I set the bowl beside me. It was a nice gesture by whoever left it. It isn't Welcome Wagon, but it will do.

However, I wonder who did leave it. I have no neighbors. A hiker would not be bearing gifts for unknowns. Then I remember the candle wax on the floor in my bedroom and the blanket and pillow that were in the other room. Maybe the devil worshipers sent a peace offering.

I walk to the screen door to see if there are any tracks. I look but see only one sign that indicates there's been any foot traffic. Across the drive going off into the woods, one side of a bush is darker than the other—the dew has been shaken from its leaves on that side. Oh, well, I welcome all gifts. I am about out of the pies and cakes the widows and single women at church brought me.

I RETRIEVE A LEGAL pad from the second bedroom and start to write down numbers. I am a very organized man. A thousand dollars a month to live on. I have to make a budget and live by it. I turn open the pages of *Walden* and look for Thoreau's accounting of his living expenses.

A hundred and fifty years ago, it was much cheaper to live in dollars and cents. On the other hand, it was more difficult to accumulate the dollars and cents. But I can't believe what Thoreau has documented. His food, part of which he grew himself, cost him a mere twenty-seven cents per week over an eight-month period.

He built his cabin for a little over twenty-eight dollars and spent an average of a quarter per week on clothes. His lamp oil cost two dollars for eight months.

I write the figures down and am ashamed of myself. My one thousand dollars per month that I have allotted for living expenses is more than the philosopher spent in his entire two-year stay. Well, I have needs. And there's been a great deal of inflation since 1845. But perhaps I can get by reasonably well on less than a thousand a month. And if I do, I can use the remainder for further investment or to help those who are less fortunate.

Then my finger falls on a passage from *Walden* in which Thoreau decries do-gooders.

"There is no odor so bad as that which arises from goodness tainted. It is human, it is divine, carrion. If I knew for a certainty that a man was coming to my house with the conscious design of doing me good, I should run for my life."

Was the man who left me the persimmons and walnuts trying to do me good or just being friendly? I don't
know. I don't know who he is.

I get my mind back in gear and start to write numbers for my monthly budget.

Food:	$220
Clothing:	40
Gasoline:	50
Propane:	30
Health Insurance:	85
Auto Insurance:	32
Book Club:	12
Law License and tax:	40
Land tax:	20
Lamp oil:	12
Continuing Legal Education:	30
Cabin Maintenance:	60
Furniture purchases and maintenance:	50
Gifts, church tithes and Benevolence:	130
Miscellaneous:	100
TOTAL	$ 911

A lot of this is but a guess and a prayer. I figure $50
per week for groceries. Clothing will probably not be $40
each month as I don't have to try to impress anyone in the
wilderness. My health insurance, auto insurance, land taxes, law license and taxes, and continuing education are pretty well set. I have to pay my lawyer license and tax and go
to a two-day seminar each year if I want to keep my license.
Although I don't anticipate going back into that drudgery, it
would be a lot more difficult to reapply and go through the
process than to pay the taxes and keep it active.

Katy would not allow me to stop paying tithes to our church. I do that in her memory. A tithe is a tithe is a tenth of my income—$100 with the remainder for gifts and a helping hand where I see a need. With the miscellaneous thrown in, I am only eighty-nine dollars below my income. That will not be much to invest or otherwise squander. I can do it. If Thoreau could do it with much less, I can do it with my budget.

I READ *WALDEN* FOR another hour and the New Testament for an equal amount of time. I start my book shelf project and make much progress in the second bedroom. I saw and hammer and lay out the shelving on the floor to be lifted to the wall in one piece once it's put together. All my tools are man-powered. The only exceptions are that I brought along a gas-powered chain-saw to cut wood for the stove and a string trimmer to cut the small amount of grass around the cabin. I really detest the noise of engines spoiling the sounds of silence in the mountains, but I must make allowances since I am alone and there is no one to cut wood with a two-man crosscut saw.

After lunch, I walk down the mountain on my property toward that of the Big South Fork trail. I want to check out for myself if the bowl, fruit, and nut offering came from a hiker. Vines, bushes, and high grass hinder my pursuit until, in walking laterally to find an opening, I happen onto a narrow foot-trail that has been trodden often enough through my property to bare the earth.

When I find the hiking trail, I walk in the direction of the river gorge although I don't expect to go that far. It's good exercise and the afternoon is pleasant—and so warm that I work up a coating of perspiration. I turn and look back. Going downhill is easy. I just don't want to go so far that my walk back will be too tiring. When I stop, I hear a crunching of twigs out of sight behind me. It's just one sound and then silence again. I have noticed squirrels in the distance from the path so I give it no thought.

I walk backwards a few paces. An old legend says that Indians often turned and walked backwards when they were in strange territory so that when they returned along the same trail they would recognize the area and know they were not lost. When I turn forward again, I feel eyes on my back as though there's another hiker behind me. I glance back and see nothing. My hand runs down to my waist and feels the .45 revolver that is holstered there. It's for snakes. I carry a hunting license just in case I'm ever asked by a ranger why I'm carrying the gun. Crows and snakes—if they pose a threat—are always in season although I've never shot either.

The trail levels out and I've gone as far as I'm going today. A large boulder is to my left. I walk there, look around it for snakes, climb up, and then sit down. The moss-covered northern side is soft to the touch of my hands, and the massive stone is as cool as a giant turtle that has come up out of the water. I try to absorb its chill and look away in the distance to where I get a glimpse of the river. The river is quiet and still to my view although I know that it has a fast current and much whitewater. Here it appears more like what I would see on an artist's canvas. The sound and fury await a closer encounter.

I DON'T PASS ANY hikers on my walk back. My paranoia about snakes must be expanding to having me believe that someone is following me. I decide to drive to Jamestown to buy food for the week, shop for some used furniture, and call to leave messages for my children that I am safely ensconced at the cabin.

Near the town, on a beautiful carpet of green, a nursing home sits to my right. It's another building I had not noticed on my drive up when my mind was centered on the mountain and my cabin. Old men and women are sitting outside near the driveway peering off toward the road and the mountains. They're awaiting their children's visits which they must think come too infrequently. It occurs to me that I should stop there on my drives to town and make friends with someone. I have plenty of time. Maybe someone would enjoy me reading to him. I read well. I know they are more alone than I. They believe their loved ones will visit. I know my Katy is gone.

IN JAMESTOWN, I FACE the harsh reality that $50 does not go far in the grocery store. I buy a lot of fruits and vegetables that need no cooling refrigerator—that I don't have. My meats must be of the canned variety or else cooked on the day of their purchase. I buy a steak for tonight. Celebration. Soap and paper towels and aluminum foil are sold in the grocery store and eat up a lot of my food budget. I mentally calculate the amounts as I go, nodding at each five dollars' worth. When I get to $45, I quit. With the sales tax, I will be to my limit. Four bags. In the future I can figure eleven dollars per bag.

At a used furniture store, I buy a rocker that fits my body nicely. I pick out an inexpensive kitchen table and four chairs, a couch that might be considered by some to match my recliner close enough to allow beside it, and a dresser and chest for my bedroom. I'll need more, but that can wait.

A junk and antique shop sits on the main strip. With no electricity at the cabin, I do need one thing in order to keep my clothes clean—a wash tub with a wringer. Fortune smiles on me. Just the one I need is lying against the side of the building. I put on my best bargaining hat and approach the shop, averting my eyes from the object of my desires, and instead I inquire about other pieces lying about. Too much interest in the tub will transform it from junk to antique status in the owner's eyes.

I lay aside an old hammer and crosscut saw to buy—which I don't need. Then, with a sideways glance, I appear to notice the tub.

"Haven't seen one of those in a spell," I say.

"Nope. Just got that one in last week. A real beaut."

"Hey, I have a sister who's having a birthday soon. I'd like to get that for a gag gift if it's not too much."

"A hunnert."

I shake my head. "She's not worth that much," I say and start to pay for the hammer and saw.

"The tub or your sister?"

I look toward the old shop owner and get the drift of

his question. "Neither," I answer and smile.

"Fifty, then."

I shake my head and pull two twenties from my bill-fold. "Forty."

"Sold."

Then I wonder if he would've taken thirty or twenty-five. I load my purchases in the trailer and wave at the shopkeeper as I pull out. I'm going to like to visit town once a week. Down the road, I turn into the parking lot of a hardware store.

I pick up a few nails and screws that I noticed I need-ed while unpacking my tools.

"Haven't seen you here before," the clerk says, want-ing my history and pedigree, I'm sure. Everybody knows everybody in the small-town, rural South. I thirst for some company anyway and am glad to talk a bit.

"Cody Rogers," I say and extend my hand across the counter. "I just moved into my cabin up on the mountain near the Big South Fork. Getting settled in."

"How long you up there for? A week? Two?"

I shake my head. "Till I get my answers."

The clerk blinks his eyes and leans closer. "Whut?"

"I don't know how long. Maybe a year. Maybe two. How long did Thoreau live at his cabin at the pond?"

"Don't reckon I know any Thoreau. Whut pond?"

"I was just musing," I say and take my bag of nails and screws.

"Whereabouts are you up there?"

"Off of Mt. Helen Road."

He shakes his head. "That's rough area up there. Who all's living with you?"

"Just me," I say and smile.

He shakes his head again and looks away. "Mighty lonely place."

"It depends," I say. "Loneliness is in the head. I have a lot of things to think about."

"Sho nuff," he says and looks over my head toward another customer. "What do you do for a living?"

"Nothing. Small pension," I add, not wanting anyone

to think that I'm independently wealthy and have gold stored at the cabin. I pause and then ask, "Do you have any .45 cartridges and twelve-gauge shotgun shells?"

He nods and retrieves a box of each from beneath the counter as though it's a frequent request. I don't need any, but it'll be good if word gets out that I'm armed. I'm less likely to be bothered by the criminal element.

I MAKE MY CALLS to my children from a pay phone using a pre-paid calling card and get machines at both houses. I sound as cheerful as I can and give them a minute's worth of details each. Maybe they won't worry. I retreat to my Jeep.

When I near the nursing home on my drive back, I slow and then wheel my Jeep and trailer into the parking lot. I get out and stretch. The late afternoon sun is still warm. A breeze is bringing the hint of fall down from the mountains. I had better check in at the office so that the management won't think I'm here to kidnap somebody or to relieve them of their wealth—I'm certain the nursing home has already taken care of that.

"You want to read to somebody?" the woman at the desk asks and wrinkles her brow. "You don't got any relatives here?"

"No, I'm living up on the mountain. Thought someone who didn't have many visitors might like to have somebody to talk with, and I could read a book or story to them."

"Whatcha say your name was?"

"Cody Rogers. William Cody Rogers."

"Just walk along outside there and see who you see. Ask them yourself. I'll put your name down here in our guest register."

I start to walk away.

"Hey, by the way . . . " she motions me nearer. "A lot of these folks can't understand much. They might think you're a relative of theirs or such. Don't give them any sweets. Lot of diabetics."

I hadn't thought about giving them any food. But I did have a bag of Tootsie Rolls and Hershey Kisses in my grocery bags. I'm a chocoholic.

I walk slowly, trying to see who has guests and who doesn't. Two older men are sitting on a concrete bench at a picnic table. I walk over to them. One—a chunky black man—is wearing a baseball style cap with a Volunteer logo turned sideways on his head so that the bill is over his left ear. His companion—a taller white man with a stubble of several days growth of beard—sits crosslegged while his hands fidget with a large straw hat on his head. They both look at me when I approach and sit down beside the black man. He smiles while the other squints his eyes. I'm afraid that he's trying to recognize me and becoming frustrated because he can't.

"Hey, fellows. You don't know me. I live up on the mountain." I point to their left. "I just stopped by to say hi."

The black man holds out his hand and I shake. He has a strong grip.

"Doc Jordan, they call me, and my friend here is William Purcells."

"Cody Rogers," I say and look at William. His light blue eyes are clouded, his lips are thin across a background of toothless gums. He looks straight at me but says nothing. "Do you have many visitors?"

"No. We don't have no family," Doc Jordan says and turns toward William. "We've known each other a long time, so we sorta hang out together."

"I just moved in up on the mountain for a while. I don't have any friends here either—no family—and I thought I might stop by about once a week and talk—maybe read a story or book to you two if you'd like that."

"Oh, yeah, we'd like that. Bill, here, likes to be read to. He's not much of one for talking. You can call me Doc. Everybody else does."

"Good, " I say. "What do want me to read?"

"Bible'd be fine. Won't be long till we meet our maker. Might as well know a little bit more about what He's trying to tell us."

I retrieve a large print edition from the lobby and

spend the next half hour reading to the two. William Purcells—Bill—never says a word. He nods occasionally. Doc smiles and says *amen* every few verses.

I leave them and know that I feel better for the experience. I promise them I'll visit again in a week.

BY THE TIME MY Jeep and trailer are unloaded, twilight is deepening and the symphony of insect instruments begins to fill the valleys and hillsides. I cook my steak and eat it with rice and a salad on my just-purchased kitchen table.

For dessert I decide to have three Hershey Kisses and a cup of coffee. I walk to the front porch and sit in my new rocker next to the bench where I sat this morning. After I finish the kisses, I wonder how tart a persimmon would taste after the sweetness.

I reach for the bowl that I left on the end of the bench. It's gone. But arranged in two neat rows are the remaining persimmons and walnuts.

5

Today I am going to talk to God. I've been at the cabin for a week and a day now. Things are settling in. I've been back to Jamestown to Foodland for my weekly shopping outing. I ate at a restaurant while I was out. I stopped and looked around Ace Hardware where they sell electric generators at a reasonable price. I don't need one and don't want one. I was just curious.

At the nursing home, my second visit with Doc Jordan and Bill Purcells was enjoyable. They both have a bit of weakness in their mental abilities to go along with their physical ailments. Bill still didn't talk but seemed to enjoy my reading.

"Where do you live now?" Doc Jordan had asked me.

"Up on the mountain off of Mt. Helen Road," I said.

"Mount Saint Helens? Didn't it blow its top back in the eighties?" Doc Jordan asked.

"Not *Mount Saint Helens*," I said. "Mt. Helen Road."

They just shook their heads and smiled.

I LOOK ACROSS THE kitchen table to where a package lies. This is the first intrusion of modern gimmicks into my peaceful life. And the worst is that my children brought it to me yesterday.

"Dad, it's a cell phone. With the batteries, you can use it anytime. Just charge up the battery in the cigarette lighter on your Jeep when you take your drives into town," my son told me.

He had turned it on to check the signal. Excellent. They gave it to me as a gift because they wanted me to be able to call in case of an emergency. What if I fell and couldn't get up? I relented and accepted it graciously. I just hope no solicitor calls.

Now, back to God and me. I have read the entire New Testament during the past week along with the Psalms. I read the story of David who was "a man after God's own heart." I studied the accounts of Abraham, Jacob, and Moses. I know the kinds of people God works through and I'm ready to ask him a few questions. I stayed away from the story of Job.

I have also completed one more read of *Walden*.

"I wanted to live deep and suck out all the marrow of life, to live so sturdily and Spartan-like as to put to rout all that was not life, to cut a broad swath and shave close, to drive life into a corner, and reduce it to its lowest terms."

This is me. I want to know what life is about. Why is the best taken when you're so near to enjoying it the most?

For this same week, I have played a game of hide and seek with the one who left me the bowl of persimmons and walnuts on my first night. The second morning the same bowl was back, sitting just inside my front porch by the door. Again, there were walnuts and persimmons. Three of each. That evening, after I had removed the fruits and nuts, I set the bowl outside the door on the step. I laid three Tootsie Rolls and three Hershey Kisses inside the bowl and watched for my benefactor to appear until I went to bed. He didn't show.

The next morning, the bowl was back inside with the same type offering. The candy was gone. I played the game the whole week—once getting a glimpse of a leg disappearing through the bushes just as night turned to gray of morning. The contest would have been fun except it made me painfully aware that I was being watched by someone who could sneak up on me at any time. He was definitely a woodsman—but so far, he was friendly.

I began my purification ceremony last night. God doesn't just talk to anyone, anytime. I took a cold shower. I'm thinking of a way to have hot water for my shower, but it's cold for the time being. Fasting and prayer go together in God's word. So, I started both after dinner. Fasting has been easier than praying. Perhaps it is because I began it on a full stomach.

Since last night's dinner, I have drunk only water. Of course, it's only 8 a.m. I skip my coffee and, instead, sip cool spring water. This is one thing upon which I disagree with Thoreau. He despised coffee. I love it. Need it. Am addicted to it. But as a part of my fasting, I give it up.

My grandfather showed me the most beautiful place around here when we were building the cabin back in 1957. He was a great hiker. The place is not far in miles; probably three. It's just that the way there is down one mountain, across South Fork, and then up the other side to the very top. Back then, he let me play in the river. It was low, barely knee deep, strewn with rocks and boulders. At the top of the other side, he led me to a rocky bluff that had a view in all directions. We sat and watched the hawks soar on outstretched wings in the updrafts. My grandfather told me the hawk's eyesight was at least a hundred times better than ours—that the hawk had seen our every footfall.

"About like God," I said.

"Very near so," he replied and pointed to another one in the distance.

We stayed until sunset. When the orange ball was cupped by the blue hands of ridges in the distance, we started back. I tired. He carried me across the river so that I wouldn't fall in the dark, and walked ahead of me back up to the cabin, watching for snakes.

That's where I'm going to talk to God. I've read about the mystery of mountains in the Bible. Moses went to Sinai to get the law. He looked over into the promised land from another. Jesus talked with Moses and Isaiah at the top of a mountain. His most famous sermon is called the Sermon on the Mount. God must like mountains. He gave us Tennesseans plenty.

When I finish my spring water, I gather the things I will take. I pack light. I'll take my New Testament and Psalms, *Walden*, a blanket, and a pair of rubber-soled wading shoes. I take no pillow, for I will sleep as Jacob did with a rock for my pillow. My dress will be hiking boots, khaki pants, and a long-sleeved blue denim shirt. I will leave my pistol in the cabin. It's not appropriate to approach God with a weapon. I carry it only for snakes. The Big South Fork people have posted placards on the trails that say to watch for timber rattlers and copperheads. The signs also say that snakes are more likely to be encountered at night when they're out eating than in the daytime. They add, somewhat oddly, to report to a ranger the location of any snakes encountered. Why? Maybe they will map the area of most snakes and plot them on a chart. I will be walking in daylight so I'll just be careful where I step.

As noon approaches, I tidy the cabin and go down my mental checklist to be sure I'm taking what I need but no more. The last things I put in my knapsack are four pints of bottled water that have been cooling in the spring behind the cabin. Lunch briefly flits through my mind, but I resist the temptation by leaving. I lock the doors and step onto the front porch where I remove the three walnuts and persimmons from the bowl and replace them with chocolates. I place the bowl again on the top step leading to the porch and let the screen door slam behind me.

After a half mile moving down the mountain at an oblique angle, I stop and lean against an outcropping of stone. The shade of the thick growth of trees has kept me relatively cool. I pull one of the pints of water out and have a deep drink. I can see the gorge below me through a break in the forest, but it still appears a long way. I think I'm in good shape, but I wonder about the climb on the far side. I haven't been to that point in forty years. If I get lost in this wilderness, nobody will ever find me. I will be a bleached skeleton, my bones scattered by scavengers, before I'm found. I look back toward the cabin. Perhaps I should have brought the cell phone. No.

The gorge appears to be where God took his finger

and gouged out a trough between the mountains for the water to flow north to Kentucky.

All of this—the blue sky, the green forest, the clear and frothy water, the gray boulders, the hawks, the call of other birds, the soft earth of layers of decayed leaves, and the rock ledge I lean against—I find exhilarating. I have never had any trouble believing that there is a God. There has to be a creator behind this creation. My problem is in learning the exact essence of His being.

"The fool hath said in his heart, There is no God."
"The heavens declare the glory of God; and the firmament showeth his handiwork."

I'm a bit surprised that I can quote some of the words of David's psalms. But they are mine as much as his. I feel I'm becoming closer to God in this short distance from the safety of my cabin. I have placed my life in His hands and shall go up onto the mountain. I straighten back up and resume my pilgrimage toward the river.

Big South Fork is formed three or four miles upstream where New River and Clear Fork merge. The Big South Fork is actually the Southern prong of the Cumberland River which it joins in Kentucky before flowing back into Tennessee. It's difficult to fathom that the same water that flows through this wilderness in all its majesty will, two or three days later, meander through Nashville and become polluted with sewage and other pollution until it empties into the Ohio near Paducah, Kentucky. Man makes a mess of God's creation.

Another half hour and I am to the bank of the river. The water is low, but there's current enough. Rocks jut out of the water, and the flow creates little eddies and whirlpools near them. I strip down to my shorts, take my wading shoes out of my sack, and pack my hiking clothes within. I believe I can make it across the river without falling down on a slick rock, but if I do, my clothes will be dry inside the plastic bag in my knapsack. The worst that could happen would be for me to fall, lose a grip on my bag, and have it float off out of my grasp. I cannot imagine talking to God in my underwear.

I tuck the bag under my arm and wrap the strap around it. My bag and I shall not be parted.

The cold water takes my breath when my foot is engulfed. Then another, and finally I am calf deep. The coolness travels up my body like tallow up a candle wick. Goosebumps populate my arms until I reach the sunshine a few yards from shore. The river here is less than fifty yards wide, captured on both sides by the abutting flanks of the mountains.

My footing remains steady, but I walk slowly, always looking down. A few minnows swim by, and I can see the copper-colored stones on the bottom. The deepest I wade into is thigh high. My underwear doesn't even get wet.

At mid-stream, I near a huge boulder and decide to rest upon its flat top. The September sun is warm, bordering on hot. Once I've safely placed my sack with my clothing and water on top, I look around. There is no human in sight. I feel safe in stripping off my underwear and being completely nude—except for my rubber-soled wading shoes—in this creation. I lay my underwear on top of the sack and then squat inch by inch like a frog into the water on the downstream side of the rock.

I shiver until all my body is covered except for my head and neck. I brace my feet against the big rock and lean my head back onto a smaller one behind me and turn my face toward the sun. My thermometer must be in my head because, despite the cold water, warmth envelops me. I lean my head forward and blow bubbles in the water. Suddenly, I am ten-years-old again. I lie back, hold my nose, and let the river flow over me. There's gurgling in my ears, and I open my eyes and look at the ridges through the prism of water. All the Earth is a kaleidoscope. I am baptized in the river of life—the Big South Fork.

When I can hold my breath no longer, I raise up, shake the water from my eyes, and look to both sides. If there is a more enjoyable feeling this side of good sex—or medium sex—I can't imagine it. My thoughts flutter briefly through courtrooms of the past, and I laugh aloud when I imagine addressing a jury in the nude. Until Katy's death, I was working all my life so that I could enjoy such sensations in my retirement. Now, because of her death, I lavish them on myself early—but alone. Where is the justice in all this? Another question for God.

After a half hour of absorbing the sun and the cool water, I climb the boulder and lie supine in the sun. I look down and see that my maleness has shrunk to turtle—baby turtle—size in the cold water. It doesn't matter. There will be no woman after Katy, just as there was none before her . . . except in the spring of 1968. Then a vision of Ginny flashes before me. Nashville. The Parthenon. The newspaper. Ginny.

I drift off into a few minutes nap until I turn and catch myself before falling off the rock. My body is dry, and it's time for me to climb the mountain. I ease down from the rock, still nude, and carry my belongings carefully to the other side. There I dress, put on my hiking boots, finish the first pint of water, and look up toward my destination. The rock bluff hangs out from the sheer cliff eight hundred feet above me and a mile to my east. Before I start up the flank of the mountain through the trees and viney growth, I sit for a minute and read from Psalm 24.

"The Earth is the Lord's, and the fullness thereof; the world, and they that dwell therein.

"For he hath founded it upon the seas, and established it upon the floods.

"Who shall ascend into the hill of the Lord? or who shall stand in his holy place?

"He that hath clean hands, and a pure heart; who hath not lifted up his soul unto vanity, nor sworn deceitfully.

"He shall receive the blessing from the Lord, and righteousness from the God of his salvation."

Clean hands and a pure heart? My body feels clean, refreshed, and spiritual after my wash in the river. But where did the thought of Ginny come from? A pure heart?

TWO STOPS, TWO HOURS, and a pint of water later, I reach the summit. Ahead of me a hundred yards or so is the beginning of the outcropping of rock that shall be my haven for the night. Hunger gnaws at me now. It's hard to put out of mind. On the trek up, I passed at least three persimmon trees, but I resisted the temptation to shake refreshment from their limbs. I stop and open my third pint of water. Now I've consumed more than half of my supply. My journey back to the cabin tomorrow will be a dry one unless I refill the bottles from the river.

I'm sure someone at some time has set foot on this bluff that has the perfect view of the river and the hills beyond, but if it's been during the last forty years, there's no sign of it. No Coke cans, no cigarette butts, no potato chip bags, no plastic bottles that held water, and no graffiti. This must be what Adam saw in the Garden of Eden if he had mountains.

I set my bag down where the rock starts and edge out toward the sheer drop-off. My fear of heights meets my vertigo and pushes me down to my hands and knees where I crawl the last five yards until I'm within an arm's length of the edge. I look over to where I was lounging in the river hours ago and it looks ages away. A hawk, like my grandfather and I saw years ago, hangs almost motionless in the air at my level but a hundred yards out between the mountains.

In the distance on both sides of the river are bluffs near the mountain tops but none with as good a view as mine. From here I will be able to watch the setting sun, and from here I can turn and watch the rising sun. The river makes two bends beneath my view and stretches for two miles or more downstream and upstream before disappearing into the furrows of ridges.

From this height, the huge boulders in the river look like pebbles, and the trees along distant ridges are reduced to no more than broccoli stalks. Seen from the heavens, the Earth must appear to be no more than a rock with a mossy growth and several large mud puddles occupied by microscopic-sized ants. I read someplace that a man's body is exactly at the mid-point in size between the largeness of the universe and the smallness of sub-atomic particles. Maybe if God and I are just shooting the breeze, I can ask Him about that too. But first there are more important questions. Tops is, "Why did Katy have to leave?"

I sit and read, waiting for some miraculous appearance. The only sound that intrudes that is not made by nature is from a passenger jet high above that leaves a vapor trail against the otherwise cloudless sky. I've ridden those too. If someone up there is looking down, he doesn't see me and probably gives those below no more than a glance. There's too much important going on like the latest news in the *Wall Street Journal*. Or what the President is doing today. When will they learn? " 'There is nothing new under heaven. All is vanity,' sayeth the preacher." And I say, "Amen."

I haven't seen a newspaper in over a week. I haven't watched the evening news or listened to the radio. If I did, I would probably hear of the Congress and President arguing, a foreign despot making threats, an earthquake in some country, a flood someplace else, a shooting in Nashville, a preacher being accused of molestation, and on and on and on. After fifty-one years, there is no *news*. It's the same ole, same ole just plugged in with different names and different locations. Instead of reading a newspaper, I'd be better off observing a caterpillar on a leaf, creating a poem, or baking a pie.

A pie. My stomach aches at the thought of food. Fasting is not easy, especially with a hike down one mountain and up another thrown in. How Jesus was able to do it for forty days, I have no idea. The little bit I have done does show me one thing. It clears the mind and allows it to concentrate on other things—things higher, things dearer, and things greater.

I consider the mountains I see rolling ahead of me. Some people like the ocean, some the mountains, some the plains, and some the great rivers. I relish them all and compare them to a woman's body. The ocean is the heart—always beating, always a rhythm that is restful and sure. The ocean is eternal. When it quits, so will the Earth. The plains of the west are the smooth stretches of abdomen. The Rockies are her knees steeped up with her lying on her back. And, of course, the mountains of the east, the Smokies, the Cumberlands, and all the Appalachian chain are her rounded breasts. And here I sit in the land of milk and honey.

I settle into reading and praying, waiting for the appearance.

"Ask, and it shall be given you; seek and ye shall find; knock and it shall be opened unto you . . . .

"The foxes have holes, and the birds of the air have nests; but the Son of man hath not where to lay his head.

"Take my yoke upon you, and learn of me; for I am meek and lowly in heart: and ye shall find rest unto your souls."

I look up and realize I have been here at least two hours. God walks on slow feet. Not even a mouse has scurried across this rock face since I sat down. Any breeze there was has died. The sun hangs just above the horizon ready to give up its light for the day without a whimper. I stand to let the rays touch my face. I am the last thing the sun strikes on today's visit to the Big South Fork.

I walk to my knapsack and drink the last of the third pint of water. I move the few feet to the woods and relieve myself of the remainder of the water that has passed through me. When I turn back, I take my knapsack with me to be my pillow. I have forsaken Jacob's example of using a rock. My body is purged, my mind is open, my spirit soars. I am ready to listen when God is ready to speak.

Darkness comes swiftly after the sun is swallowed up. The rock is warmer than the air which cools rapidly. If God hadn't designed the Earth with great oceans to moderate the dissipation of heat, the difference in temperatures from day to night would be hundreds of degrees rather than a mere thirty or so.

Then there is the fact that the Earth also has a molten core that provides for part of the heat so that we're not solely dependent upon the sun to warm this huge mass of rock. The layer that we sit upon, farm, mine, and anchor our houses and buildings to is like the eggshell to the egg. We're sitting on a crust of ground that keeps us from falling into the liquid rock core. Occasionally the core pours through in the form of volcanoes and heated geysers. Man stands around and marvels at these—steam coming from the Earth and white-hot liquid rock. The marvel is that God has planned it to be contained so well.

The lesser light—the moon—rises behind me. The light of the night. It's influence on life on Earth is not fully appreciated. Besides light, it gives us the movement of tides and even influences the flow of rivers. How has it kept circling the Earth at the perfect distance for so long? And why is it seen the great majority of time at night instead of during the daylight if there was no plan behind it being hung where it is?

I lie back onto my knapsack as the stars appear one by one until there are thousands. This is something I never saw in the cities. The vastness of their number and their light is unnoticed where there is artificial light, but here it is as though diamond dust was thrown against black velvet. Occasionally it appears one falls off—a meteor streaks across and dies out. Night was given to man for contemplation. Our minds expand to meet the ballooning of the universe, and it is only then that we realize the size of our place in it. Small.

We don't think about that as much as the ancients did because we are not exposed to it. We hide in our houses in front of the television and beneath artificial light. Our world centers on us. Outside in this wilderness, it's brought back to me that this bit of matter that I call a body is puny, insignificant, just a speck on a rock.

A crunch of brush behind me brings me back to the here and now. Some animal is out night-feeding. I hope it's a deer and not a bear. I have no fondness for wrestling bears—especially on this rock cliff. I am no Samson or David. I reach toward my pillow—my knapsack—but remember that I did not bring a flashlight or even any matches. I am in the dark in more ways than one. The soft moonlight illuminates me but not the thing that was the source of the noise in the woods. The bear, or whatever, can see me, but I can't see it. I hunker down. God will protect me. He is testing me. He will speak when He knows I'm sincere. I lie back and pray out loud.

"God, why did you take Katy? Why am I left alone in the years when we needed each other most? Speak to me and tell me what use you have for me for the remainder of my years without my helpmeet that you gave me."

God doesn't answer, but there's no more sound from the woods either. At least my voice has driven away whatever animal it was. I hope.

"If you will not talk to me directly, send me an angel like you did to Abraham, Lot, and Jacob. If I am not Moses whom you talked to straight forward, at least send me a messenger with your word and instructions for what I should do."

I lie back and cover myself with the blanket. The fasting was stressful, and I have rock for a bed. I must suffer if I'm to learn. I try to keep my eyes open, but I catch sleep tugging them shut.

When I first wake, the moon is straight up. It is not the light that startles me but the absence of sound. The crickets, cicadas, and all the night insects who play their dissonant chorus have stopped. I press the button on my watch that lights the dial. Now, if anyone ever asks, I know that the insects call it a night between 2:30 and 3:00 in the morning. I have yet to hear a word from God. My eyelids are like they are weighted with sandbags and they close again.

They ease apart when the first streaks of dawn drive the stars and moon away with gray light. I doze some more, awaiting the sunrise.

When I wake next, I have not moved. I can see streaks of sunlight on the mountain top straight ahead of me over the point of my boots. My body feels as though it is welded to the rock. I am old, stiff, and brittle. I roll my eyes to my left without moving my head to see if the sun is peaking above the horizon. I don't see it. But I do see two lengths of rope lying within two feet of my left ear.

They are as thick as my wrists and as long as my arm. Then I see the slits of eyes. Snakes. I don't move a muscle. Timber rattlers. We stare at each other. I'm close enough to recognize all the markings the books warned about, and at the tips of the tails I see the little knobs. I can't count the rattlers. Concentration has fled. Brother and sister or husband and wife. They've eaten well over the night, I hope, and are just digesting their food. When the sun's rays strike them, their bodies will warm and they will start to crawl.

I pray that this rock is not where they spend the whole day. They lie between me and the forest. I will not jump off the cliff because of two snakes. They still haven't moved.

Then I feel pressure on my left ankle and the sensation of a movement easing up and across it. My skin turns as cold as the river I lay in yesterday. I shift my eyes to look down between my legs. I don't see his head, just the back of the rattlesnake that has found my ankle an obstacle to his going from one place to another. His markings would be colorful and something to study up close—through a terrarium if I had a choice.

He stops. Probably senses the heat. He doesn't move again. Probably warming himself. My fingers on my right hand inch toward my belt where I carry my gun . . . except when I'm going to talk to God. It's at the cabin.

I feel a tug at my pants cuff where the snake has put his head. He wants to go up my pants leg where it's warmer, but he stops momentarily. I pray that I can hold my water.

My eyes drop back to the first two. They haven't moved. Then I see a shadow emerge from the forest behind them. All the light is behind him, but I'm sure it's my angel.

He looks like a boy—barefooted with stringy hair. He crouches as he walks without noise or vibration toward me. His steps are slow and soft. Then I see he is not looking at me but at my two friends to my left. He leans over when his feet are near their tails and with two sure, but small, hands grasps the snakes behind their heads.

He smiles and carries them off toward the forest.

"Come back," I want to say but don't. The movement at my pants leg has renewed. In a few seconds I am going to have to kick and see how fast an old man can jump straight up. I will not let him crawl all the way up my leg and feast on my private parts. Cold scaly skin moves across my bare ankle and up my leg another inch.

The youth is walking back. He motions to me to be quiet—as though I need any reminder. He has seen the snake and is on his way to get it. Then he bends before he reaches it and snatches another one that was out of my line of sight. It is bigger than the other two. He carries it to the woods while perspiration runs down my forehead to my eyes.

On the next trip, the boy goes around my head and toward my feet from the right side. He obviously has a better view of my visitors than I.

Please hurry. My eyes are fastened to his face. He smiles when he sees my predicament with the snake that's entered my pants. He shakes his head briefly, but then bends down, and with one swift snatch pulls the snake off my cold leg and away from my pants. He holds him up to his face and smiles at the snake. The snake opens his mouth and what passes for a hiss escapes.

The boy is not bothered. He carries this one off. I'm afraid to move. There may be more.

Now he's back and standing over me.

"That's all of them. You can move now."

I roll over to a seated position. My pants are wet where I couldn't hold my water.

"Are you an angel?" I ask.

The boy smiles. "No, I'm Toby Siler. My Pa says I'm the son of the devil." He reaches into his pocket and brings out a Tootsie Roll. "You want a candy?"

6

Heat and cold. They're not a problem if they're in the right place. That's true of a lot of things. It's been a week now since my visit to the mountain. I've cut wood and stacked it. Trailer after trailer full of firewood for my stay through the winter. Now I'm writing down the things I'll need to construct my inventions to hold cold and hot water. They're really not my inventions—just my modifications of old standbys.

Toby has helped load wood, carry wood, stack wood by the cabin, and otherwise made himself useful. While I'm sitting here on the front porch with my cup of coffee writing things down, he's in the spare bedroom that I'm turning into a study. He helped me lift the shelves into place and now he's stacking my books on them. I showed him how I wanted them—the *National Geographics* on the bottom three rows, leaving room along for additions I hope to get, my law books at eye level, and my collection of mystery novels over them.

Toby is ten-years-old. He lives down the road about a mile with his parents. He's an only child. That's his story.

I know he's an angel sent by God to give me some answers. When? I don't know. Where? I don't know. But they're bound to come. God just didn't want to talk to me in person. He sent an angel instead. Years ago I didn't believe in angels. I didn't really believe God spoke to us in any way except through the Bible. However, the more I read the Bible, the more I see angels mentioned. In Psalms, David said:

"What is man, that thou art mindful of him? and the son of man, that thou visitest him?

"For thou has made him a little lower than the angels, and has crowned him with glory and honor."

And in Hebrews, the writer says:

"Let brotherly love continue. Be not forgetful to entertain strangers: for thereby some have entertained angels unawares."

I am entertaining an angel. I'm as sure about that as I am about anything.

As part of my now departed law practice, I learned to write down bits of evidence that added up to form the whole. Sort of like putting a puzzle together or solving a mystery. God has left enough out about Toby for me to know he's an angel.

First, this is the early part of October. Any ten-year-old boy would be in school. It's the law. Second, he was the bearer of the persimmons and walnuts. It would be almost impossible for a human to set those bowls inside my door without me hearing. Third, he showed up when I was in greatest need. That's angelic.

Next, I don't know any ten-year-olds or many men of whatever year who would pick up four rattlesnakes in a row and gently put them back down where they were out of the way. He looked the snakes in the eyes and smiled.

Lastly, I have not disputed it to his face, but I've been over these mountains for years, and no one lives in the direction where he says his house is located. Would parents let their little boy spend hours and hours at a stranger's house? Or let him follow him all night to the top of the mountain?

He leaves near dark and walks off. He tells me he doesn't need me to walk him home. As a matter of fact, it would be better if I don't. I nod my head. Yes. I can't go where his home is. I watch as far as I can. Then he disappears into the forest as those dead baseball players did in *Field of Dreams* when they walked off into the corn field.

I'm going to go along with the ruse and see where it leads. God is teaching me to be patient.

Toby comes from the study and stands in the door frame scratching his head.

"Cody, have you seen Portia since you've been here?"

"Portia. Who's Portia?"

"She's my possum. When I used to sleep in here, she'd come visit me at night. She showed me where all the good persimmon trees were. Have you seen her?"

I scratch my head. I hope I haven't hurt an angel's opossum. "I met her my first night here. I put her outside in the back woods. I didn't know her by name. She fainted when I shined my flashlight in her eyes."

"Scared her. She always came to me in the dark. No flashlights."

He comes and sits beside me.

"Toby, did you say you used to sleep here?"

"Yeah. Some nights in that room where I'm working now. Had a pillow and blanket."

"I cleaned that out the first day I was here." I pause. I don't know how much to ask a being like Toby. I guess he'll stop me if I get into an area I'm not supposed to know. "Did your parents know you were sleeping here?"

He nods but doesn't look up. His legs are swinging like pendulums from the bench.

"They didn't care?"

He shakes his head. "As long as I get my chores done, they don't care. I like the woods."

"Do you go to school?"

"Home schooled."

I nod. It's a good answer. No angel would be registered with a school system. I reach over and rub his head. His hair feels just like a human's.

He looks over to my yellow pad. "What are you drawing?"

"This is going to be my water heater. And this is going to be my spring house." I point to my rough drawing of circles of black hose housed in a wood frame. I had figured three hundred feet of one-inch-diameter hose laid in tight circles inside a wood box and attached to the roof and water pipe would give me solar heated water. I'm tired of cold showers, and I have a Southern facing roof where I could put it.

The spring house will be concrete blocks laid on their

sides in an area where I have dug out the bank of the spring behind the cabin. Then I will lay other blocks around to form a small block house about the size of a large desk. The cool spring water will run in from one side, maintaining a depth of about a foot, and then out the other. I will put milk, juice, and other foods that need to be cooled there and retrieve them as needed. My grandfather had one, and I'm just reinventing what the pioneers used before refrigeration.

The hot water on the roof I will run into a holding tank above the shower stall. I figure I will have ten gallons of very warm water by noon on any day that it's not cloudy. A quick five or ten-minute shower with hot water will be a treat. When It turns cold, I'll know it's time to get out. Until now, I've been heating water on the stove when I wanted to wash with warm water. This will save energy.

"You think it will work?" Toby asks.

"I think so. What do you think?"

"Yeah. Let's build it."

I'm sure now. "We'll have to go to Jamestown and get the materials. You want to go?"

"Jamestown? Where's that?"

"The nearest town. You never been there?"

He shakes his head and looks down.

"If it's okay with your parents, you can go."

"They won't care."

If he was really a ten-year-old, I'd make him bring me a written note before I take off with him in my Jeep. But knowing what I know, we load up and go.

HE'S WIDE-EYED WITH his face up against the windshield as we drive down the mountain and into the more populated areas of Fentress County. We turn at the intersection in Allardt, and he waves at everybody he sees.

"Sit back and put that seat belt on. It's the law. Angel or no angel."

His hands are on everything at the building supply store where I purchase blocks, plywood, two-by-fours, and my long lengths of hose. I drive to Ace Hardware and look at the gas-powered electric generator. I read the label to see how many electrical outlets, the amperage, and the hours it would run on five gallons of gasoline. Nights are getting longer, and I don't read well by the kerosene lamps. But I don't need this convenience. Toby and I walk back to the aisle where he has picked up a new pocket knife.

"You want that?"

"Can I?"

"Sure, you've worked hard for me. I'll pay the clerk."

When we get back into the Jeep, I notice a Dollar Store on the next block. Toby has worn the same pair of jeans every day that I've seen him. It's probably standard angel issue for the mountains, but I want to be as benevolent as I can.

"Would you like some new jeans and shirts?"

He shakes his head. "I don't think I should. My folks wouldn't like it."

"Aw, come on. It's pay for your work." I take him in and he reluctantly tries on new clothes. He turns and grins at me when he sees himself in the mirror. On another counter, I see a name brand of athletic shoes. I sit him down and find the right size. Socks are purchased. I end up spending two months of my clothing budget on Toby. It's okay. I don't need anything.

I TURN INTO THE drive to the nursing home and see Doc Jordan and Bill Purcells sitting in their normal space at the concrete picnic table. I stop on the circular drive near them and get out.

"Come on, Toby. I want you to meet some friends of mine."

"Hi, Cap Cody. How's the volcano?" Doc Jordan asks. Bill salutes but says nothing.

"It's fine. Just rumbling a bit," I say. It's no use explaining again that I live off of Mt. Helen road and not Mount Saint Helen. "This is my friend, Toby."

"Fine looking young man," Doc Jordan says.

I go and retrieve the large print Bible from the lobby and return to read to them. Toby is sitting crosslegged on the ground.

"Aren't you afraid you'll get grass stains on your new jeans?" I ask.

"Naw," he says, picks a blade of grass from in front of him, and begins to chew. Toby looks back and forth at the old men. Then he blurts out. "What happened to your skin to make it that color?"

I swallow hard and look at Doc who blinks and then smiles. I look at Toby. An angel should know the answer to that question if anybody does.

"God just gave us a little more color after he made the pale folks. We're the new and improved version," Doc says.

"The bottoms of your hands are a different color," Toby adds.

Doc turns his hands palms up. "I've just about worked the color out of them."

Bill is chewing tobacco without teeth and suddenly spits a stream of juice to his side.

"I can do better than that," Toby says, and spits between his teeth almost ten feet.

For the first time that I've seen, Bill smiles. Doc Jordan laughs.

"Why do you wear your cap sideways?" Toby asks.

Doc's eyes reach upward toward the bill of his cap. "So's people think I'm looking at 'em when I'm not."

Toby nods and picks another blade of grass.

"I like this boy, Captain. You need to bring him with you all the time."

After I read the story of Samson to the two old men, Toby and I start to get back into the Jeep. Toby turns and spits again. Doc Jordan slaps his knee and doubles over with laughter while Bill spits out a tobacco juice stream to his side.

Near the cabin, I turn to Toby. "You haven't seen black people before?"

"You talking about like Doc?"

"Yeah."

"He's not exactly black—just a little more color than me. That's what he said." He looks out the windshield.

"No, I've never been to Jamestown. Is that where all the dark ones live?"

I shake my head. "No." I look back to him. "Where all have you been?"

"Just up and down the mountain. We go once a year to Newport."

"Do you have television?"

"What's that?"

AT THE CABIN, TOBY helps me unload the supplies I will use to make hot and cold water. He eats the evening meal with me and then goes back to work stacking the books on the shelves. I sit and have a cup of coffee on the porch. Maybe he's not an angel. Today I will follow him when he leaves and see where he lives.

A half hour later, Toby stands over me in the doorway again with a bundle in his hands. Five books wrapped with a red ribbon.

"Where do these go?" he asks.

I reach out and take them. I haven't seen them in years. One of my children must have put them with my other books when we were loading up. I untie the ribbon and lay out the volumes on the bench beside me.

"I've got to go. I'll put them up tomorrow. Thanks for the clothes and knife, Cody." He is out the door and into the woods before I remember I am supposed to follow him.

My mind is on the journals beside me. I don't want to open them. They are my distant past.

When I was twenty-one and all the world was new, I believed that an individual could make a difference. These are journals of my six months in Nashville. From January 1968 through June of the same year, I wrote down my thoughts, observations, and philosophy on these pages. Highs and lows. Beginnings and endings. Love and the loss of love. Animal and spirit.

A volume each for January through May. I wrote a lot then. I'm afraid to open them now for I know they will sound foolish and childish. And I know Ginny will be there . . . in the spring of '68.

7

Sunlight filters in through the mist in gold and green when I walk the dirt road the next morning in the direction that Toby said he lived. He always takes a shortcut through the woods, but he told me he lived on the other side of the road not far away. I don't know what "not far" means to a boy or angel of his age considering he followed me three miles down one mountain and up the other. He's not one to give distance in terms of miles.

"Not too far," is the only way he describes anything to me. One day we went hiking on a trail that I didn't know existed. He told me it wouldn't be far to the trees where he harvested the nuts and persimmons. An hour later we were still walking. He's a woodsman of some talent. Besides his ability to carve bowls from slices of walnut logs, he is an accurate thrower of the green-hulled nuts. He displayed his prowess by knocking a squirrel out of a tree thirty feet above our heads with the first throw. Then he went and picked the dazed rodent up and placed him back on a limb of the tree. I see a *Field of Dreams* in his future.

A logging truck approaches. About one a day comes out of the mountains with logs three or four feet thick stacked on them. To me they look like severed arms and legs. They are clearcutting some of the forest just a few miles up the road. One side of the road is Big South Fork and protected. The other side is not. Thoreau and I would lead the trees in a phalanx of walking green heads from one

side of the road to the other where they would be protected—in the perfect world. Now, however, I just wave at the
truck driver. He waves back, but looks at me strangely as
though to say, "What are you doing on *our* road?"

Dust swirls up behind the truck, and I walk to the
center of the road and down the tracks it has just made.
Diesel fumes linger in the fall air where whiffs of evergreen
had been before. The lumber people have invested heavily
in harvesting the trees, and people like me who build great
houses are part of the reason. There's a market for the arms
and legs and trunks of the hardwood that just passed me.

*"There is never an instant's truce between virtue and
vice."—Walden.*

Another fifteen minutes and I notice a slash of gravel
that leads off to the right, down a flank of the mountain, and
around a bend. I stoop down and see tire prints where the
gravel meets the dirt. A hand-lettered sign a few feet down
warns: "Privite Proparty." Another one says: "No Trispass."
And a third one makes it clear: "Trispasers Will Be Shot!"
I find the exclamation mark redundant.

I will walk as far as the signs but no farther. My .45
pistol is at my side but the last thing I want is to get into a
gun battle.

When I reach the sign that warns I will be shot, I can
barely see the corner of a building just around the next
bend. There's a plume of smoke curling up above the trees
but I can't see the chimney. I think I hear voices. They're
ahead of me, so I will go a bit farther, but easily to where I
can turn and walk—or run—back quickly.

I step to the curve of the bend and look around the
last tree obstructing my view. A hundred yards away I can
make out a woman in a dark dress that comes to the ground.
She is speaking to someone who is taking a bath in a tub
that is sitting outdoors beside steps that lead to a weather-
worn shack. I believe it's Toby. I hear his voice in a pleading tone talking to the woman.

"I didn't mean to. I told him, 'No.' "

Then his voice fades as the woman is facing him and talking. She's pointing her finger and gesturing toward the side of the house.

I raise up from where I've been bent over eavesdropping and feel a presence behind me. I know I've been caught, but I'm afraid to look. When I barely turn my head, I see the shadow first. There's nothing I can do but 'fess up.

When I turn, I pretend that I knew he was there all the time. This must be the author of the sign. I'm six feet one inch and weigh about a hundred and ninety pounds. This man is at least six-five and probably outweighs me by eighty pounds. He belongs on the line of a professional football team. He wears a long leather coat and hat that shades his brow. His eyebrows look like three fuzzy black catorpillars that have met in the center of a highway. His skin is light and his eyes are blue. Beard and mustache hide the skin from the nose down. I have time to notice this because I have lost my voice, and he doesn't care to speak.

His coat is pulled back at his hips to where I briefly see a sawed-off shotgun holstered at the right and a hunting knife big enough to gut me with one swipe on the left. He lets his coat fall over his weapons and crosses his arms at his chest. I put out my hand to shake, but he leaves it hanging there like a limb that needs pruning.

"Cain't you read?" he asks with no humor in his voice.

I want to say back, "Can't you write?" But I resist and instead say, "I'm a friend of Toby's. Is he your boy?" I wait a second for a response and then add, "I'm your neighbor, Cody Rogers."

"No trespassin'," he says and spits. "You're not my neighbor, and I hain't your'un. The youngin' don't need your handouts. You'd better learn the way of the hills if'n you want to live up here . . . or anywhere." He spits again. "We respects people's privacy. You hear?"

I nod my head affirmatively. "I'm sorry, Mr. Siler. I was just checking on Toby. I'll be going," I say and start to walk around him. I am outmatched in height, weight, strength, youth, firepower, and whatever other category I can think of. He could kill me here, and nobody would ever know. I am a trespasser carrying a gun.

"Wait, let me see your pistol."

This is tough. Do I want to hand him my own gun and be completely helpless? I gently take it out of the holster and offer it to him hoping for mercy. "I didn't come to shoot anybody. I always carry that," I say while he eyes it up and down. He hefts it up and looks down the barrel. Then he squeezes off all six rounds striking a tree twenty yards away each time. He formed a perfect circle with the holes. Now I know. My gun will be found in my hand when they find my body. He will tell them he shot in self-defense. They'll look and see that I did, indeed, empty all the rounds in the .45.

"Good gun," he says and hands it back to me. "You better get on home."

"Yep," I say and walk away, counting each step until I'm sure I'm out of the range of a sawed-off shotgun. He wouldn't shoot me in the back since it would be hard to argue self-defense. So, I don't pull a *Lot's wife* and look back. My eyes seek the road and the safety of my cabin. He is definitely a hill person. There is no valley blood coursing through his veins.

Back at my place, I read Thoreau's chapter on "Brute Neighbors" in *Walden* but find he is not talking about the kind I just encountered but, instead, the insects, birds, mice, and other animals that inhabit the territory around his cabin.

While I am recovering from my meeting with Mr. Siler, my heart still races from a combination of fear, anger, and the exertion of returning to the cabin faster than I left. I turn to other reading to calm myself and pick up the bundle of journals that I left on the bench the night before. The temptation will not flee. I must read what my world was like in 1968. I begin with the first of the five—January.

I ARRIVED IN NASHVILLE on New Year's Eve without any plans for where I would live or where I would work. I was a journalism graduate and had just finished my first semester of law school. I thought I could get a job as some kind of reporter for either the Nashville *Tennessean* or Nash-ville *Banner*. I had a suitcase full of clothes, a small televi-sion, a 1967 Ford Fairlane with a nice 289 V-8 which I owed on, and two hundred dollars—my entire savings. I knew no fear or was too ignorant to recognize it.

An ad in the paper led me to a basement apartment in a house on Orleans Drive off West End Avenue less than a mile from Centennial Park. Half of my savings went for the first month's rent. When my landlady asked me my occupation, I told her I had hopes of being a reporter for one of the local papers.

"Huh! You're not one of those boozing reporters are you?"

"No," I had said. "I hardly touch alcohol."

The place was dark and dreary with tile floors throughout. I had forgotten about the need for linens and sheets until I saw the bed. I rushed to the nearest store that was open on the eve of the new year and spent another fifty dollars for necessities and food.

The new year of 1968 came in with the largest snow of a season which would have much snow. I settled down to make a plan for seeking employment the following day. There was another apartment on the same level of this old house that had been converted to many living quarters. Muffled voices emanated from that direction but I couldn't detect the exact location until I got down on my hands and knees and opened the base cabinet door below the kitchen sink. Then I could see light slanting through the joints of the cabinet coming from my neighbors' apartment. I couldn't imagine what they saw when they looked toward the back of my sink. Perhaps there was more wall there than I could see from my perspective.

The University of Tennessee played Oklahoma in the Orange Bowl in Miami on New Year's night. I sat and watched it alone and cheered on my Vols. They eventually lost by a score of 24-26.

The next day I was up early, dressed in my best suit and tie, and was at the personnel office of the local papers when they opened. Oddly, the two competing papers were housed in the same building on Broadway. When I walked in, I turned right instead of left. Right led to the *Banner* while left led to the *Tennessean.*

I was hired on the spot. I later learned two reporters had left with the end of the year, and my hiring had to do not so much with my qualifications as it did with my being a warm body who could type. My services were a subject of debate and wrestling as to who got first dibs on me. Again, it was not my talent that initiated the battle, but the fact that I was there and could go to work immediately.

I felt a bit like the slaves must have felt when watching masters bidding for their bodies. I ended up with a benevolent older reporter who would teach me the ropes of covering Metro Government, as they called it, since Nashville was one of the few places in the country where city and county had already combined their services and oversight.

While I was learning my way around Nashville, writing obituaries and going to Metro Council meetings, the majority of the world was engrossed in greater happenings.

Lyndon Johnson was named man of the year for 1967 by *Time* magazine in its first edition of 1968. My mother called with the news that another of my high school classmates had been killed in Vietnam. The Tet Offensive began and the USS Pueblo was captured.

In my journal, I ruminated about my student deferment in the draft. It would end if I didn't return to school after another semester. War protests were growing more frequent although I hadn't joined them. A journalist is an observer and reporter, not a participant.

I close the journal for January, 1968, because my eyes keep drifting up to the road. I want Toby to come walking down here and explain to me about his father. If Toby isn't an angel in the heavenly sense, he is still one to me.

By noon he hasn't arrived, so I begin to erect my solar-powered water heater on the roof of my cabin. I make a six-foot-by-six-foot frame out of two-by-fours. Then I loop the hose into tight circles until it is all coiled and fit snugly into the frame. One end I attach to the pipe with water coming from the spring and the other end to piping that goes to my shower.

At the shower, the reservoir that sits on top will now have two sources of water coming into it. One will be directly from the spring and one from the heated water from the black hose. It's a primitive way to do it, but it'll work. A ten-gallon hot shower is better than no hot shower at all.

Then I walk behind the cabin to where I have already begun to dig out for my spring house. I carry the concrete blocks one by one to the bank of the stream and begin to place six on their sides in the midst of the stream pool that I've widened. They sit about ten inches below the flow of the stream.

The other blocks I stack on edge around the others to make a little house about three feet high. On the upstream side, I leave an opening of half a block's size to allow water to come in. On the opposite side, and one block layer higher, I form an opening for the water to flow out. Without the blocks being sealed or put together with mortar, water flows out through the seams and seeps out through the blocks themselves. But I don't need to catch the water, just slow it down to where there is a continuous cooling pool. This I have accomplished. A two-by-four and plywood roof built with hinges to open tops off the project and I sit to rest.

The early October sun still brings out a sweat when I exert myself. I take my shoes off and cool my feet on the upside of the stream. The coldness moves up my body until I begin to shiver. I look at the cabin, to the roof where my water heater is absorbing the sun's rays, and then down the slope of the ridge and see a deer scoot off through the trees. This is the life.

At four o'clock, I go in and take a shower to try my hot water invention. The water begins hot for about two minutes and then begins to cool in degrees from hot to warm to cool to cold. It's an invigorating shower that brings a glow to my skin and a sense of accomplishment to my mind. I feel as pure as a newly baptized child. I dry, dress, and sit on the front porch with Thoreau and the Apostle Paul.

Paul tells me to be content in whatever state I find

myself, while Thoreau says:

> *"Man flows at once to God when the channel of purity is open. By turns our purity inspires and our impurity casts us down. He is blessed who is assured that the animal is dying out in him day by day, and the divine being established."*

I close up the books and meditate. I have opened the channel of purity with my spring house, and here in the mountains I feel as close to God as I ever have. Whether the animal in me is dying out, I don't know. And whether I'm totally content, I'm not certain. When I get the answers, I will be nearing the next level of perfection. I close my eyes and see Katy, and then I see Ginny walking up next to her.

I GO TO THE kitchen and start dinner. Thinking too much can be spooky.

I eat alone at the table where I have four chairs. It's quiet, too quiet. I find I miss the companionship of the ten-year-old.

At sunset, I am washing my dishes in the sink over cold running water when the screen door on the front porch bangs closed. I hear the padding down of feet running from the porch to the front door. I grab a towel and dry my hands, turning at the same time to meet my visitor.

Toby stands in the doorway bent slightly forward with the load he's carrying. His hair hangs in a ragged wet mat all around his head. His eyes and nose are red. There are the tracks of tears all the way to the corners of his mouth. Then I notice that his shoulders and feet are bare. He's sniffling.

He holds all the clothes I bought him with both arms in a great wadded up heap in front of him. He throws them all into a pile on the floor . . . and then I see that he is wearing no clothes. He cups his little hands to hide his nakedness.

"Pa said to tell you I don't need any clothes from you!" he shouts and cries at the same time. "They said if the clothes they got for me ain't good enough, I could go naked for a few days and see how it feels. They whupped me because of you, Cody."

With that he turns, and a latticework of red streaks and welts over all of his buttocks and upper legs strike me like a red hot poker thrust into the pit of my stomach. I haven't said a word since he walked in. My eyes focus on the severity of his assault. Streams of blood have puddled and dried all along his buttocks and legs like a blotchy mapwork of torture. Blue is beginning to take the place of red in broad stripes like the clothing prisoners used to wear. He turns back toward me.

"Your dad did this to you?" I ask as though there could be some other explanation.

"My Pa told my Mama to do it. He wants you to see what you caused. You hurt me, Cody. I told you, 'No' in the store, but you wouldn't listen. I hate you! I never want to see you again."

Before I can say anything. He turns, runs out to the front, and disappears through the forest toward his house, bare soles of his feet waving at me while I stand on the steps. I sit down there, bend my head, and feel hot drops of tears hit my hands. Then it begins to rain—a cold, pelting rain that washes the tears from my hands.

8

The social worker looks at me through a valley formed by mountains of files on each side of her desk. I am the first customer, client, complainer, or whatever at the Human Services Office of Fentress County in Jamestown the next morning.

Her eyes glaze over after the first three sentences as though she has heard this story a hundred or a thousand times. I tell her about the wounds that I witnessed on Toby Siler the night before from a beating his parent or parents inflicted on him.

"Toby Siler," she mumbles and rolls her eyes to the ceiling. "Those Silers are strange folks. You ever meet Toby's father?" she asks.

I nod my head slightly. The fingers of my hands are laced together under my chin. I hold them tight so they won't shake from my fear and hate.

"You need back-up, a lot of back-up, if you ever go to do anything up on the mountain at the Silers." She looks at me and shakes her head again. "You say you live on the mountain too? Since when?"

"A little over two weeks."

"And he ain't burned your house down yet?" She coughs out a little cackling laugh and then catches herself when she sees my serious expression hasn't changed.

She thumps the files on her right. "I've got too many cases, Mr. Rogers. Besides, corporal punishment by parents is still allowed in Tennessee."

I open my mouth to speak but she trots ahead.

"And there is a fine line between correct corporal punishment and child abuse."

"This is definitely child abuse," I say.

She sits there for a minute shuffling files and then looks me in the eyes. "Let's say you're right. Mr. Siler is guilty of child abuse. We go up there with police back-up and have a little war. Then we take Toby away." She turns a pencil in her hand. "Where do we put him? He has no other relatives. You want him? You think you can take care of him . . . and be safe from Mr. Siler?"

I shake my head. "That's not my problem. I want the child to be safe. You have foster parents."

She shakes her head. "No one will take Ben Siler's child. It's like volunteering for a death warrant."

I leave the office feeling dirty—dirty, not just for me but for our system that can't protect children. Then I feel dirty for myself for the question she asked me. "You want him?" I am the problem. I am why he was beaten. I'm a do-gooder that Thoreau said to flee from. I wanted to buy him nice clothes. He told me not to, but I wouldn't listen. Mountain life is different from valley life.

My anger has not subsided when I stop at the hardware store and buy me a high-powered rifle. I'm not a deer hunter, but if beastly Ben Siler ever comes in my sights, I will kill him.

When my anger cools from white hot to smoldering, I stop at another hardware and building supply store to inquire about the cost of roll insulation. When we built the cabin, we had no thought of insulation or even that someone would live there on a permanent basis.

Now, it will be harder to install in the walls, but I have plenty of time. Mountain winter will be here in less than two months with the cold drafts finding their way through the planking. The ceiling will be easy, as the attic is bare of any flooring. I can just roll the pink stuff out like on the commercials on television I used to watch.

I get the price of the rolls of insulation, walk over to rub my hands over the gas-powered portable electric generator, and then leave for the cabin to get the measurements I need to make the purchase.

Although my last visit was just two days ago, I circle

through the nursing home drive and stop where Doc and Bill are seated.

"I hope Toby didn't offend you," I say to Doc and glance over to Bill who is looking away toward the mountains.

"No, Captain. That's a smart little boy. How's he doing?"

"Well," I say and hesitate. "He's done better, but he'll be okay."

"He sick?"

"No. Just some trouble with his parents."

"Boys will be boys, Captain."

"Yeah," I say. "I've got to go." I walk away a few paces and then turn and walk back. "Doc, I don't mean to be rude, but why do you call me *Captain*? Do you remember my name is Cody?"

"Oh, yeah. I remember that. But I was brought up that all white men expected black folk to respect them. 'Give them a title,' my mother told me. 'It makes them feel good and doesn't hurt you.' Captain's a pretty high rank. That's what I call all the white men . . . except William here. I just call him Bill. We've known each other a long time."

"Thanks, but you don't have to call me *Captain*. I'm just plain Cody. I don't need a rank."

"That's fine, Cody. I call all white men *Captain* until they give me permission to do otherwise."

"Permission granted. But you don't need it. This is a different age from what you grew up in."

He looks at me and then at Bill. "Is it?"

OVER THE NEXT WEEK, I remove the interior walls board by board. When I've exposed the spaces between the wall studs, I place the insulation in, staple or tack it into place, and then replace that section of boarding. It's a delicate and tedious job. The wood has seasoned to a hardness approaching steel over the last forty years, and the nails squeal in a tense chord of resistance as they're pulled out by the gripping claws of the hammer. I do my bedroom first and then start on the kitchen and living room.

I leave the study for last because I can't go there without thinking about Toby having slept there with his little blanket and pillow. I always listen for his return but have yet to see any sign of him since he was here naked a week ago.

When I tire from the tediousness inside, I go into the forest to cut and stack more firewood for the winter. I saw only the trees that have died and are ready to fall. My conservationist side tells me not to take the living ones. My real purist wilderness friends would tell me not to cut the dead ones either—let them decay and enrich the forest floor with the leaves. However, I need heat. So, my Jeep and I make daily foraging runs over my fifty acres. We pull the logs to a place where I can drive the trailer before I saw them into lengths for the stove. My Jeep goes anywhere over my land. If I happen into a ditch from which it cannot pull out on its own, I have winches on the front and back with a hundred feet of steel cable on each. I hook up to a sturdy tree and am out in no time. Sometimes I just get into difficult places so I can use the winch to get out.

IN THE EVENINGS WHEN I relax, I go back to *Walden*, the Bible, and my journals of 1968.

In February of 1968, in Nashville, I was becoming a more astute observer of city government and began to write some good play-by-play of the council meetings.

I could never feel safe and calm in the house on Orleans Drive because of the sounds and voices coming from my unseen subterranean neighbors. When the couple fought, they fought loudly. And when they made love, it was a noisy, moaning, pounding madness that I experienced vicariously through the vibrating wall. When it was over, they smoked. I didn't, and I found it hard to sleep. I had yet to meet any girl or woman in Nashville. So, I moved to an upstairs apartment two miles from downtown, off of Eighth Avenue South, on Benton Avenue.

The downstairs was occupied by a daycare where fifteen to twenty pre-schoolers spent the day. I awakened each week day morning to their exuberant entrance, but their sounds were neither bitter nor lustful as my previous neighbors' had been. Their noise was better than an alarm clock and their vitality instilled in me the energy to make it through the day. My apartment was one great room that served as bedroom and study with a bathroom off the back. There was no kitchen, but I wasn't yet into cooking. I had a refrigerator where I kept sandwich meat, drinks, and ice cream.

Four-year-old Frances always watched me come down the stairs, sleep still tugging at my eyes. "Have a good night, Mr. Rogers?" she would ask. Then when I patted her on the head, she would say, "Have a good day," long before "Have a nice day," became the cliche of our time.

On the national scene, the New Hampshire primary was drawing the interest of several Republicans. Richard Nixon, out of politics since 1962 was battling with Nelson Rockefeller and George Romney. The quixotic Eugene McCarthy mounted a vocal challenge to LBJ.

For me, Valentine's Day passed without a love interest. There was more snow in Nashville, and the weather was getting more news coverage than politics.

THE FOLLOWING MORNING, I resume the pulling of nails from the wall boards. I'm halfway around the living room, working my way toward the study. I have a heap of boards neatly stacked along the wall a few feet away where I will work next after putting insulation where they were taken from and replacing them. Halfway down the wall, I come to a cross member that's been hidden by the boards. Sitting on it is an old Coke bottle placed there forty years ago by me, my father, or my grandfather. Dust layers it like old memories.

I take it and sit down at the kitchen table. Then I brush off the bottom, hold it up to the light, and look at the markings on it to see where it was bottled. This is what my father and grandfather taught me. Before they ever took a swig from a Coke on any trip, they would tip it up to see where it came from. You can't do that with two-liter plastic bottles. It was a refreshment I remembered. We had a washtub filled with ice and "dopes" as we called the carbonated beverages in my youth. I preferred the Dr. Peppers while Dad and Grandpa chose the Cokes or RC Colas.

I sit here at a table with four chairs. Then I remember what Thoreau said about his cabin.

"I had three chairs in my house; one for solitude, two for friendship, and three for society."

When I clear the dust from the rest of the bottle, I see a paper rolled up inside and the mouth is sealed with a candle that has been heated until the tallow melted around the lip. I take my pocket knife, carve through the wax, and retrieve the rolled up document from inside.

My heart starts to thump when I see Grandpa's large writing on the yellowed paper. My father and grandfather are now sitting at the table with me although they've both been dead for years.

"To whoever finds this: This is a fine cabin. We built her well. The roof was nailed on hard. The stone laid for the chimney with precision and care. The hearth stone was a chore to drag down, but she's anchored and won't move.

"If you find this, it means you're tearing the place down or remodeling it. If you're tearing it down, I hope you'll replace it with something as well built. If you're remodeling or adding on, don't make it too big or too fancy. It is just a cabin after all. The mountains, the forests, and the rivers are the important part. Get out and see them. That's all I got to say.

"If you can locate William Cody Rogers of Knoxville, give him this note. He's my grandson that helped build this. It was a great summer we had in 1957.

"Sincerely, Cody Beeler Rogers."

"A written word is the choicest of relics. It is something at once more intimate with us and more universal than any work of art."—Walden.

9

It's Halloween night and I'm sitting here in the dark on my front porch. I figure if Ben Siler is going to burn my cabin down, this will be a good night to do it. It could be blamed on vandals who come out on nights like these. They wouldn't know someone was living here, so the pile of charred bones the authorities would find in the rubble would be more accidental than premeditated. If they found the culprits, which they wouldn't since it would be Ben Siler himself who did it, it would be a hard homicide case to prove. Siler would probably report it himself. "A person must be weird to live up on the mountain all by himself," he would say and spit a stream of tobacco juice as they combed through the ashes.

But I'm prepared. My Jeep and trailer are pulled around to the back of the cabin out of sight. He might, in reality, just want to drive me away. Burn the cabin while I'm gone. Across my lap lie the rifle I purchased and my shotgun. My .45 is holstered at my right side, and on my left is a knife as big as his.

In my hands, I hold two cables with buttons at the ends. One is hooked to my new gas-powered electric generator which is also at the side of the cabin. When I press the button, a battery-powered starter will kick the generator to life instantaneously. The other cable is to an electrical switch which will turn all the spotlights on with one click. I've installed sixteen—two at each of the four corners, two facing straight toward the front, and two each to the two sides and back.

I've tested it on a dark night like this for a few seconds. When I hit the switch, the area around my cabin looks like an airport landing strip or where a space ship has landed with an out-of-this-world glow. I went out and stood on all sides and turned the lights on. It's blinding. I'm proud of my ability.

I bought the generator to power inside lights for a couple of hours each evening since darkness is coming earlier and earlier. I need light to read by, to see my food at dinner, and to wash the dishes. I still don't have a radio or television and don't intend to purchase either.

Tomorrow is the first day of November. If I live through the night, tomorrow I will climb the ridge overlooking the Silers' shack and see what I can see. I have to know that Toby is still alive. If I die in the process, it will be a death well spent. If I kill Ben Siler tonight, I will liberate the child and mother tomorrow. Nobody will convict me for his shooting if he is on my land with a torch and bottle of gasoline. It's the law of the mountains—and I'm learning it quickly.

I've finished my insulating. The cabin is tight and warm. There's already been frost and a flurry of snow, though none stuck. But I can sit in front of the stove, read, and feel toasty warm. All the books and copies of *National Geographic* are neatly arranged. Toby had almost completed all the work before he left. I've added a bed and dresser to the study in case he ever comes back and wants to sleep over. I retrieved his little blanket and pillow from the box that was going to the dump. I use my cell phone to check in with my children once a week and to call my old law office so that they can keep me on the letterhead. Both my children will visit at Christmas if not sooner.

A mist moves up the mountain from the river. It comes through the screen wire like sifted flower and attaches to any vertical object or makes its way out the far side. This is as dark as it will get here. It's cloudy. No moon or stars present their soft light, and the fog makes it a sticky darkness. The only place it could be darker would be in a cave, and there are no caves in the Big South Fork region. I've been in Carlsbad Caverns when they've turned the lights off. Darkness grips you by the throat and sucks the breath out of you.

I pull my heavy flannel shirt around me. I hear only its rustle and my heavy breathing. It's scary to lie in wait for an arsonist. I listen for my friends—the insects of the night—but there is no chirping, no grating of legs together, no flutter of wings, and no call of tree frogs. The cold has driven them under cover, but not too far. They're just a layer deep now and will come back out for a bit in the warm sunshine before making a final retreat in the face of winter's volleys.

Now there is the sound of tires against gravel and I see the flash of headlights against the cut in the road a quarter mile away. It could be Ben Siler and his big pickup with the oversized tires. It slows, but my heart beats faster as the truck nears my driveway. The headlights are killed and it turns in slowly. It creeps down the short, gravel bed like a large turtle going to water and stops about twenty feet from the porch.

I lay the rifle down and place the shotgun next to me. I keep my right hand on the cables while I reach for my flashlight with my left. There're too many things for me to keep up with. I'm afraid I'll stumble and Ben will gut me with that knife of his.

It is a pickup truck. The fog moves over it like a sculptor's hands over clay. My eyes adjust to the dark figures that are jumping out of the bed of the truck. Long hair, skinny. There're four. Now there's two more from the cab. When the door opens, the inside light shows that they're looking for something.

"Where's the matches?" I hear one say.

"Jason, you light them all while Cathy holds them," another one whispers.

All six are gathered around the front of the truck. A match is struck. The one with the match reaches out to the one holding something . . . candles flicker to life. Each of them takes one until there is a procession of six. They all wear hoods. When the candles are all lit, the youths line up and step toward my porch. They start a low chant, rhythmic, and bow their heads. The first one reaches up, opens the screen door, steps in, and walks toward the door to the cabin.

When three are in, I shine my flashlight in the eyes of the leader.

"You here to worship me?" I shout. "How about we go to Hell!" With that I press the buttons in my hands. The light knocks the three still outside to their knees. I swing my shotgun around and fire a blast safely away from the creepy kids, but they don't know it. They hear only the thundering roar.

They scream, crawl to the door and out toward the truck, throwing down their candles as they scramble back to the truck like roaches in the shock of light. The cab that held two on the trip down now holds four on the escape out while the other two vault into the bed and lie as low as snakes. Another blast is fired over their heads for emphasis.

I see the tail lights of the truck going down the mountain at a pace too fast for the curvy road. I push the buttons, and the cabin, once again, is cloaked in a blanket of black mist. I stand and walk to where two candles on the floor of the porch burn weakly. I pick them up and walk out to be sure no other is left burning.

When I'm assured all is back to normal, I go to the kitchen and bring another cup of coffee to the porch. Just because I drove the devil worshipers off, doesn't mean Ben Siler won't be by later. It's a good trial run though. And I'll repair my shotgun blasted screen in the morning.

10

When I stoke the fire in the stove the next morning, sparks fly up the stovepipe in a refreshing swirl. It's cold outside, so I pull a chair up toward the opening of the stove and leave the door agape to watch the wood flame up while I have my coffee. Except for the teenagers, I had no other visitors last night. I scared them away and hope I frightened some of the foolishness out of them to boot.

In the mail I took from my box in Jamestown is a circular about a continuing education course in Nashville. It is a two-day conference that would give me all the credit hours I need to keep my law license in good standing. It's in two weeks. I only have one calendar at the cabin since there's not much need for one, let alone several. I fill out the form and write a check for the fee. To get it there in time to assure my proper registration, I'll need to go toward Jamestown and mail it at the first public drop box in Allardt.

By the time the conference arrives, I will have spent almost two months at the cabin. If I wait any longer, bad weather may interfere with any plans that take me down from the mountain. Besides, Nashville will be a good place to visit. I wonder what has happened to the places where I lived in 1968? And I wonder about Ginny. But more, I wonder if she wonders about me. I will read my journal for March of that year before I go. Then in Nashville, I'll retrace our tracks from April and May.

With all the filling out of the forms, watching the fire, and thinking about Nashville, the last half of my first cup of coffee has cooled. Then when I walk out onto the porch to throw the remains out the front, the bowl is sitting just inside the door. In it are six walnuts and six persimmons, these a little darker and softer than my first ones six weeks ago.

My hand is trembling when I pick the bowl up. I stick my head out the door and then step fully out. The fog veils the passages between the trees. I look up toward the top of the oak that shades this side of the cabin and see the sun streaking through the red and gold leaves at the crest. It's cold, but I'm warm.

Finally I get my nerve and yell, "Toby! Toby! Come inside. I got your bowl. There's some chocolates to replace the walnuts and persimmons." I stand and wait, looking from one side to the other. When he doesn't want to be seen, Toby can melt right into the scenery.

From the kitchen, I take the Hershey Kisses and Tootsie Rolls and put them into the bowl. I roll the walnuts and persimmons onto the counter top. With a hot cup of coffee, I go out, set the bowl on the first step on the outside, and then go back onto the porch to sip my coffee and watch for the boy. I shiver in the coolness once the first rush of warmth subsides. I hold the warm cup in both hands and soak in the liquid heat.

In a few minutes, the tousled head peers in through the screen at the very lowest point. The eyes are wide and look at me unblinkingly. "You mad at me, Cody? For me hollerin' at you? I'm sorry. You ain't gonna whup me, are you?"

I'm frozen by the sight and the words. Then I shake my head from side to side. Finally my tongue warms to the occasion. "Toby. Come in. I'm glad you're back. I'm the one who should be apologizing."

"Apolo . . . what?" He steps onto the porch with the bowl of chocolates.

"Apologize. Saying you're sorry. I should be the one saying I'm sorry. I was the reason your parents beat you."

He shakes his head. "No. I didn't mind them. That's why they whupped me. I get whupped when I'm bad." He unwraps a Kiss and puts it to his mouth. "You want one?" He holds out another foil-covered candy to me.

"No. Just coffee. You want a Dr. Pepper, Toby?"

"A what?"

"A soft drink. A Coke."

He shakes his head and bites down on the chocolate. "No. I just drink water and goat's milk."

"That's all?"

He nods his head and swallows.

"I don't want to get you in any more trouble, but do you want to try a soft drink. It's not against your religion is it?"

"Religion?"

"Church. Jesus. God. What religion are you?"

He shakes his head. "I don't know."

"Do you ever go to church?"

"We go to snake church once a year."

I remember the ease with which he relieved me of my serpentine visitors the night I went to the mountain and the morning I woke in horror.

There's more snake handling lore in the Appalachians than there are actual snake handlers. It's a small group that travels the South from West Virginia and Kentucky, through Tennessee, into the low hills of Georgia and Alabama. Their faith is strong although, I believe, misplaced. They drink poisons and handle rattlers and copperheads.

Again, it's a mountain religion that's different from the valley faiths. Those people feel the Spirit, while the valley people talk about Him. Their numbers do not appear to be growing but probably dwindling as more die from the bites and the younger ones fall to the lust of video stores and tanning salons. The population of heaven will be as small as the suburb of Waco where the Branch Davidians made their stand if you have to handle snakes to get there.

"Do you handle the snakes at the church?"

"No." He laughs. "That's crazy. We sell them the snakes we've caught during the year. Them people do like snakes. I catch them to sell and so does my Pa."

I nod my head. I don't believe you can support a family on the income of snakes. The Silers appear to be living even below my standard except for the expensive pickup truck and tractor I saw parked at the corner of their house right before I was caught by Ben.

"What else does your father do to make money?"

Toby unwraps another Kiss and bites off the sharp tip. "He farms. Raises alfalfa in our greenhouse."

"Alfalfa?"

"Yeah. He sells a lot of it to other farmers who come to pick it up. Grows real tall where we water it and tend it."

"I didn't see any greenhouse when I walked down your drive. Where is it?"

"Way back behind the next hill."

"Oh," I say. I get up and open the screen door. "Let's go get you a Dr. Pepper from the spring house. It'll be cold as ice."

When we get there, Toby helps me lift the top back and looks at all my juices and food I'm keeping cool in the pooling cold water.

"You got a bunch of stuff. When you gonna eat all this?"

"Along," I say and reach for two bottles of Dr. Pepper.

When we're back in the kitchen, I open the bottles and hand one to Toby. "You sure you've never drank a soft drink before?"

He nods his head. "Just water and goat's milk."

He holds the bottle up and examines the dark amber liquid through the light coming from the window. Then he turns it up to his mouth and takes in a mouthful. He swallows, his eyes roll wide in his head, his head rocks forward, and he spews the drink all over me and the floor. He grabs his throat and gasps for air. Tears fill his eyes. "Whatcha tryin' to do? Kill me? This must be poison. It burns my throat like fire." He spits out the rest onto the wood floor.

I smile when I remember that it's his first carbonated drink. I guess if you've never had a swig of that kind of beverage before, a big gulp would feel like a blaze. He starts to run out the door, but I catch him by the shirt. "No, Toby. I forgot to warn you. You have to drink it slow. Real slow." I turn him toward me, pick up his bottle, wipe off the neck, and turn it up to my own mouth. "See. It's not poison. You've just got to get used to it."

I hand it back to him and let him sip it slowly. He sits down at the table and finishes the bottle.

FOR THE NEXT WEEK Toby is over at the cabin every day. We strike a bargain. He'll wear the new clothes when he's with me and will change back to his old ones before he goes home. On two nights, he sleeps over in the new bed I bought. He tells me that his parents don't care. As long as he gets his chores done, he's on his own, and they'd just as soon he was out of their hair. He's a pleasure for me to have around.

He loves my *National Geographic* collection. He sits for hours and looks through the issues. He'll bring me one that has an owl, an otter, a hawk, a mountain scene, a river, or something else that seems familiar to him. He'll sit and tell me where we could go and see similar things in this region of the Big South Fork.

In Jamestown, I take him by the local schools' office and inquire about his education. They inform me that he indeed is in a home schooling program that has been approved by the state. I shake my head in disbelief that they don't want to test him and that he could be home schooled by his parents. I buy the textbooks that the schools use for the first five grades and check out other colorful ones at the library. When I approach a used bookstore on our way home, I stop and buy others. The whole back of the Jeep is filled with books and study helps. I have time. I'll see to it that he really is home schooled.

When we start through the books, I quickly discover that he is not past the first grade level. He is enthusiastic and bright, and his only failing appears to be that he has not had the opportunity to learn from books. He knows a mountain more than me about the habits of animals, where the good berries and nuts are in these hills, and every creek and valley for a five-mile radius. He even tells me there is a cave not far away. All the guidebooks for the Big South Fork say there are no caves because of the geology of the area, but Toby insists there is one. And he'll take me to it. I balk and tell him we'll do it later. We have to get him educated with "book learning" first.

"I have to go home early today," Toby tells me near the end of the week. "We're pulling some of the alfalfa from the greenhouse out to dry tonight. It's the last of the crop."

I nod my head. November. Alfalfa in a greenhouse. I watch him sprint away after he changes clothes. Then I take a pair of binoculars I've stored in the study and proceed to follow toward his house. The way Toby described the location of the greenhouse, I should be able to get a look from the top of the hill that looms above the Silers' house. I carry my .45 and shotgun so that I can say I'm hunting squirrels if I happen into Ben again.

Off the dirt road and to the right, I walk up the flank of the ridge amidst newly fallen leaves that cushion my feet in a bed of copper and bronze. I slip once and again as the leaves have yet to be pulverized and their layers are not compact. The last two weeks of October and the first two of November have seen the colors peak. Katy would have loved sitting and watching God paint each leaf with a tiny brush. Now they are half fallen where they will serve a more practical need to fertilize the forest floor.

When I near the top, I lean against a maple and watch as leaves parachute down in arching resistance to the pull of the ground. My breath steadies, and in another hundred yards, I glimpse the slender shaft of smoke coming from the Silers' chimney. I lie down on the leafy knob of the ridge and bring my binoculars to the bridge of my nose.

Aha! I see him. Like a bear standing on his hind legs, Ben Siler walks between the greenhouse and a nearby shed. All three of them are working, carrying long stalks with leaves from where they were grown to hang them in the drying sunshine and air of the open shed. Except for the size of the stalks, it would look like any other Tennessee tobacco farm family.

I adjust the power of my binoculars. This isn't tobacco . . . or alfalfa. As tall as giant sunflowers, the stems bear the unmistakable shapes of marijuana leaves. It must be the last harvest of the year. Toby carries one plant across each shoulder while Ben carries four on each. The plants

are a good ten feet in height. Toby and his mother can barely balance them without dragging one end or the other on
the ground.

"Keep them in the air!" Ben shouts at Toby and his
wife. I lie still and count. They finish when I reach ninety-
eight. I do some mental calculations. That's at least a hundred thousand dollars in "street value," as the cops say.

Ben Siler is a grower and wholesaler. He probably
has to sell for much less to the street vendors. I grit my
teeth. Now I'm angry—not so much about the marijuana.
That's bad enough. But with that much illegal money, they
still let Toby run around in worn out clothing and shoes.

From here, Ben Siler makes a perfect target, if I only
had my rifle. I'm not a killer though, and besides, I only
brought my shotgun and pistol. He's not in their range.

It's dark when I get back to the cabin. I light a few
kerosene lamps, start dinner, and then switch the electric
generator on so I can have more light to eat and read by. I
strictly limit my electric consumption to two hours per night
and burn only six sixty watt bulbs in all throughout the cabin. During the last week, while Toby's been around, I haven't had a chance to read any more on my journals. Now,
though, I open March, 1968.

More snow fell in Nashville during the first three
months of 1968 than had since the turn of the century. It
was during a snowfall one evening in March that I met
Ginny. When I wasn't covering council meetings for the
Banner, I often drew assignments when the older reporters
begged off. I was new, single, and twenty-one. That auto-
matically made me eligible for the late-night committee
meetings of some organization or other.

LBJ's Great Society was still struggling along as
though it could make some difference in the midst of the
Vietnam War. There were urban renewal and community
action committees. It was at a community action committee
that I first laid eyes on Ginny. It was not love at first sight.
She looked like a skinny, long-haired, serious girl who
thought she could save the world. I did not even make a

note in my journal of our first meeting, but I remember it well now for what developed afterwards.

She was a Vanderbilt girl working part-time as a staffer on the local committee. That was unusual in itself as most Vanderbilt girls, then, didn't work at anything part time—they generally partied on daddy's money.

She had power to her voice, but it was also as alluring as the call of the Bob White in a farm lane. Although skinny and with hardly a hint of breasts, her movements were fluid and as graceful as a ballerina. I was captivated not by what I considered then to be beauty, but by the power and force of her presence. She looked me in the eye when she spoke as though she could read my mind.

When it snowed that night during the meeting, her ride didn't show up. We walked out together while she was trying to bend the ear of this reporter. I'm sure it was not a spark of romance that caused her to ask me for a ride but the hope that she could say more about her cause. Hers would be the last words I heard that evening and therefore the most fresh when I wrote the story for the next day's paper. I quoted her.

Then, on the first day of spring, we had the deepest snow of the season, wet and weighty, burying the early flowers of spring. I was caught at her apartment. The power went out, but we discovered more of each other.

On the last day of March we lay on her couch and watched the statement made by LBJ on television that he would not run for re-election. Ginny began to cry when I said I thought it was only an early April Fool's joke. She was probably one of the few who wept at the announcement. It meant the end of the Great Society and the beginning of an even meaner and more bitter time. She seemed to sense it.

Ginny came to me in the spring of '68 and was the love of that season of the year and that season of my life—as much as Katy would be my summer love.

11

T oby and I are up on the roof early one morning a few days later before the sun arches over the nearest mountain. A stone in the chimney blew down on the metal roof last night. The sound shook me out of bed. I rolled to the floor, grabbed my arsenal, and turned all the spotlights on.

When I went out, the wind was strong. I knew then that it was probably a limb that had broken from a tree and fallen onto the cabin. But with dawn's light, I looked up at the roof and saw the stone that had slid halfway down.

A little mortar mix and we're in the repair business. I find an old trowel in a base cabinet near the sink. I don't know if it's one my grandfather used in building the chimney, but it well could be.

Toby is up here like I was when it was built, so I decide to let him etch his name in a mortar joint with a nail. "T . . . O . . . B . . . Y," I say to help him along. Although he knows many words, his spelling and penmanship are near non-existent. With my help, he scratches the letters out—all in big block upper case. I then add the day, month, and year in numbers.

"Cody, do you know our names sound alike?" he asks.

I lean forward, put an arm around the side of the chimney, and look him in the eyes. "You're right. Cody and Toby have two letters in common."

"In common?"

"The same letters. O and Y."

"Spell your name for me, Cody."

"C . . . O . . . D . . . Y," I say.

"And mine is T . . . O . . . B . . . Y?"

"Right."

"I like that."

"What?" I ask.

"We're almost the same."

I MAKE A DEAL with him. He's to watch the cabin while I'm gone to Nashville, and I'll bring him something back . . . that he'll keep at the cabin. What does he want?

He shrugs his shoulders. "You got me the knife. I don't need anything else."

I think about his arm and accuracy with the walnuts. "What about a baseball and glove?"

"Okay," he says. He looks down and then back up to me. "What's that?"

I clinch my jaw. I want to grab my rifle and run up the mountain and gun down his father . . . a father who has robbed his son of his childhood. Instead, I say, "I'll show you when I get back."

I look at him and smile, and then add, "Don't let them candle-burning creepies bother you."

"They won't. I was sleeping in my room one night when they were burning candles in the other. They didn't know I was there. Portia was there with me. I started moaning and scooted Portia out the door toward the room where they were. They got real quiet. When they seen that moaning possum, they were out the door and gone." He smiles until his teeth show.

MY JEEP'S BIG WHEELS roar over the highway toward Monterey, and it is not until then that Toby's words sink in. He has become almost a man in his tender years because of necessity. He was wrong about us being almost the same. At ten, I couldn't find my way without my father and grandfather. At ten, Toby does—because he has to.

Near Nashville, I-40 widens to three and then four lanes in each direction. The other cars and trucks now have more room to pass my slow-moving vehicle—whizzing by on their way to important destinations. I notice about an equal amount of traffic coming toward me in the lanes on the opposite side of the highway.

Why do they want to go that way and we on this side are in a hurry to go the other way? Everybody is on their way to going someplace else. Going is a life of its own. Going is a diversion to keep us from finding who we are and to whom we belong. What is my place? And who is my family? I'm still working on these. I'm not sure whether the distractions of Toby and his problems and my meeting of Doc and Bill are aids or hindrances in finding the answers.

In my two months in the cabin, I have found that my lack of going—except where I go for my food and supplies—has given me the opportunity to think about who I am and why I am here.

Now, if the traffic coming towards me, and my brethren and I on this side of the road traveling west, would have stayed where we were, we may have been just as well off. Of course, then I couldn't go to this conference in Nashville, and someone on the other side couldn't go to some conference in Knoxville.

All the gas and oil that we burn in these travels is another thing. How many million gallons or barrels do we use every day? There is no conservation here. It's as though we believe there is an inexhaustible supply. I think that we shall run dry at this rate of consumption during the next hundred years. But what do I know? Thoreau thought that society would eat less meat and even quit eating meat.

"Whatever my own practice may be, I have no doubt that it is a part of the destiny of the human race, in its gradual improvement, to leave off eating animals, as surely as the savage tribes have left off eating each other when they came in contact with the more civilized."

His words in *Walden* were written a hundred and fifty years ago, and now we're eating more meat on the average per person than then.

When I compare our sprawling metropolitan areas to the old town squares, there is something to be said for the way of life a century ago. Then merchants lived above or near their stores while the professionals populated houses within walking distance or a short buggy ride of their offices. The farmers and cattlemen lived on the outskirts of town and made their monthly or weekly visits to the town square where they bought their victuals and heard the latest gossip.

Now we choose residences far away from our jobs so that we can forget our employment when the day is over. We say, "It's just a short commute by interstate." This could be ten or a hundred miles.

Past the airport, a sign directs to Briley Parkway. The highway that necklaces Nashville with the Opry complex hanging from it like a diamond pendant is named for the person who was mayor during the spring of 1968—Beverly Briley.

Now the Nashville skyline looms ahead of me, changed dramatically over the past thirty years. It's taller and wider than the spring skyline I remember. Then, the Life and Casualty tower was the tallest, but it did not cast its shadow over the Capitol to the north that sat like a Roman temple on the hill overlooking downtown. Now the skyline looks like something you would see on a space odyssey with sharp spearpoints glistening skyward on the flanks of the Batman Building that reaches up like a serving fork impaled on its stem.

I'M DRESSED IN MOUNTAIN attire of jeans, flannel shirt, and boots when I reach my conference in the convention center. I receive a few sideways glances from the assembled attorneys asking with their eyes what a person like me is doing here. My two months' growth of beard and moustache with my hair reaching past my collar hide me in a head that no one recognizes. It's just as well. I don't want to spend the day explaining to everyone what I'm doing now. Especially, since I don't know what I'm doing now.

I glance around and am thankful that I've gone to the cabin and am no longer counted as one of these beings who cannot loose themselves from beepers attached to their belts at one side and miniature cell phones at the other side. When the lectures begin, my attention is drawn away from time to time when a beeper vibrates a lawyer to life or his phone signals him that he is so important that someone can't live without hearing his voice for a day.

What happens when death snatches him away from the land of beeps and rings? Who will remember him then? Will they just go to the next in line at the law firm for their important question?

Most of these think that their influence is like a cannon ball thrown into a small pond in terms of waves that they make. In reality, we are all like pebbles thrown into the ocean. There are few who will miss us, few that we influenced for good or bad, and few who will wake up at night and think of us. Mainly family—and probably few of them.

WHEN THE LECTURES ARE over for the day and before I go to the hotel, there are three places I must visit. The first two are the ones where I lived in 1968. Then when it's dark, I want to go to Centennial Park and the Parthenon to see if the spirit of Ginny still walks there. Outside, I look up at the sun and know that I only have about two hours before the November night comes down like a window shade.

Out Broadway past 16th Avenue and the home of country music, West End Avenue begins and I pass Vanderbilt on my left and then Centennial Park on my right. I take a glance but don't stop. Another half mile or so should get me to the intersection of Orleans Drive. A left turn takes me to the V where Orleans wraps to the right and where my apartment in the basement of the old Victorian house should be. I park and walk up the familiar steps and beneath the overhanging tree limbs to get a view of the house. I'm greeted by a vacant lot. The steps and walkway lead to a bare spot where grass has not had time to grow. Even the surrounding grass is dead now in November's chill. I look around with my imagination and remember exactly where my door was. I walk there and stare ahead, walking through my apartment in the cells of my memory.

A stray kitten wanders out from the shrubbery, mews, and rubs against my leg before moving on. They've bulldozed it down and replaced it with nothing. I look toward the rear to where my noisy, passionate neighbors were. There wasn't that much distance between us. I turn on my heel to do a full circuit of it. I close my eyes and breathe in deeply. Then I exhale. That's all. It's gone.

I return to my Jeep and head for 8th Avenue South and then to Benton Avenue where my room above the daycare was. I pull to the curbside of the address and am shocked again. It's still here—and still a daycare. They've enlarged the outside play area and fenced it in better. Pea gravel has taken the place of grass. It's very recognizable. I can still touch something that had to do with my past. I stand on the sidewalk and admire it until someone opens the front door and walks down to where I stand. He is black, short, and stocky with a broad face and short hair. His lips barely quiver in a nervous smile while he looks me up and down here. "What do we have here?" he must be asking himself. "A homeless man wanting a meal or a place to stay?"

"I lived here in 1968," I say. "I haven't been back since. I wanted to see what it looks like. If it was even still here."

"That so?" he says in a slightly British accent. "I was born in 1968. Nigeria. I've been here seven years."

We talk here on the sidewalk. He and his wife run a non-profit daycare. Most of his clients are poor and black. Their ancestors for the most part have been here since slavery. This provides the working poor a place of reasonably priced daycare.

"Forty children on average now," he tells me.

I describe the upstairs apartment where I lived.

"Not much different. My wife and I live in the upstairs. What do you do?" he asks.

I can think of nothing else, so I tell him I am a lawyer.

He looks at me again. "We have big problem with government tax people in applying for exempt status. They keep asking more and more questions."

"That's their job," I say. "They can't approve you on the first application. It would prove that they're not needed. They've got to prove their worth, so they send you more paper, more forms. You send it back. They send you more. You play their game for a year until you're broke from lawyer fees, and then they approve you."

He frowns. "You know these people?"

"No. Not personally. I know their kind. Bureaucrats. It's a game."

"Game?" he asks.

"Yes. Big game," I say.

After I convince him that I can not be of any help in his application, I drive off with him still standing on the sidewalk, rubbing his chin, and contemplating what I've just said.

In a few minutes, I park near the Parthenon in Centennial Park. This replica of the one in Greece was built for the state's centennial in 1896, although it was a year late in its completion. This sand-colored monolith with its forty-six Doric columns was meant to express that Nashville was the "Athens of the South" when it was built. Nashville then was a genteel Southern town with more colleges per capita than any other Southern city.

When I came here in 1968, it was similar. It was the second largest town in the state with Memphis being the largest.

Now, though, Nashville has left part of its intellectual Greek heritage and moved on toward that of Rome and its circuses. The city is known now more for its country music, professional football, and professional hockey than for its educational system or colleges. Vanderbilt is still here, along with many smaller colleges, but there's more disappointment that Vanderbilt cannot compete with the state university in football than an appreciation for what it is.

As Athens was home to the first modern Olympic games in 1896 when this Parthenon was underway, so Nashville is now home to the games and diversions that our population lusts for.

When Elvis died, Memphis began its decline in population, and a few years ago Nashville surpassed it. Now Nashville wants to chase Atlanta to become the New York of the South rather than relish its Southern tradition. Thus, the grasping skyline.

Parthenon in Greek means the virgin's place. It was

with this significance that Ginny and I made it our main place of recreation in 1968. We were both virgins—not physically but in spirit and mind—in that year which would try our understanding. I reach to the seat beside me and take my journal for April 1968.

We walked here around the grounds of the Parthenon on the first day of April in the evening and then went inside to view an art show. Ginny was concerned with the national picture. Nixon had won the New Hampshire primary to end Nelson Rockefeller's and George Romney's hopes of gaining their party's nomination. Ginny wanted to leave and go help Eugene McCarthy in his quest now that Johnson was pulling out. The war had not gripped her yet like it had many. She was more concerned with improving the lot of all the citizens in our country.

After April Fourth came with its killing of Martin Luther King in Memphis, it was almost as though Ginny became a different person.

For the next week, I was at the newspaper practically all of the time. I would talk to her in snatches. She holed up in her apartment. "What's happening to the country?" she asked over and over.

A curfew was declared by Mayor Briley for Nashville. "Negroes Riot in North Nashville," a headline in the *Banner* read. The railroad tracks were the dividing line, it seemed. My own paper was making it sound as though it was *them* against *us*. The Tennessee National Guard was called out for patrol duty along with state troopers.

I was in an outer office of the mayor's suite at the Metropolitan Courthouse when the squat mayor walked in and showed all of us from the press that he was carrying a gun. He pulled back his suit coat to reveal a holstered small pistol on his belt. He smashed out a cigarette in an ashtray, looked up at us assembled there for a news conference, and said, "Just in case *they* try to take the courthouse."

I didn't laugh out of respect for my elders, but the thought of the mayor trying to repel any attempted takeover with his pistol seemed far-fetched. From what I observed, the tension was overstated.

After a week, Ginny and I were together again. She clung to me more than ever, always trying to convince me that I had more than an obligation to tell the story. I should be an activist—not just an observer. Her committee had no meetings for the month. King's death ended, for the time being, the sense that black and white could work together here for society's betterment.

Ginny became physical, sexual, as though April would be our last month together. She wanted to make love any place and every place except the normal bedroom. We did it against the cold stone of the Parthenon floor late at night. At the Capitol, we lay together near the tomb of the building's architect on the north side. Ginny said she liked the contrast of cold stone and hot bodies.

She wore long, loose dresses, sandals, and no underwear. When she was in the mood, and she was in the mood often, she would lift her dress and straddle me. She liked being on top. She liked control. I wasn't choosy.

After we had made love in all the out of the way places she could think of, she asked me, "Can you get us into the mayor's office late some night? Can we do it on his desk? You know some of the custodians, don't you?" I went through the motions of acting like I would check it out, but we never made it to the mahogany desk of Beverly Briley.

Then she decided that the grounds around the Parthenon would be our special play area. We started on a project of making love under each tree on the south and east side of the temple. She said it would be our "altar of licentiousness. Sex is our opium and our offering." I told her I thought she was reading too much. We didn't invent sex. But it was as though we thought we had. We both had some experience before we met each other—I suspected that Ginny had a lot more than I—but April was one hot month.

In my journal, I began to make notes that were a code for me in case someone else should ever read my words. I would write "two trees tonight" or "three trees" or sometimes just a "single tree." I accused her of being a nymphomaniac. She smiled and said, "No, a nympho can't be satisfied. I just like to be satisfied real often."

The Capitol steps and Ginny remain in my mind more than the Parthenon. It was just one time at the Capitol—many, very many, near the Parthenon. On that dark evening, a cool breeze lifted up and blew her hair while she was sitting there moving rhythmically. Her hair danced back and I could see the moonlight in her eyes. She stared away to the north and only occasionally looked down toward me. Then she glanced around—and sure that no one was too near—lifted her dress off, raised her arms, tilted her head back, and felt the wind across her body.

Her breasts were as small as plums. She would lean over and tease me with them and then sit back up. Then she finally bent over wrapped her arms around me and began to cry. It killed the mood.

"Why are you crying?" I asked.

"Because soon, I'm going to have to go and leave you behind. I love you, Buffalo Bill Cody Rogers," she said, wiped the tears away, and sat back up. I didn't ask her any more that night. I could tell that was all she wanted to say.

Ginny and I did things in reverse order. The natural progression should be love growing into a sexual relationship, I was always taught. For us, our sexual closeness developed into love as the month grew on. It gave us relief and hope. The year had been hard so far. Ginny revived her optimism in the days ahead until April ended. We did a forest of trees.

I close the journal for April and reach for the one for May, but a patrol car pulls up behind me. I look at my watch. It's late and the officer reminds me. I move on.

THE NEXT DAY WHEN the conference ends, I drive toward my cabin without ever opening May and reliving our last full month together. There's still just a bit of sunshine left when the Jeep begins the climb up Mt. Helen Road toward home. I look to the east and watch large clouds crawl along the mountain peaks on gray-gloved fingers that stroke the tree tops. If they were a bit heavier and it was a few degrees colder, snow would probably be falling. But it's clearing behind me and the sun streaks them with orange and gold.

My two suitcases are filled with my clothes and my purchases for Toby. I splurged. I bought two baseball gloves, a bat, and a dozen baseballs. When I got to thinking about baseball in the mountains, I realized there were no level places around to play. He and I will play catch, but when we miss a pitch, it may go a hundred yards down the mountain before stopping. I can't wait to throw to him. We might get in a little catch before dark.

I call out to him when I enter the porch. "Toby, it's Cody. I'm home. I got you something."

There's no response. He may have had to go home. Everything appears in order as I walk through the living room and look over to the kitchen area. Two kerosene lamps burn on the table. Then I hear a low moaning coming from his bedroom. He's trying to play a trick on me with Portia like he did on the devil worshipers.

I turn the knob and open the door just barely wide enough to peek in. Toby is lying on his bed with his old blanket clutched to his mouth. His body is contorted into almost a circle, his knees are pulled up and his sobs are louder now. He wipes the blanket at his eyes, and even in the dim light I can see they are streaked and red. His face is puffy.

I drop the suitcases and rush to him. "They beat you again?" I ask and pull his shirt up. Then I pull his pants down over his buttocks to see what has happened to him. There are no marks.

He turns to me but his eyes are still closed.

"What's wrong, Toby? What are you crying about?"

He opens his mouth to speak and I see blood inside. I reach down and turn his lower lip out. He's chewed on it until its raw. I run and get a wash cloth and soak it in cold water. I return and sit him up beside me on the bed while I minister to his mouth. "What happened?"

Finally his eyes blink open. There are no whites. "Pa kilt my mama," he says and collapses onto my lap.

12

The deputy sheriff looks over the desk at me while I go through the story as I know it—as it was told to me by Toby before he ran back to his house last night. The deputy then leans back, looks at the ceiling, and rolls a yellow pencil between his fingers. Occasionally his head jerks and he reaches up to his collar to tug at it. While I do my monologue, the jerking head becomes a bit distracting. It's as though I'm talking to a man who just escaped a hanging—but not by much.

Ben Siler killed his wife in a drunken rage. He backhanded her, sending her across the room with her head striking an iron stove. Her neck snapped, and blood ran from her mouth. Toby ran to her and tried to revive her. She never made a move.

When Ben knew for sure she was dead, he pulled her body outside, stacked wood on it, poured gasoline over the wood, and threw a match to it. Toby saw it all. When he burned as much as he could, Ben dug a trench with his tractor's front-end loader and pushed the remains in there. He poured what Toby described as lime on the little bit left and covered it up. He raked gravel and straw on top to make it look as though nothing had happened.

All of that took place within and hour and a half. Toby had a mother one moment. She was dead the next. And there was no remembrance of her before her body had time to cool.

I couldn't keep Toby at my place. "I've got to go back to Pa," he had said. "He'll kill me and you both if he finds me here."

The deputy never looks down when he speaks.

"So the boy tells you this?"

"Yes."

"Did you go look for yourself?"

"No. I've met Ben Siler before. He has a non-human side. He beat his child, killed his wife, and raises marijuana."

The deputy leans over at the mention of the illegal crop. "Marijuana? How do you know? That ten-year-old tell you that too?"

"No. I saw them harvesting it."

"When?"

"About a week ago."

"Why didn't you report it then?"

"I reported the child abuse and nobody did anything. I asked about Toby's schooling and nobody did anything. Why should I think you'd be interested in marijuana?"

"Television, man. Those stations from Nashville and Knoxville like to see stalks of marijuana in the backs of our pickup trucks. We say we confiscated such and such amount. It makes good television. They film us burning it at the dump. We do it every summer and fall."

"Is marijuana more important than a woman getting killed?"

"Naw. But you saw it with your own eyes. The other is hearsay. You wait here. I'm going to talk to an assistant D. A., and see if he wants to talk to you."

I look through the wanted posters for a half hour before the deputy returns with a neat looking young man who appears to have just graduated from law school.

"Mr. Rogers, I'm Stan Goddard. I'm an assistant D.A. Deputy Crawford here tells me you're reporting a murder and a marijuana grower. Can you tell me a little more about it?"

I go through the story as I know it once again. He makes notes on his yellow legal pad and nods as I jabber along.

When I finish, he looks up. "Mr. Rogers, why did you wait a week to report the marijuana?"

I tell him the same thing I told the deputy.

"Well, we have to have a pretty strong case of probable cause to go onto someone's land and do a search. The hearsay of the boy probably won't get us by the judge. But even though you're late with your report on the pot, he might give us a look around on that. Probable cause is a legal term—"

"I know what it is. I've been a lawyer longer than you've been born, I expect."

"You're a lawyer?"

I nod my head.

He looks me over, smiles, and asks, "What are you doing up on the mountain?"

"Trying not to be a lawyer," I say.

"Oh," he says and looks back to Deputy Crawford. "You know the area, don't you, Henry? You know where Siler lives? You know where Mr. Rogers lives?"

The deputy nods at each question. "We'll need more than a piece of paper if we go on Ben Siler's land. Better round up all our people and half of Scott County's."

The assistant turns back to me. "Go on back to your cabin, Mr. Rogers. It will be tomorrow or maybe the next day before we can get a search warrant. We may want you to ride along in the back of a cruiser to point out where you saw the marijuana. Is that okay with you?"

I think back to my encounter with Ben Siler. If we're unsuccessful in finding enough for the law to arrest him, he'll see me in the back of the car and come after me when they're gone. Yet, I suppose if they show up without me, he'd have a pretty good idea who sent them. I shouldn't act like a coward. "Yeah, I'll go. But if he killed his wife, I'm worried about Toby between now and when you go up there.

Can't you do it any sooner?"

"We'll try for tomorrow. If his wife is dead, she ain't going to get any deader. If he meant to hurt or kill the boy, he would've done it by now."

"But the boy's the only witness. Otherwise he could just say his wife died in a freak fall, and he disposed of her body in his own way—the way of the hills."

The assistant shakes his head. "I know, Mr. Rogers. But that's the best we can do."

LATE THE NEXT AFTERNOON, six patrol cars line up on the road at my drive. Two of them are 4-wheel drive Jeep Cherokees. I'm sitting on the porch reading when Deputy Crawford walks toward the door. His head jerks about every six paces as though he's counting off so many feet. He doesn't see me through the screen wire. When I speak just as he is ready to knock, he grabs his collar and tugs where the knot of his tie meets his neck.

"We got the gang up, Mr. Rogers. We're ready to take on Ben Siler. What about you?"

I walk to the door, open it, and step out. "You still want me to go with you?"

"Yep. You know where the weed was. General Goddard is up there and thought it would be good for you to go along. You up to it?"

"Sure. Do I need to take a gun?"

"No. If Ben takes all of us out, you wouldn't have a chance anyway."

I look up the road and see Goddard dressed today in camouflage with a sidearm holstered at his belt. When I get to where Goddard is standing, he hands me a bullet-proof vest and helmet to wear.

"Just in case," he says and helps me to adjust them to my frame and head. I strap on the helmet while he looks at me and smiles.

"Do I look that bad?" I ask.

"You look like that shot of Michael Dukakis driving the tank. You remember that? I was in high school then."

"Yeah, I remember it. I was for him, but that did him

in. Who could imagine him as our commander-in-chief after they saw that dumb photo?"

GODDARD CARRIES A BULL-HORN and walks behind one of the Jeep Cherokees when it enters Ben Siler's drive. Two of the squad cars stay on the road. All of the deputies—eighteen in all—carry shotguns and are wearing the same type of vests as I, except they look better on them. I'm in the back seat of a squad car that is the second behind the Cherokee. Another of the 4-wheel drive vehicles is behind us.

"Ben Siler. This is the law. Come out. We have a search warrant for your place. This is the law," Goddard says over the bull-horn in the direction of Ben's house. We round the curve and I can see fifty yards ahead the bath tub I had seen Toby and his mother at before. No one is there now. A few chickens run when the noise interrupts their feeding near the steps to the gray-boarded house. The big pickup is aimed toward us. The glass is darkly tinted. Beside the house, the blue and gray Ford tractor stands with the front-end loader almost touching the side wall boards. The greenhouse and pot storage shack are not visible from our vantage point.

When we're about twenty-five yards from the door of the house and our pace matches that of molasses in the winter, the truck bounces and starts toward the lead vehicle at about the same pace we're moving. Goddard and the deputies all scramble to take cover behind our four cars on the narrow drive.

"Siler, stop that truck! We have a warrant. We'll blast it!" Goddard says from a squatting position behind the front Cherokee. I lean down to get behind the seat and out of clear view but continue to squint over the seat.

The truck stops, and on the passenger side the window is rolled down. Toby leans out from the waist and waves his arms. "Don't shoot!" he yells as loudly as he can. "It's just me and Pa."

Goddard and Crawford turn to the other deputies and tell them to lower their guns.

"We don't need any blood shed," Goddard says over the speaker, "we just need to talk with you, Ben. Cut the engine and get out. You don't want your boy to get hurt."

My hands are rolled into tight fists now. Ben doesn't care about Toby or else he wouldn't have him in there with him.

Now the truck stops at the same time as our procession. It, alone, mirrors the movement of our caravan. Toby still leans out, his hair waving back and forth as his head jostles from side to side.

"Ben Siler doesn't care about anybody," I tell the driver. "He'll use Toby or anybody else as a shield. Tell them not to shoot. Toby will die, and it'll be my fault."

He nods. "We know what we're doing. We all've been trained in hostage situations."

"You haven't been trained with the likes of Ben Siler," I say, and he nods again. Goddard is still talking through the loudspeaker. Then the truck's driver's side window rolls down and the barrel of a rifle or shotgun angles out toward the sky. The deputies hunker down.

The truck door opens, and Ben Siler steps out. He never points his rifle toward the deputies, but he holds it straight up as though to let us know he isn't cowered by our numbers. Then he bends over and gently lays the rifle down, unbuckles his belt, and lets his sidearms slide to the ground. He takes his coat off. Finally, he unsheathes the big knife and throws it to his side. It sticks in the ground. He holds his hands up to show he has no more guns.

The deputies and Goddard come out from behind the cars and two of them walk toward Ben. I can't hear now as Goddard hands him a paper and speaks to him up close. Then I hear one word from Ben. "Pot!?" He looks toward my car and I can almost read his lips when he asks Goddard where the one is who said he was raising marijuana. His voice is getting louder now and I don't need to read his lips.

He starts walking toward the row of cars, looking in each squad car until he gets to ours. I sit back up straight. I'm not afraid of Ben Siler—at least not now, not with eighteen deputies around. He looks in and at first doesn't recognize me. My hair, beard, and helmet mask me. Then it clicks, and I can tell he knows who I am. He points a finger at me before three deputies step in front of him and herd him back to where Goddard is walking around the house.

Five minutes later, I am standing in the middle of the spot where the shed was that I saw them carry the marijuana into last week. There's nothing here. The shed is gone and so is the covering over the greenhouse. A bare metal frame made of steel piping stands like a skeleton of a great praying mantis between the two hills. But there is no sign of the illegal crop. One of the deputies brings the dog that has been trained to sniff out drugs. He doesn't signal at anything. I'll give it to Ben that he knows his business.

We all walk back toward the house and the convoy of sheriff's patrol vehicles. I walk across an area covered with fresh straw and gravel. This is Toby's mother's grave. I know it, but we traipse across it as though it is no more than a hog lot.

Crawford and Goddard wait until I'm near to ask Ben about his wife. They were here for the marijuana and found nothing. Now they're fishing for a murder. Maybe he'll accidentally say something that will let them bring in their dozers and push up the earth to find the remains of Mrs. Siler.

"Where's your wife?" Goddard asks without hesitation.

"Why? You want to search her too?" Ben asks.

"No. Just curious. With all of us here, I haven't seen her stick her head out the door."

"She caint," Ben says.

"Oh. Why's that?" Goddard asks.

"She's gone to Atlanta for treatment."

"Atlanta? Treatment? What for?" Goddard asks.

Now there are two dogs with the officers. They're still circling the house, the other outbuildings, and over the path we took to the greenhouse.

"She has some kinda cancer. Just found it. I couldn't leave right now. So she's gone by herself. If you don't believe me, ask Toby here," Ben says and looks at the boy who holds on to Ben's belt. His head is cast down.

Goddard gets down on his knees and looks at Toby.

"Son, is that right? Is your mother gone for treatment in Atlanta?"

Toby shrugs his shoulders and then looks up.

"Yep, Mama's gone . . . for treatment. Cancer. Atlanta. It's just me and Pa now."

THEY LET BEN GO his way. When we're back to the drive to my cabin, Goddard retrieves my bullet-proof vest and helmet and takes me aside.

"That second dog we had out there wasn't looking for marijuana. That one's trained to sniff out bodies. The handler took him all over the plot but didn't get any hits. I told him to stand over that area you described where the fresh straw and gravel were. Nothing. If Siler's wife's body is there, he's done a great job disguising it to where the dog couldn't sniff it out."

"He's cunning," I say. "What can you do now?"

"We'll check all the Atlanta facilities that treat cancer to see if Mrs. Siler is down there. Ben couldn't give us a name of the place. But we can't arrest him for that."

"Can't you go in and doze up that area and see what you find?"

"You know better than that, Mr. Rogers. The boy says she's in Atlanta. Now we don't even have a ten-year-old who would be a witness. Until he's ready to turn on his daddy, we don't have anything to go on."

"He's scared," I say. "If we had him away from his father, Toby might tell you the truth like he did me."

Goddard shakes his head. "I don't know. Children have wild imaginations. Maybe she's dead and maybe she's not. Besides, there's no statute of limitation on murder." He starts to walk back to the cruiser but turns a few paces away. "I'd keep an eye out for a while if I were you, Mr. Rogers. If Ben is a killer, he probably wouldn't mind adding your scalp to his collection."

I wave him away, but when he's about to open the door to the car, I yell after him, "If I die under mysterious circumstances, you better know it's murder!"

Goddard nods his head. Then they all leave, and I'm alone here with my nearest neighbor—nearest whatever—being Ben Siler. Why wouldn't Toby tell them the truth?

AN HOUR BEFORE SUNDOWN I take my rifle, attach the scope, and place six cartridges in my pocket. I strap on my .45 and holster my knife on the opposite side of my belt. If the law of the hills predominates, I will take the law into my own hands and deliver Toby from a certain death at the hands of his father. It's just a matter of time before Ben kills him too. Once he starts to think that Toby is the only witness, the boy grows older, and the killing still gnaws at his memory. It's better that I be arrested for murder and put away than for Toby to die so young.

I walk back up the road, looking through the scope occasionally to be sure I can sight a hundred yards away. I head off up the hill from where I spied them carrying the marijuana last week. My breath now comes in great heaves as my body adjusts not only to the heavy exertion but to the effect of becoming a killer.

When I lie down on the slope in the bed of leaves, only the hulk of the piping of the deserted greenhouse and one outbuilding are in view. Through the scope of my rifle, I can see three chickens pecking along the path where the fresh straw is. I put the cross-hairs on one and insert a bullet into the chamber of the rifle. There would not be enough chicken left to make a cup of soup if I shot her with this rifle.

In a half hour, Toby comes around the curve in the lane carrying something in his hands. I look through the scope when he stops and kneels at the spot of the gravel and straw. I take the bullet out so that there will be no accident where I kill Toby. He has a wooden bowl like the one he left me with the nuts and persimmons. There's something red in it. It's too late for flowers, and then I make out that it's a red ribbon that he places on his mother's grave—and the bowl with walnuts.

Then he sits there crosslegged with his head drooping down until Ben rounds the curve and sees him. The father walks quickly over to Toby, stops, and takes in the scene. Then he kicks the bowl to the side of the lane and into the woods. He picks up the ribbon and wads it into his pocket. Toby stands and turns when Ben orders him back to the house. Ben shoves Toby in the back and the boy stumbles to his knees. Then he gets up and runs off toward the house.

Ben kicks the remaining walnuts from the grave and starts to walk back toward the house himself. His back is a broad target. I bring the rifle and scope up to where the cross-hairs are on the middle of his back. My breathing is heavy and the cross-hairs dance with the trembling of my hands. Before he gets to the turn, I take a deep breath, center on the target of his back, and squeeze the trigger.

Click. Nothing happens. I took the bullet out and forgot to put it back in. Ben pauses and looks around as though he heard the sound of the firing mechanism. Then he walks on out of sight before I can load.

13

The remainder of November slides by at a snail's pace. Each night I go to sleep with one hand on my .45. I wake, it seems, every fifteen minutes, awaiting the inevitable confrontation with Ben Siler. Will he kill me without waking me? Or will he terrorize me and torture me before he does me in? Those are the only questions. Already the torture and terror are apparent.

I stay at the cabin more than ever, afraid to venture far away, for I know he is a much better mountain man than I. My trips into Jamestown for groceries and supplies are hurried runs. I haven't visited Doc Jordan and Bill all month. They must think I have forgotten them. I haven't. I'm just afraid my cabin won't be here when I get back if I'm gone too long.

My concentration when I try to read has fled, so I don't read much. I flip through my collection of *National Geographic* and look at the pictures. I haven't read any more of my journals from 1968 since my trip to Nashville. If Ginny could see me now, I'm afraid my appearance would frighten her. When I look in a mirror, my hair and beard remind me of pictures I've seen of Rasputin or the last days of Howard Hughes. I should trim my hair and shave a little before I take on all the characteristics of the mountain man I'm beginning to look like. At least I do trim my fingernails and toenails. I wash and bathe as well as I can. My water heater on the roof is of little use during these days when dirty steel wool scours the sky and rolls up from the river.

When I pulled the trigger and the chamber was empty, I knew that I had deserted the precepts of my valley heritage of letting the authorities handle matters and had taken on the law of the hills—settling our own differences. Ben

Siler is turning me into someone I don't want to be. The cabin and mountains were supposed to be a refuge from the evils of the gluttonous and materialistic society. I came to the cabin to contemplate why my dear Katy had left me so soon and to figure out God's scheme in this matter. It was to be a period of reflection and renewal. Instead my cabin is my cell of solitary confinement where my mind cannibalizes itself, eating up all the good morals that I ever had and swapping them for a rule of might. I want out of here, but I don't want to be driven out by someone like Siler. I have too much pride for that.

I try to put Toby out of my mind and imagine that he's doing okay. If I imagined anything else, I would go crazier than I am now.

I so fear that Siler will do something to my cabin that I met my children for Thanksgiving at the Holiday Inn in Crossville rather than have them come here. I listened for word from them that I was on the way to being a grandfather but there was no such forthcoming news. Both my children asked me whether I'd had any visitors. I stared at them. Did they know about Toby and Ben? No. They couldn't have. I told them about the teenage devil worshipers, and we all shared a laugh over our turkey and dressing.

Today I am going to see Doc and Bill. I will not tolerate being a prisoner any longer. And soon, I will go back to the mountain and speak to God again. The angel he sent me has Satan for his father.

Before I go, I determine to read a bit of *Walden* just to show myself that I can put my mind to good use rather than fretting with worry. A short passage strikes me:

"We read that the traveller asked the boy if the swamp before him had a hard bottom. The boy replied that it had. But presently the traveller's horse sank in up to the girths, and he observed to the boy, 'I thought you said that this bog had a hard bottom.' 'So it has,' answered the lad, 'but you have not got halfway to it yet.'"

This reminds me of how Toby always says, "It's not

very far," to someplace that I find later is a half day's journey. It also brings to my mind that perhaps I have not
reached the bottom of the miry pit into which I've stepped in
taking on Ben Siler. What I will find at the bottom, I don't
know. I close the book, put on my coat, and head out the
door to go down the mountain to see Doc Jordan and Bill
Purcells.

       NO ONE IS SITTING outside the nursing home when
I arrive. The chill and dampness have driven even the har-
diest indoors.
       The receptionist looks up when I ask for the room
number of Doc Jordan or Bill Purcells.
       "Are you a relative?"
       "No. I live nearby and have been reading to them
when I get a chance. I'm Cody Rogers."
       "You live on the mountain, don't you?" she says and
lets her eyes roll up and down my body. I suspect she is
saying it more from my appearance than knowing who I am.
       "Yes, up off of Mt. Helen Road," I say.
       "I'm sorry, Mr. Rogers. Doc Jordan and Bill Purcells
are no longer with us."
       "What? They both die?"
       "Mr. Purcells passed on . . . ," she says and looks
down at her calendar. She tells me the early November date
and I remember that was when I was gone to Nashville.
"Doc Jordan had me to try to contact you. But you don't
have a phone listed and no one wanted to go up to the mountain to find you. Doc thought you might want to come for
Bill's funeral."
       I nod my head. "Yes, yes, I would have. If I had
known."
       She taps her pen on the desk.
       "What about Doc Jordan? Is he still here?"
       "No. He's no longer with us either."
       "He die too?"
       "No. He moved back to Crossville."
       "He get better that quickly? Or did he transfer to
another nursing home?"

She looks up and down the hallway where wheel-chairs are moving by slowly.

"No. Doctor Jordan was only here because he wanted to be near Bill Purcells. You don't know their story, do you?"

I shake my head. "No, I definitely don't."

"Bill Purcells worked for Doctor Jordan all his adult life. Everything—yardman, handyman, cook, driver—you name it, and he did it. When Bill got sick and bad off enough to come to the nursing home, Doc wouldn't let him come by himself. He moved into a room here. He knew Bill didn't have long to live."

"You mean you can live here if you don't need to?"

"Honey, if you gots the money, we have the rooms."

She takes a phone call while I register this new information.

"Is Doc Jordan really a medical doctor?" I ask when she gets done with the call.

"Oh, yes. Rich. No family. Just him and Bill. Did you know Bill was deaf?"

"No, not really," I say. "I knew he never talked to me, but I thought that might be some other kind of condition. He always looked at me when I read."

"He was reading your lips. Doc could sign to him. They were real close. Best friends over the years."

"Do you have Doc Jordan's address? I'd like to go see him."

IN CROSSVILLE, I DRIVE out to one of the resorts on a private lake and stop in another circular drive. This is where Doc Jordan lives according to the nursing home receptionist. I should have called before my visit.

When I ring the doorbell, I'm greeted with a voice over the intercom. I recognize it as Doc's.

"Doc, it's Cody Rogers from Mount Saint Helens. I've come to read to you." I can hear the laughter on the other end, and in a minute the door opens. Doc Jordan stands before me with a pipe in his hand, dressed in a shirt, tie, and matching trousers. A vest of dark red and gray plaid sets him off as a retired professional.

"Captain Rogers—Cody, I mean—come into my study and have a shot of winter cheer."

He leads me through a spacious house that is dark for the most part. He must at one time have done a lot of entertaining. I glance into the dining room and see a table that could seat sixteen. We walk on through to a study and sunroom toward the rear. There's a desk, a chair behind it, two in front of it, and walls lined with book shelves. His desk is heaped up with letters, cards, and envelopes still unopened. To the side, a computer screen has gone into saver mode with fish swimming as though in an aquarium.

"I got behind on my correspondence while I was with Bill at the nursing home. They told you he passed on, didn't they?" he asks and I nod. "The nursing home called and said you were coming to visit."

"You're really a good actor in addition to being a good doctor," I say and smile. "You look a lot different without that cap pulled sideways on your head."

He laughs. "Well. I had to fit in. You must fit in, but you have to remember who you really are too. Didn't want them to know I was a real doctor. Everybody would want an opinion. I was just there for Bill. He was a great guy. He took care of me for so many years that I couldn't desert him in the end. There's a time for turning loose and moving on though. When he died, I knew it was time to come back and be who I really was."

We talk and I have a glass of wine. He tells me his life story. He has delivered more babies than he can count. The letters and cards are from former patients wishing him well or informing him of their becoming grandparents or such. He's created a large and distant family.

Finally, he asks about Toby. "How's that boy who wanted to know about my cap and the color of my hands?"

I tell him the sad story.

"Well, Cody, you just have to be ready. God's not through with you yet. There's going to be some way that you can help that boy. I don't know how, when, or what. But in the meantime, you've got to take care of yourself. You said your wife died. You've got to move on."

I look out onto his broad yard that tapers down to the lake, now slate-like in the gray day. "What about going back, Doc? Do you think it would be wise for me to try to find this woman I was in love with thirty years ago before I ever met Katy?"

He takes a draw on his pipe. "That's a tough one, Cody. She's probably married. She may be dead. You may have been just a fling to her. Your imaginations now may be very one-sided."

"Yeah," I say. "Maybe delusional."

He blows out a puff of smoke that hangs above us before dissipating. "However, if you're willing to accept that those things may have occurred, I'd say go for it!" He smiles broadly.

IN CROSSVILLE, I STOP at a drug store and buy an assortment of toiletry items—cologne, toothpaste, and shampoo— before stopping at a motel. For two hours, I sit in a bathtub full of hot water and soak until my skin wrinkles and softens. It's so good to have a hot bath when you haven't had one for several months. Oh, for the physical pleasures of indoor plumbing. I check the phone book and find a hair stylist who is still in. I go for a haircut and trim of my beard.

After my hair is fixed and I look in the mirror, I decide I now look more like a college professor than a madman—if there's any difference. I'm ready to go find my Ginny.

First, I stop and buy me two new outfits to wear when I go on my journey. With clothes shopping done, I stop at a convenience store before going back to the motel. I buy a dozen Krispy Kreme donuts.

Back at the motel, I soak long into the night in the tub that I keep refilling with hot water, watch country music videos on cable television, and eat the whole dozen donuts. I have fallen into the decadent life-style of our age—but just for one night.

Finally in bed, I fall into a delicious sleep. It's time to move on.

14

now dusts the mountain like powdered sugar the morning after I get back to the cabin. I have a few things to put in order before I leave to find Ginny. One of the first things I have to decide is where to look first. In 1968, when she left Nashville at the end of the third week of June, she was going home to Louisville, Kentucky. She left on a Greyhound bus on the day before summer began. Our romance began and ended in the spring.

I go and pick up the May journal. I didn't keep one for June, 1968, because things spiraled out of control too quickly. But during my first week away from Ginny, I did go back to the May journal and wrote in the blank pages the happenings of June—at least my version of them. Ginny may have disagreed.

After the curfew was lifted and things began to return to normal in Nashville, Ginny went on a new binge of sorts. Her committee disbanded for the time being. She dropped out of Vanderbilt and became a letter writer. She wrote to every political figure and general for whom she could obtain addresses. "Stop the war!" was her message, but she said it with more verbiage. I knew because she often showed me the letters before she mailed them. She would ask for my comments and editorial opinion but ended up writing them the way she wanted.

Her attitude toward me seemed strained in one sense but closer than ever in another. She asked me to run away to Canada to avoid the draft one day. The next she asked me to go with her to join McCarthy in his campaign. And if I didn't like McCarthy, she was willing to go with Bobby Kennedy. Anyone, she said, was preferable to Humphrey or Nixon.

When she was not writing her letters, she was tutoring male students who were in danger of losing their student deferments from the draft because of their grades.

When I declined her invitations to go to Canada or hit the campaign trail, she urged me to be more outspoken in my writing for the newspaper about the war. I tried to explain that the Metropolitan Council, from where I mainly reported, had nothing to do with war policy. Only if the Viet Cong invaded West End Avenue and Centennial Park would the council and Mayor Briley take a stand. Ginny did not like my attempt at humor. Where did I stand on the war? she wanted to know.

I explained that the Rogers family had given a son, a brother, an uncle, or a cousin in every war since the one that began our country. Our land grant in East Tennessee was ours partly because of some ancestor's service in the Revolutionary War. So, it would be difficult to run away. I still had my student deferment, but I wouldn't for long if I didn't return to school. I was struggling with whether I should return to law school, stay in Nashville and await my inevitable draft notice, or run away with Ginny. I was too young to make such deep decisions, but I had to, eventually.

Meanwhile, Ginny and I continued to frequent Centennial Park on every night that it wasn't raining, or she would hear about other out-of-the-way places where we should make love. I was a willing participant in all of this. It held us together. We would argue in the afternoon, and then make wild love late at night. It was quite a relationship. I began to think I was becoming more like my first noisy neighbors.

With the coming of June and my knowledge that law school would be starting back up in Knoxville, I finally told her I was going back to school. I could serve my country better with education than I could in Vietnam or in Canada. Maybe someday I would be one of the politicians Ginny was writing to. I asked her to go with me. And I think she was seriously considering it until Bobby Kennedy was shot in that kitchen of the hotel in Los Angeles.

With that, Ginny decided she would have to be more of an activist. She would join up with some alternative campaign and do battle with the establishment. She was hurt when I wouldn't join her. So, on the day before summer began, she headed to Louisville and I drove alone to Knoxville to begin summer school.

I saw Ginny only one time after that. There were never any letters or phone calls. When I saw her—and I wasn't for sure it was her—it was on a television screen in August of the same year. The scene was the confrontation between the police and the students and protestors at the Democratic convention in Chicago.

While I sat and watched from the safety of my room near campus in Knoxville, I saw the police pulling a girl along by the hair in Chicago where all the protestors were shouting, "The whole world is watching!" The camera closed in for a shot, and I believed that was Ginny they were throwing in the police wagon to take to jail. I got down on my knees in front of the screen and watched. She was defiant until the end, sticking her arm out the door until it was shoved back in and the door slammed.

"Ginny, Ginny, Ginny!" I cried over and over that night. I stayed up until the station went off the air, hoping they would show that scene again so I could be sure. They never did.

I put the journal away and start packing. With Doc Jordan's encouragement, I will begin my search for Ginny. I will be gone for up to a week and pray that my cabin will still be standing when I return. If it's not, I figure it's God's way of telling me I shouldn't be here. Before I go, though, I will walk to the mountain top one more time to talk to God about all of this. I will see if he sends me another angel. With December's cold, there should be no worry about snakes or other cold-blooded creatures. This time I will fast for a day before I go to the top, but I will carry with me two

Thermos bottles of coffee and my .45 pistol holstered to my side. I think God knows why.

Strapped to my back are two sleeping bags and my rubber hip waders. I begin my walk at noon. Darkness will come an hour and a half sooner than it did when I went before. It's too cold to sun myself on the rock in mid-stream of Big South Fork. The water feels like flowing ice through my waders. I'm careful of my steps. A fall would plunge me into hypothermia.

The leaves are fallen from the trees—skeletons reaching toward Heaven. Up and ahead, I get a better view of the rocky ledge that projects out over the gorge. It will be my home for tonight. I have never been there in winter. I expect the view to be about the same but with less vibrant colors. I walk better in the biting cold than I did in the warmth of the last trip. I wear enough clothes to keep me warm as long as I'm walking, and I build up a thin lathering of perspiration under my layering.

The sounds I hear are my own breathing and the creaking of the cold trees when they're shaken by the wind coming up from the valley. Squirrels here aren't afraid as most of this area is not open to hunting. I hear them in the leaves as they're scavenging for nuts to put away for the winter. If I knew how to interpret their gathering, I'm sure there would be some sign as to how severe the coming winter will be.

When I'm to the place where Toby stepped out of the woods and saved me from the snakes on my last trip, I catch myself looking behind every tree as though he will be there again. It's like when Katy died. I would look at something and turn to tell her about it, but she wouldn't be there. It happened over and over. Or I would say to myself, "I'll have to tell Katy about that when I get home."

I take off the load from my back and make my bed for the night. The wind dies down. I crawl to the ledge on my hands and knees and look over. There's no one for as far as the eye can see. There are no hawks. In the distance three dark crows fly to a pine tree on a bluff.

The sun goes down without the beauty of a fall sunset. It's as though it is snuffed out by a gray glove of an unseen hand, and with the other hand the canopy of blackness is pulled up from the east.

I honor my goal of keeping one Thermos of coffee for the morning but go ahead and finish the first. When I've found a short piece of an old log that I will use for a pillow, I settle down to prayer and meditation. I close my eyes for a half hour or so and just listen to the blood flow through my veins and feel the cold air search for my exposed skin. There is no song of insects. They rest, awaiting the resurrecting spring.

When I open my eyes, the night is fully upon me. The sky is clear like before. There are stars but no moon. This brings out the stark contrast between the pinpoints of light and the black velvet they rest upon. If anything, the winter sky is more sharply defined than the fall and summer sky. Perhaps it is the lack of moisture in the atmosphere. It's as though I'm surrounded, and I could reach out and touch them—just as Katy tried to do on that night in the hospital when she reached for the moon.

Now I begin to talk out loud in case God can't hear my thoughts.

"God, Father, Yahweh, Allah, the Great Spirit, or whatever men have called you through the ages. I know you are the one and only God. You have made me. You have a plan for me. I need to have you speak to me and tell me that plan. Where do I go from here?

"I have lost Katy. I have lost the angel you sent me—Toby. But I'm sure you know his name. I have lost my buddy Bill Purcells, and my friend Doc Jordan has gone back to his home in Crossville.

"Father, I came here to ask You about Ginny."

I stop speaking for a minute. What does God think about me forgetting about Katy so soon and talking about another woman? I'll ask Him.

"Father, do you think it's okay for me to think about Ginny this soon after Katy's leaving? August to December. It's been five months if you count both August and December. Yet, this is just the first week of December and she died pretty late in August.

"Anyway, Father, should I begin to look for Ginny? I've got my bags packed, and I'm ready to take off tomorrow unless You tell me differently."

I pause and listen for an answer. I cannot hear the stars singing. I only hear a slight breeze lapping against my ears.

"Father, Doc Jordan said to 'go for it.' He's a good man. I think he's right. You know I'm having a hard time with all these people being taken from me, and I feel a little guilty about Ginny. I left her as much as she left me. That was a long time ago, and I know we both have changed. But we had something back in 1968.

"She and I were close. Well, I guess You know that if you saw us in Centennial Park. But I've asked your forgiveness for any sexual indiscretions we had a long time ago. Remember?

"Now, I want to find her because I remember that I did love her. Is that okay?"

The sound of my voice seems to evaporate as soon as the words are spoken. I stare up into the vastness of the universe and wonder where God is hiding. Is He listening to some child's prayer instead of mine? A hungry man somewhere? A woman giving birth? Someone more worthy? Am I being selfish to bring this to Him now when there are so many more things in the world that I should be praying for?

I close my eyes again and remember the passage from *Walden* where Thoreau is telling about each person marching to his own drummer.

"Let him step to the music which he hears, however measured or far away. It is not important that he should mature as soon as an apple tree or an oak. Shall he turn his spring into summer?"

Shall I turn my spring into summer? Ginny was my love of spring and Katy my summer love. They were different and both very important to me in their own ways. Now I'm in the fall of my life without either. Katy—I can't bring back. Ginny?—well, that's the question.

Then I remember that Ginny always wanted me to read to her from the Song of Solomon when I read the Bible aloud. She'd pick out the passage, point to it, lie back in my arms, and tell me to read. She told me this was my love song to her.

"Behold, thou art fair, my love; behold, thou art fair; thou hast doves' eyes within thy locks: thy hair is as a flock of goats, that appear from Mount Gilead.

"Thy teeth are like a flock of sheep that are even shorn, which came up from the washing; whereof every one bears twins, and none is barren among them.

"Thy lips are like a thread of scarlet, and thy speech is comely: thy temples are like a piece of pomegranate within thy locks.

"Thy neck is like the tower of David builded for an armoury, wherein there hang a thousand bucklers, all shields of mighty men.

"Thy two breasts are like two young roes that are twins, which feed among the lilies.

"Until the day break, and the shadows flee away, I will get me to the mountain of myrrh, and to the hill of frankincense.

"Thou art all fair, my love; there is no spot in thee."

Then she would turn her head to me, open her eyes, and ask, "Do you want to watch the deer feeding among the lilies?"

WHEN I AWAKE THE next morning my breath has frozen in crystals on my beard. I bring my hand up, wipe it across my face, and look at the speckles of ice as they melt. Before I turn over, I raise my head to look down toward where my booted feet make towers beneath the sleeping bag. There are no snakes, but I want to be sure.

The sun rises above a thin layer of misty clouds. The morning star is just fading out against the blue sky. There is no snow, but a deep frost that rode up on the mist of the stream far below rests on everything that hasn't been stroked by the sun's rays. Only the dark trees escape the artistry of the crystals. They stand in formation with their roots dug in beneath the white blanket.

I turn over and sit up in one motion. Beside me is the Thermos of hot coffee. I pour a cup and scoot to the edge where I can see the Big South Fork beneath me snaking through the gorge and carrying a shroud of fog along its spine. I turn to the north and look in the distance at the range of hills rolling away like a gray washboard. Somewhere beyond my sight is Louisville and Ginny.

I HAVE FINISHED MY bottle of coffee by the time the roof of my cabin rises to eye level. I rest for a minute against a tree before walking the final quarter mile. When I turn to walk again I begin to hear thumps in nearby trees. A few more paces and another thump. Squirrels dropping husks of nuts, I believe. But then when I get to where I have a view of the front steps of my cabin, I see the source of the noise.

Toby is sitting there and springing his sling-shot into life every few seconds. Pebbles sail through the air to the nearby trees in his practice. As I near, I'm sure it's him. He has on a frayed old toboggan and a large corduroy jacket that hangs loosely to his hips. His hair snakes out from beneath his head covering.

He smiles when he sees me. "You been to the mountain again, Cody?"

15

My packed suitcases have remained in my bedroom for the past two weeks since my return from the mountain. My search for Ginny must wait. Toby's return signals to me that I must stay with him for as long as he needs. When another disaster happens and he runs back to his father, I will go to Louisville. But for the Christmas season, I cannot desert my young boy.

His mother's death has not come up at all in conversation. A therapist might say he is repressing it. I fear if I bring it up, I will lose him to another run for home. Instead, we spend our time on other things. A half dozen baseballs have been lost down the ravines as Toby and I play catch and I let him bat the balls. We still have another six that haven't been lost. He has quite an arm, as I suspected when I saw him hit the squirrel before. With the right training, Toby has the prospects for a college scholarship.

To that end, we spend hours each day studying the books I have bought. He begins to read and spell better. He loves books. When he learns that the words come to life when he knows how to read, he devours every one he can find at his reading level.

The next time we're in Jamestown at the used bookstore, Toby finds one that he asks me about.

"Cody! This one has your name on it," he says and points to a picture storybook about Buffalo Bill Cody.

"Yeah, Buffalo Bill was a performer who traveled the world putting on wild west shows," I tell him. "Sometimes, I think I was named for him. My mother called me Buffalo Bill Cody Rogers when I missed supper-time and she had to yell from the back stoop for me."

"Anybody else call you that?" Toby asks.

I pause and think back. "Only Ginny," I say in a whisper.

"Ginny? Who's that?"

"A friend of mine from a long time ago."

He turns the pages and his eyes open wide. "Wow! Look at those horses . . . and that pistol," he says and points to two pages of colored drawings. He brings the book up near his eyes and studies the gun. "I've seen a gun like this, Cody. You know where?"

I take the book from him and look at the illustration of the .44 caliber Navy Colt revolver that's shown. It became popular in the Civil War. "No. Where?" I ask.

"In that cave I told you about. Can we go there and let me show you?"

"Toby, there are no caves in the Big South Fork area. But let's get you the book, and I'll walk with you tomorrow to where you *think* the cave is."

ONE THING ABOUT TOBY is that he never forgets my promises. The next morning we are on the trail early seeking what he says is a cave. It's cold and the clouds roll in at treetop level. We take three biscuits with bacon, a pocket full of Tootsie Rolls, two Dr. Peppers, and a Thermos of coffee. When Toby says, "It's not too far," I know to pack lunch.

An hour later, a few snowflakes filter down. We take turns catching them on the back of our hands and looking at the crystal formations. "They say that no two snowflakes are exactly alike," I tell him.

Toby turns and wrinkles up his forehead at me. "How do they know? I've seen some heaping big snows. Have they looked at every flake?"

I shrug. He has a point. There's a "heap" of snow that falls around the world during a year. Maybe each snowflake has a twin some place like they say about humans. Or maybe the old saying is just speculation, the same as saying everyone has different fingerprints. We will never know for sure until we examine every one—an impossibility.

In another hour, the snow has fallen enough that we

are leaving tracks in it where we step. Toby puts up his hand and stops.

"There it is," he says and points off to the right.

I look but see nothing. "Where?" I ask.

He takes my hand and leads me to where I finally see a small hole where the face of a rock cliff meets the ground. Brush and dead weeds cover most of the opening. But even when Toby clears that away, the hole is barely big enough for a man to squeeze through.

"Come on," he says and slips through the opening that he says he's familiar with.

I take off my coat and bulky sweater and am able to barely slide through. The opening drops about four feet and then angles off to a level floor. Still, the ceiling is only high enough to crawl on hands and knees. I follow Toby's beam from his flashlight into a chamber that widens and is of greater height. I shine my own flashlight around and guess the room to be about the size of a two-car garage.

None of the light from the opening enters this room. I put my hands down and take off my gloves. The floor is dry. I shine my light around the base of the whole room and then to the top to be sure we don't have any animal companions. Nothing but shades of gray and brown.

"I don't see any gun," I tell Toby.

"It's in the next room," he says.

"I don't see any *next* room," I say.

He shines his light to the far side and now I see another small opening at the base of the wall. He crawls over and slithers through. I follow on hands and knees with my yellow light stabbing at the darkness.

At the opening, I stick an arm in but can't reach the far side. I lie on my back and put my head into the hole first. I wiggle into the passage until my shoulders touch both sides. Then my claustrophobia takes over and I begin to imagine that I will become wedged into this opening with Toby on the far side. He can't go for help. We both die a slow death, and nobody ever knows. I'm still moving, though, inch by inch. I drop my coat and sweater because they're too large to pull through.

Another foot and my head emerges. Toby shines the light in my eyes and laughs. He is straddling my head.

"You look funny, Cody. I hope you don't grow anymore in here or you won't be able to get out."

The same thought has struck me. My nose scraped the top of the passage with my head flat on the floor. I hope I can get into the same position to exit. My torso emerges, and then Toby reaches under my arms and helps to pull me through.

I sit up and catch my breath. "When we leave, you're going first, Toby. If I get stuck, you can go for help." I check the base and ceiling of the room with my flashlight from where I sit. The room is about twice as big as the first one we were in. It's the size of a small apartment. I check further. No bats, no snakes, no noise except our breathing. It's cool but not as cold as outside. "Are there more rooms?"

"Yeah, but the way to them is too steep for me," Toby says. "Maybe you can try it."

I lean back against the wall still seated. "No. If it's too hard for you, I know I couldn't do it. Where's the gun you were talking about?"

Toby starts to walk toward the far side. His light flashes off the wall and I see the opening he spoke of—a small black hole. Then his beam catches a pile of rags at the base of the wall that I hadn't noticed when I shined my light around. He motions to me. "Come over here, Cody."

I stand and walk to where he is. We both shine our lights to the small heap of cloth.

"There's the gun," he says and moves the light just a few inches.

At first it looks like a piece of wood, but when I take a few steps closer, I can see the dust-covered pistol lying about a yard from the cloth. "Have you ever picked it up?" I ask.

"No. I was afraid he wouldn't want me to."

"Your father?" I ask.

"No. Him," he says and shines the light at the other end of the cloth. The teeth of an open jaw of a skull grin at me and I step back. I drop my flashlight, and it begins to roll toward the bones. I grab it before it gets there.

Toby laughs. "Scary, ain't it?"

I think I hear something and turn my light around to drive out the invaders, but there's nothing. My heart races and I drop to my knees. "Isn't it?" I say.

"What?" Toby asks.

"Don't say, 'Ain't it?' Say, 'Isn't it?' "

"Oh. Scary, huh?"

"Quite. Why didn't you tell me about this before?"

"I thought you wouldn't come."

"You were probably right."

I scoot closer to the skull and notice the shreds of cloth are from a military jacket. I can't make out whether it's blue or gray. Then I pick the gun up. It's just what Toby said it was—a .44 caliber Navy Colt revolver. Then I look at the cloth again. It must be blue. The North had more of this kind of weapon. I bring the gun and the flashlight up to my eyes. The pistol is still loaded. Only one round has been fired.

I shine my light on the skull and gently rub my hand around the cold bone. Then I see the hole on the right side. The left side is blown away.

"Who is it?" Toby asks.

"A soldier from about a hundred and forty years ago."

"Wow! Did they have a war in this cave?"

"Probably not. He could have been coming across the mountain and got lost. Or he might have been running from some Rebs. Or who knows? He must have climbed into this cave and couldn't get out. Maybe he didn't have any light."

"Did the Indians kill him?"

"No. It looks like he killed himself."

"Why?" Toby asks.

"He couldn't stand being alone. He thought he couldn't get out after he got in."

"Yeah," Toby says, "Sometimes I feel that way."

I look up to where he stands next to me and see his mouth turned down at the corners. His eyelids flicker in the soft light. I run my hand over the scrap of cloth. Maybe this soldier left some identification. Even a hundred and forty years later a descendent might like to know what happened to their great-grandpa. There is nothing more than a few scraps of leather—probably from a belt or cartridge case. A cluster of cartridges lies in the dust beneath one leather piece. I pick them up.

"You reckon he was too fat to get back out?" Toby asks.

I shrug my shoulders. "I wish he could tell us. Have you found anything else in here?"

"Some arrowheads and a big cat skull."

This time I don't question his accuracy. "What did you do with them?"

"I took them to my house."

I nod my head. It's against the law to remove Indian artifacts, especially in the Big South Fork area that is federal land. But I'm not sure that we're on Big South Fork land. We may be on lumber company property.

"How big was the cat?" I ask.

Toby makes his hands into a ball big enough to indicate a panther or some pre-historic cat. "Cody, why were the Indians and cat in here?"

"They probably weren't at the same time. They were just passing through like this soldier here. Indians generally lived in the lowlands. They came to the mountains on hunting trips or when they were run out of the valleys by the whites. There's a trail nearby that runs from east to west. They may have come in to get out of the weather or to sleep. I don't think they would've lived in here."

"And the cat?"

"Probably just looking around. A cat should find its way out though. Maybe it came in here to die."

"And they were all just passing through?" Toby asks.

"Yeah," I say and put a piece of the uniform in my pocket.

"Are we just passing through, Cody?"

I look back up at Toby. Kids can ask the toughest questions. "Yeah, we're all just passing through. But we can enjoy that passing a whole lot," I say, reach my hand in my pocket, and hand him a Tootsie Roll.

For the next two hours, we talk about Indians, the Civil War, and pre-historic cats. We take turns burning our flashlights so we both don't lose power at the same time. We have lunch here with the soldier—biscuits, bacon, coffee, and Dr. Pepper. For a while we both turn our lights off and take in the darkness. I ask Toby to imagine what it would have been like. But I find he doesn't like the darkness for very long. He already knows what it's like.

"When people die, Cody, where do they go?"

"Are you asking about someone in particular?" I ask.

"In particular? What does that mean?"

"Are you asking about anybody you know?"

"My mama," he says and takes my hand.

"Your mother is in a better place, Toby."

WHEN WE GET BACK to the cave's entrance with the gun and scrap of cloth, a snow storm has struck for sure. It is drifting down into the opening to where I can't get a grip to pull myself out. I can stand with my head out but I keep sliding back in. I push Toby out, and with him pulling me, I manage to crawl out into the white forest. I put my sweater and coat back on. The snow blows into our eyes so that I can barely see where we're walking.

"Toby, do you know your way back real well? Everything looks the same to me."

"Sure, just follow me."

The two hours' walk going to the cave turns into four hours walking back. Only the white of the snow and the bit of light that filters through guides us. By the time we reach the cabin, it's dark.

We both celebrate with a wave of our arms when we reach the porch. Snow has sifted through the screen-wire and blankets most of the area where I sat in the fall. But Toby and I sit and look out into the deepening whiteness. We both are quiet and just listen. It's as quiet as it will get on the mountain. The snow completely muffles any sound.

"I guess you're going to spend the night?" I ask.

"Yeah. I'd rather be here."

16

T
wo days before Christmas all of the snow has melted and the ground is spongy and soft. Toby has stayed most of the nights with me since he came back but also spends others back at his house. Not another word about his mother has come from his mouth since the cave. I leave it to him to bring it up since I'm not sure how to approach such matters.

This morning we dress for another little walk in the forest to find a suitable tree. There is a thicket of cedars not too far away, and the thinning of the bunch by one little tree will not harm the environment and will uplift our spirits. Toby has never had much of a holiday season I gather by his lack of knowledge of what it's all about. Whereas many moderns have become obsessed with the commercial aspect of the day, Toby has been left out on both the religious significance and the gift giving part.

I've read different stories to him and let him look at books with scenes depicting an idyllic Christmas. He's full of questions.

"Why the tree? How do they know Jesus was born at this time? If Jesus is God, how did he become a baby? Could Jesus talk when he was born?"

He nods with understanding at the manger scene. "Yeah, I've slept in the barn. Chickens and goats. They should've let him in the house."

He is excited about the proposed decorations—all to be made by us. As soon as we put the tree up, we'll pop some corn and string it with needle and thread. Then we'll hang those strands around the tree and make some chains from colored construction paper and glue. We'll find a white cloth to put around the base of the tree, and perhaps gifts will magically appear there on Christmas morning—presents he can use and play with at my cabin but not take home.

By the time I finish my second cup of coffee, he's at the door with the axe slung over his shoulder, smiling with the excitement of a child readying for his first Christmas. He always wants to help. He's not a slacker. He does all the chores that his father wants done there everyday including cooking some of the meals and washing the dishes. Then when he's here, he does the same. He thinks he has to work for everything he gets—which is a good trait in older children and adults but robs a small child of his security.

My children are coming to the cabin for Christmas Day. I told them to bring a dish or two, but I would cook the ham, turkey, dressing, and green beans. I'll also make deviled eggs.

"I have a guest I want you to meet," I told both of them over the cell phone last week.

Neither of them acted surprised. Said they were anxious to get acquainted.

Toby is excited at the prospect. When I told him I had two children coming up on Christmas Day, he said they could use his ball glove and baseballs if they wanted to. He thought they were as young as he until I told him they were old enough to have their own children.

"Oh," was his only comment, but I could see the longing in his eyes for other children to play with and talk to.

CHRISTMAS EVE COMES IN cold but cloudless. Very rarely do we have a white Christmas in Tennessee. More snow falls in January, February, and March than in December. But with the cold, Toby and I stack enough wood inside beside the stove to last us through the night and all day on Christmas.

He sits near the base of the tree and lets his eyes walk the limbs where the popcorn and colored paper hang. Occasionally he takes a puff of corn and nibbles. I try to read his thoughts, but I don't know what a ten-year-old is thinking about a holiday he's never before observed.

We've made our own manger scene in front of the cabin from old wood, with plywood figures for Mary, Joseph, and the Baby Jesus. Toby brought two of his goats over and tethered them near the scene to make it look more authentic. I tell him goats aren't sheep. And he tells me my wood figures aren't real either.

"Are you going to spend the night here?" I ask. "Or is your dad going to be mad that you're not home on Christmas Eve?"

Toby pulls his feet closer to him on the floor and looks down. "I'm going over and do my evening chores. I'll be back. I want to come back. I want to see if my goats talk at midnight."

I smile. I had read him one of the legends of Christmas is that animals talk at midnight when Christmas Eve turns into Christmas.

"I don't think you should be up that late. You'll need your rest for Christmas Day."

"Please, Cody. I want to listen to my goats talk."

"We'll see," I say and go back to my cooking. Clothes and toys for Toby are put away in my room. I will put them beneath the tree when he finally goes to sleep tonight. I had the store to wrap them in the holiday paper. I never was good at that.

He's anxious. He walks between the tree and the manger scene, carrying in more and more firewood. The cold makes the lobes of his ears and tip of his nose red. So, I read him the story about Rudolph and Santa Claus.

When I finish, he shakes his head. "Naw, that can't be true. Deer can't fly. I've seen a bunch of deer. They jump good, but they can't fly. And there's no Santa Claus."

"Why do you say that?"

"I've been just over the hill all my life. Ain't no Santa Claus ever been to my house. He wouldn't visit all the other kids in the world and leave me out, would he?"

"It may have been too hard to find you up here in the hills," I say, trying to give Santa Claus the benefit of the doubt.

Toby shakes his head. He goes back out for another load of wood.

When he leaves for home a little later, I go to my room and unstack the gifts in the closet. I put tags on each—most from me to Toby. Then on the basketball and goal set that takes up the whole inside of the space, I write a note from Santa Claus. "Sorry, I missed your house all these years. But I saw you at the manger scene this year when I passed over earlier. Merry Christmas to you, Toby." Then I sign in large bold script "Santa Claus."

It's dark when Toby comes back from his house. The cabin smells of cedar, hot chocolate, and steaming food. After dinner of some ham, dressing, and green beans, I turn the spotlights on to illuminate the manger scene.

We go to the front steps with a mug of hot chocolate and a bowl of popcorn. The goats munch on some corn we scatter and then hunker down near the Baby Jesus. Toby and I sing all the Christmas songs I know. Toby is enthusiastic but slow to learn the words. He likes "Jingle Bells" and "Silent Night" the best.

I relent and tell him he can stay up until midnight to see if the goats talk. But when they go to sleep and the hot chocolate does its work, he eases over into my arms and dozes off. I carry him to his bed, cover him up, and kiss his cold cheek.

I walk back outside and sit by myself on the steps. I know this Christmas will go down as one of the most memorable ones ever. There's just one person missing.

"Katy, I wish you could be here for this Christmas." I look up at the dark, cold night and speak again. "I know you are here. I wish I could see you. This boy, Toby—I don't know what to do with him. I take it one day at a time. I'm afraid to grow too close. He could be gone anytime. Sallie and Johnny are coming tomorrow. It's the first Christmas we haven't had you here. I miss you so. We'll say a prayer of thanksgiving for you. But, Katy, please talk to God for me and let me know what to do about this boy. I tried to talk to God myself, but He won't talk to me. I asked Him for an angel, and instead I got Toby—who's an angel okay, but he has worse problems than I do. Send help, please."

At midnight, I listen for the goats to talk, but they are as silent as the night. I go in, turn off the spotlights, and look back out. Starlight and moonlight turn the night into soft hues of dark blue. Somewhere Santa Claus is making his rounds. I am his helper. I go to my room, bring all the gifts to the tree, and then go to bed.

THE TINY STRING OF bells tied near the manger scene tinkle in the wind early Christmas morning and a couple of small limbs fall onto the metal roof of the cabin. With that noise, Toby awakens and runs outside, shouting as he goes, "I heard Santa Claus, I heard Santa Claus, I heard Santa Claus!"

I am up and standing at the front door when he walks back. His eyes are wide as saucers and his smile is filled with teeth. "Did you hear the deer on the roof? Did you hear Santa's sleigh bells?" he asks.

I nod and smile.

Toby ran out the door so fast that he did not see the heap of gifts at the base of the tree. When he steps through the door, he sees them.

"Cody, how did Santa get in? You have a fire going. He couldn't come down the chimney."

"I left the door open," I say.

He looks at the tags on the presents. He lets out little gasps each time he sees one with his name. He gently takes each and puts them in a pile by themselves. His eyes strain at the names of Johnny and Sallie. "Is that your other kids?" he asks.

"They *are*," I say. It's difficult to correct a child's English on Christmas morning. Then I think. He said "other."

While he's opening one after the other of his gifts, I

watch and pour us both some hot chocolate. It's strange how just one word can make my day. *OTHER*. He thinks of himself as one of my children. I'm happy. I'm sad. Happy that he can consider me a father but sad that he needs to.

WE ARE OUT SHOOTING basketball on his new goal set when the Jeep Cherokee edges into the driveway from the road. My son and his wife are in the front, and my daughter and her husband in the back. Toby and I wave but keep throwing the ball up while they walk toward us with a basket full of presents.

"You weren't supposed to bring gifts," I say. "You know I don't need anything."

"Yeah, but it's Christmas, Dad," Sallie says and hugs me. Then my son grips me in another hug. I've forgotten how big he is.

"This is Toby," I say and introduce him to all four. "He's my guest I was telling you about."

"Oh," my son says and shakes hands with Toby. "Do you have any other guests?"

"No. Who were you expecting? Santa Claus?" I say and laugh.

"Santa Claus has been here," Toby says. "He left me this ball and goal."

AFTER DINNER WHEN JOHNNY and Sallie's husband go out with Toby to play some more ball, I tell Sallie and Johnny's wife about Toby.

"What're you going to do, Dad? His father sounds dangerous. You've got to get off the mountain."

I shake my head. "No. If he were going to do anything, he'd have done it by now. I came here for some answers, and I'm going to stay until I get them."

"Any of your friends been up to see you?" she asks.

"No. It's pretty isolated. I go to Jamestown. I've been to Crossville. Nashville for a couple of days. I really like the simple life up here. I only have the electricity on because you're here. Otherwise the generator is turned off except for a couple of hours a day. I left it on last night until midnight to light up our manger scene."

"Are you ever going to go back down to civilization?"

"I've been thinking about that a whole lot. We're valley people by heritage. And mountain life is different. But now I can't go back because of Toby. He doesn't have anybody else. What would happen to him if I left? Besides, I figured I would stay at least two years like Thoreau did at Walden Pond. Have you ever read *Walden*?" I ask.

"Only when I was required to."

"What do you read?"

"Mainly study guides and lesson plans now. I read some mysteries occasionally."

"Well, you ought to go back and read *Walden*. And have your students read it too."

THE VISIT SEEMS TO pass so quickly. My two grown children leave before the sun goes down. They visited their in-laws on Christmas Eve. Now they are going off for a week to the beach before their schools start back. They are not into the rustic life that I have chosen. I wasn't either at their age.

Toby carefully puts his toys, the basketball, and new clothes into his room before he leaves to go do the chores at his house.

"I've got to spend the night at my house, Cody. Pa says I'm spending too much time over here. But I'll be back. I want you to show me how to shoot that dead soldier's pistol."

"Are you coming back tomorrow?" I ask.

"I'll try. I want to shoot some basketball and throw some baseball with you. I know you like to play," he says and walks off through the forest, leading the Christmas goats behind him.

FOR A WEEK NOW I haven't seen Toby. Last night I put batteries in my portable radio and listened to Tennessee play football in the Sugar Bowl. There was a time when I didn't miss many games. New Orleans was a favorite watering hole. But now the crackle of the announcer's voice seems a hundred years away.

This has been the saddest week. The weather is dark and dreary. No glistening snow. Just a great coat of gray moss as clouds move over the hills. They have as much personality and color as slugs on the front steps. Gift giving, laughter, and the scent of cedar have all departed the cabin. I took the manger scene down this morning and stacked it against the back wall. Maybe we can use it next Christmas if I'm still here.

I'm sitting on the front porch late in the afternoon when a speck of color moves up the road along the side of the mountain. Yellow. It's a car or truck that I haven't seen here before. It's going very slowly, stopping and starting every little bit while making the ascent. It's not Ben Siler's big truck, and it's not the little pickup of the devil worshippers. Not a police or sheriff's car and certainly not a logging truck.

When it gets to where my drive is, it stops and the driver gets out. A Yellow Cab! The black driver wears a chauffeur's cap. He pops the trunk open. Lost and a flat tire, I think. I step outside to help him.

When I get near the road, the driver has deposited three suitcases beside the car and has gone to the far side to open the door for his fare. The passenger comes around and looks down toward my cabin. She hands the driver three hundred dollar bills and then looks me in the eyes.

"Buffalo Bill Cody Rogers. Aren't you going to invite me in? I've come a long way."

"Of course, Ginny. I was expecting you," I say and take one of the suitcases while the driver takes the other two.

17

O f course, I *wasn't* expecting Ginny to appear in a Yellow Cab. My words an hour ago were the first thing I could think of to say at such a strange moment. Akin to, "Doctor Livingstone, I presume." An understatement of which my English ancestors from Yorkshire would have been proud. Ginny always was headstrong, brash, forward, unafraid, and whatever other words that could be found to describe a woman who came of age during the sexual revolution of the '60s and the women's movement that followed.

That she appeared on my doorstep in a Yellow Cab at the least expected moment should have come as no surprise. Yet, for the past hour, few words have passed between us. I busy myself with carrying her suitcases into my room, straightening the room, and changing the sheets on the bed for her to have tonight. Then I begin to think that with three suitcases Ginny is planning on spending more than one night. I give her a tour of the cabin and the surroundings. She nods and smiles approvingly—I believe. Then I pull a chair up for her in front of the stove and open the iron door. We both sit here in silence watching the wood flame up and then die down to burning embers.

"That's life," she says.

"What's that?" I ask.

"We're like the wood. We burn brightly when we're

young and on fire. Then, as we grow older, we turn to glowing embers."

"There's still fire there, though." I take my poker and
punch at the orange, radiant chunks with black fringe. They
turn and light up. "All it needs is a poke."

"But what you did will make them turn to ash sooner
than if you left them to their glowing sadness."

"Yeah, but they'll flame out instead of smoking out."

Ginny looks beyond the stove to the chimney. "It
looks like there was a fireplace there one time. Why did you
close it up?"

"When we built the cabin, my grandfather laid the
stone for the fireplace. When I came here as a child, we had
great fun carrying large logs into the cabin to burn in the
fireplace. We'd sit around and watch the sparks spiral up
the chimney and make wishes on them like we did on the
first star. When I turned forty and my children tired of carrying logs in, we closed it up and put in the woodburning
stove. It's much more efficient. A lot of heat went up the
chimney from the fireplace."

"And a lot of wishes too, I gather. A fireplace is more
romantic than a stove. I thought you would always be a
romantic, Cody."

"You can get the same effect with a woodburning
stove if you leave the door open and watch the wood burn."

Ginny's eyes turn toward the fire, and I stare at her
in profile. She has aged well. Her dark hair now has silver
and is shorter than she wore it in the spring of '68. She has
features that a sculptor would have been proud to have created. The skin of her face still glows in smoothness like the
first ripe peach of summer. Her eyes, chin, and nose make
me think of a Greek goddess in a contemplative mood.
Smart, sexy, and tough. Her appearance now is to what it
was in 1968 as the sunset is to the sunrise. The hope of the
sunrise reflected in the grace and majesty of the sunset.
Like the flame of burning wood to the embers we discussed,
Ginny is now a glowing angel in my sight. I still see fire
there. What does she see in me?

If she has gained five pounds, I wouldn't know where.

She is slender with the grace of the ballerina. Even walking down the drive from the road to the cabin, she carried herself like a Thoroughbred race horse.

"What brought you here, Ginny?"

Her head swivels toward me. "A Yellow Cab."

"No. I mean why? But where did you find a Yellow Cab around here?"

"Have I ever crossed your mind, Cody?"

I look down, then at where the fireplace was, then at the fire in the stove, and finally at Ginny. "Yes, I've thought about you. A lot lately."

"Really? When did you first think about me?"

"Oh, you've always been in my thoughts. But when I came to the cabin in September, a week or so later I hiked down to South Fork and then up the mountain on the far side to do a little meditation. I was out in the middle of the river on a rock sunning myself when I had this thought about you that struck my mind like a lightning bolt."

"Would that have been about the twenty-ninth of September?"

I think back. I came to the cabin on September twenty-first. My trek up the mountain was exactly a week and a day later—the twenty-ninth. "Yes. How did you know?"

"That was when I determined I was going to find you. I called your son, and he told me about the cabin. Then I visualized it and you here walking. I saw trees and rocks and water. I closed my eyes and sent you a signal, Cody. Remember back in 1968 we could almost read each other's minds? I would know when you were going to call and be by the phone."

I think back. Those details have left me. But I do remember how it was then. We were on the same wavelength. Mental telepathy. "I do. I do remember," I say and stretch my legs toward the warming stove.

"I took the Yellow Cab from Lexington. After your son told me where you were, I looked at a map, and saw there was no easy way to get to you. So, I just called a cab. It was a two-hundred fifty dollar ride with a fifty dollar tip. Do you think the tip was too little?" Ginny smiles at me and

I know what she's thinking.

It was Nashville and the time we took a cab in an early spring snow. We became so passionately involved that we didn't notice when the cab stopped. The cab driver just let the meter run until we came up for air. We were broke with the cost of the fare and gave the cabby all the change either one of us had for a tip—a nickel. He looked at it and said, "It was a pretty good show for a nickel."

"How did you know I had a son? And how did you find him?"

Ginny sighs, turns her head, and then brushes a piece of wood back with her foot, scuffing her shoe against the floor in doing it.

"Oh, Cody, I hate to tell you this. It'll give you the bighead. But I guess I will. I've kept a scrapbook on you ever since we parted. When I got back from Chicago and the Democratic convention . . . did you know I got arrested up there?!"

"I thought I saw them hauling you off on television."

"Probably so. Anyway, I was angry at you but in love with you at the same time. I subscribed to your little home-town newspaper and have been a faithful subscriber for thirty years now. I knew when you graduated. When you passed the bar. When you got married. I have cut out photos of your children's birth announcements. And I knew when . . . when Katy died."

I nod. Ginny is not one to hold back once she gets on a roll. I wonder what she thought about Katy, but I'm afraid to ask.

"When your wife died, I waited a month and called your number. But you were gone. Then it was a week or so later when I called your son and put the vision on you. Your son was real nice. He didn't mind me calling. He said he thought you would appreciate a visit from an old friend."

"That's how you described yourself to my son? An old friend?"

"Well, I didn't say *old*. I said I was a friend from 1968. He assumed that made me . . . and you . . . old."

I look out the window where the dark January night

cloaks the mountain. "If you found out where I was in September, why did you wait until January to come see me?"

"Oh, Cody, I had . . . I had second thoughts. It was a romantic impulse to find you. But then I got to thinking, what if you didn't even think about me. What if you didn't want to see anyone? You were grieving. So, I let it pass for a bit. I got my situation in order where I could come down for a week or so at the first of the year. But there've been days when I've concentrated on you and tried to send you messages. I don't know if I got through. Have you thought about me since the day you walked to the river?"

"Yes. I even went back to Nashville and checked out some of our old places. The places where I lived. The Parthenon and the Capitol."

I glance over at her. Is that a blush moving up her neck or just the reflection from the fire?

"The Parthenon. There were a lot of trees around there, weren't there?"

I nod. "Almost a forest."

"Cody, I noticed riding up the mountain in the cab that you have a bunch of trees here too."

I look out again but can see no trees in the darkness. "Yeah, but they haven't been christened like the ones in Centennial Park."

"Give them time."

Then I latch on to the words she just said—"a week or so." She isn't just going to spend the night. My mind whirls in search of what this means and in thoughts of how I can fix the cabin to be more accommodating to a lady like Ginny. We need more hot water. I can't expect her to take a cold shower. I'll go in the morning and buy a propane water heater and spend the day in plumbing work to hook it up to the shower and basin in the bathroom.

"There's also the period of mourning I knew you were going through," she interrupts my thoughts. "I didn't think it was proper to come down until you had some time alone to deal with your loss of Katy. I know I had to have some time when my husband died two years ago."

"I'm sorry, Ginny. I haven't even asked about any

family you might have. Actually, I was afraid to ask. I thought you might be married and some jealous husband would be coming up the mountain with a gun. That's all I need is another crazy man on the mountain with a gun."

"*Another*? Who's here now?"

I tell her about Ben Siler and Toby. For an hour, I rattle on about the boy I thought was an angel. His mother's death. How he has grown to be a ten-year-old without real connections with the outside world. I tell her about his room where he often sleeps and about the times when he's not here. About my worry.

"Sounds like he would be a good subject for a psychology or sociology study. Cody, if I'm taking up too much space in your room, I'd be okay in calling the cab back and going home to Lexington. I don't want to interfere with anything between you and the boy."

"No, no, no. I can sleep out here on the couch or buy another bed. Toby's been gone for the past week. He'll show up, but I don't know when. Did you and your husband have children, Ginny?"

"A boy and a girl. About the same ages as yours. Funny, isn't it—how similar we are?"

Ginny continues to tell me about her son and daughter while I take us up some dinner. She has a horse farm near Lexington, Kentucky. In addition, she and her husband published a magazine for horse owners, racers, and breeders. She doesn't say, but I suspect she has enough money to buy and sell me. I'm not a clothing expert, but the long dress she has on didn't come from Wal-Mart. Rings on her fingers catch the light of the fire and seem to intensify it. She has a subdued elegance.

"You ride horses, Ginny?"

"Yes. Did you expect anything less?"

"No," I say and hand her a plate.

"So who runs the farm and magazine while you're away?"

"My daughter. Our son is a lawyer. Can you believe he would choose such a profession?" she asks and smiles at me over the leftover turkey and dressing.

We talk until midnight. I have left the generator on so that we would have light. I explain our electrical situation to her and she nods in understanding.

"Cody, I like your cabin," she says just before she closes the bedroom door with me standing in the living room. "And I like your beard. It's very becoming. I'm glad you've loosened up over the years."

When the door is closed, I sit back down by the stove. We have become opposites. She was wild and carefree in the spring of '68. I would have never imagined that she would have ended up as a lady of means. I have left a profession that could have brought me some wealth and have become a laid back mountain man. I was uptight in 1968. However, opposites still attract even though we've reversed the polarity of the magnet.

I HAVE A FIVE GALLON pot of water on the propane stove warming the next morning when Ginny cracks the bedroom door open and peeks around.

"It's so quiet here, Cody. It's so peaceful. No wonder you came here."

"I'm heating water for your shower," I say and nod at the pan. "I'm going to make a more permanent solution to that today."

"I believe I'll have a bit of cereal before I shower," she says, carrying her own box of some healthy type bran with her. She looks around. "Where's your milk? Your refrigerator?"

"In the spring house," I say and nod out the kitchen window.

"Spring house? Oh, yes. You showed me that yesterday."

Ginny walks with me out the door, clutching the bathrobe tightly to her to keep the cold out. When we reach the spring house, I lift the roof and show her the contents. Ice has formed a sparkly layer where the jugs and bottles meet the flowing water. I pull out a jug of milk, shake it, and listen to a lump of ice strike the inside wall of the container. "This should be cold enough. You want some orange, tomato, or apple juice?"

She chooses orange, and we walk back toward the cabin. She stops and holds her hand out in front of me. She stares up at the chimney and the blue-gray smoke slowly spiraling out. Mist is lifting behind the cabin with the sun just barely rising above the far valley.

"This is beautiful, Cody. I wish I was an artist and could paint this scene."

"You stay here long enough and you could be," I say and take her hand. Except for a brief hug when she first came inside yesterday, it's our first touch. She takes hold of my hand and we walk up the steps together.

WHILE GINNY SHOWERS, I set out for Jamestown in my Jeep, pulling my trailer behind, to buy the water heater and piping to install it. She says she will make herself at home and not to be in any hurry. I pass the nursing home on the right where I used to visit with Doc and Bill. A bit of sadness pecks at my soul but is shooed away with the thought of Ginny at the cabin.

WHEN I RETURN, GINNY is sitting beside the stove reading a book to Toby.

"I see you've met," I say and nod at each of them. "Toby is supposed to read on his own instead of just listening."

"She reads so good, Cody. Her voice makes me think I'm there when she reads about it. I like her reading better'n yours."

"*Well*," I say. "She reads *well*."

"She sure does."

"Toby, how about helping me unload the trailer. I bought a real water heater and another propane tank."

The remainder of the day, Toby and I work at the hot water project. He is a bundle of energy. He and Ginny have struck it off famously.

"She's pretty, Cody," he says to me when I'm wrestling with the propane tank to put it in place. "Do you like her?"

"Yes, I've liked her for a long time."

"You gonna marry her?"

"Toby! She only arrived yesterday. It's much too early to even think about that."

"She said she's going to sleep in your room. My room is still mine. That right?"

"Yes. That's why that bed is in the trailer. It's going in the living room. You still have your room. Anytime you want it."

Toby looks up at the sun going behind the ridge in the west. "I've got to go. I can't spend the night. I want us to go hunting, Cody. Will you?"

"Sure. Just let me know when."

"In a day or two. Okay?" he asks as he walks away, looking back over his shoulder.

"HE'S A GREAT BOY," Ginny says when we sit again near the stove after dinner. "He's smart. A charmer."

"A snake charmer," I say and tell her about his coolness in rescuing me from the serpents.

"He's the nearest thing I have to a grandchild," I say. I look at Ginny. She has a soft smile creasing her cheeks while her eyes stare straight ahead at the fire. "Do your two children have any children?" I ask.

"They don't," she says. She reaches over, takes my hand, and looks into my eyes. "I have a grandchild, Cody. And . . . you do too. *We* have a child and a grandchild."

18

"H e goes thither at first as a hunter and fisher, until at last, if he has the seeds of a better life in him, he distinguishes his proper objects, as a poet or naturalist it may be, and leaves the gun and the fish-pole behind."—Walden.

Toby and I walk through an inch of snow on our hunting expedition. He carries a 20-gauge shotgun. I have given him a box of shells. We're hunting crows. I carry the .44 Navy Colt that I retrieved from the cave. I have spent days restoring its luster and making sure the moving parts are working properly. The hardware store in Jamestown was able to order me some bullets for it. I didn't want to try the ones that were near it in the cave.

Some would think a ten-year-old is too young to be carrying a shotgun. However, my father gave me a 410-gauge for my ninth birthday. Toby is much more of a mountain child and hunter than I ever was. I don't want to shoot any crows, but I do want to try out the Colt.

We walk in long periods of silence, which is good for me. I'm still working on what Ginny told me three days ago.

She was pregnant when she left Nashville in June 1968, but didn't know it for sure until July. She thought she could have lost the child in the turmoil in Chicago in August, but when she didn't, she returned home to her parents' house in Louisville. She thought about calling me but didn't want me to think she was pressuring me.

When her parents found out about the pregnancy, they insisted, and she finally agreed, that she put the child up for adoption when it was born. To that end, they kept her secreted in their large home until a couple of weeks before the due date. Then she went to Lexington, had the baby, and turned it over immediately to the adoptive parents. She saw the child just once—at birth. He had thin red hair and big blue eyes. There were no names given by either the mother or the adoptive parents.

She tried to put the child out of her mind for a quarter of a century. Neither her husband nor her other children knew that she had a child out of wedlock. When her husband died, Ginny decided to see if she could find her first child. She hired an investigator, signed all the forms to have adoption records opened, and found to her surprise that her birth child was also seeking her.

He grew up in Nashville and became a minister to the deaf for one of the large Church of Christ congregations there. He's married and has a son—my birth grandson.

When they finally met last August, the young man also wanted to know about his birth father. Ginny told him a little but not enough to identify me. She wanted to protect my privacy. She told him that she would write and ask me if I wanted to meet him. But one thing led to another and she never did. She didn't know how to tell me by letter that I had a son I didn't know about. She didn't know if I opened my own mail, or who else might see such a letter. And she couldn't bring herself to call me.

I'm delighted. My step is a bit stronger and faster today than before. I am a grandfather. Now I don't know how to tell my other children or Toby. I want to see my firstborn, but I don't know when or how. I have a twenty-nine-year-old son in Nashville. I may have passed him on the street when I went there recently. Probably not. He wouldn't have been in those places. Ginny and I could never take the place of his real parents who reared him, but there's something strong that draws me to him. How would a child with my genes who grew up with other parents turn out? Apparently, pretty well. My grandfather Cody had red hair, and now my son, Jerry, has the same. I want to meet him.

"Walk real quiet, there's some crows up in that pine thicket," Toby says.

I bend nearer the ground and whisper to him, "*Quietly.*"

"Yeah, be quiet," he says in reply.

I haven't shot anything in twenty years. When I was a boy, I hunted rabbits, squirrels, and quail. I had to be quick and accurate with the little 410. And I was no danger to anyone unless they were very close. The more I hunted, the more I came to enjoy the walking and the scenery over the shooting. I finally put down the long gun and just carried a .22 caliber pistol in case of snakes.

I expect Toby will do the same as Thoreau said of most mature men. They become poets or naturalists. Maybe both. The older I get, the more reverence I have for all life. Unless something needs killing, I leave it alone. A spider outside the cabin can spin her web and capture the glorious morning sunlight on the dewdrops without worrying about me. A skunk or opossum can saunter across the lane with no fear.

I don't think less of men and women who hunt deer or other animals. I see enough deer carcasses by the roadsides to know that their population could stand a little thinning. And if I were hungry and couldn't afford food, I could still hunt for meat for the table. However, all life should receive some respect and reverence.

Then when Toby pulls back his cap, I see a bruise on the side of his head. There are some animals who need killing. He aims his shotgun toward the tall pines and waits for a crow to fly out. The shotgun roars, black feathers begin to filter down, and the bird thuds to the ground thirty feet away. The snow turns crimson in splotches. The other crows fly out of the thicket in the opposite direction, cawing loudly as they go.

"I waited until he flew, Cody. I gave him a fighting chance."

"You gave him a flying chance," I say. "Not a fighting chance. He didn't have a gun."

Within the next hour, Toby bags three more. I walk

along, never firing a shot. Then when we're deep in a ravine near the river, I prop a discarded can up on a stump. I take twelve paces back and check the revolver one last time. I don't want an old gun blasting apart on me when I pull the trigger. Toby covers his ears. I aim and squeeze off six rounds. None of them hits the can, although one lodges in the stump. The roars echo along the walls of the canyon and back to us.

"Can I shoot it?" Toby asks.

"I don't know. *Can* you?"

"Huh?"

"*May* I shoot it?"

"You've already shot it. I want to."

I show Toby how to reload the pistol. He watches, rocking back and forth from one foot to the other.

"I know how to load a pistol," he says. "I've watched my Pa do it hundreds of times."

"You still have to be careful," I say and hold the gun up when I finish. "You have to be sure there's nothing behind your target that you could hurt," I continue and look toward the stump, "in case you miss."

"Like you did," Toby says and smiles.

"Yes."

He holds out his hand and takes the revolver from me. "It's heavy." He holds it with two hands and stretches out his arms toward the stump. His left eye closes, his nose wrinkles, and he aims down the long barrel. I put my hands over my ears when he begins to squeeze the trigger. The gun roars, and bits of wood fly up from the stump as the gun recoils upward in Toby's hands.

"Boy, this thing makes the noise and kicks," he says.

"You aimed low. Up and to the right."

The next shot hits neither the can nor the stump.

"Too high," I say.

Toby shakes his head and aims again, his lips thin over his teeth as he sets his jaw tightly. The gun blasts, and the can flies off the stump and tumbles in the air for twenty feet before landing.

"I got it, I got it!" Toby says and jumps.

GINNY IS PULLING THE Jeep into the drive when we get back from our hunting. She is a self-starter, a woman who is not afraid to change her ways or hesitates at driving the Jeep to Allardt. Ginny likes the mountain life she's experienced during the last few days, but she has one luxury she said she can not give up—she likes to have her hair done by a professional.

"The first shop I came to could take me," she says as she alights from the Jeep with a bag filled with things she has purchased on her outing. "Cody, you and Toby carry in the pizza and ice cream."

I raise my eyebrows. Ginny is apparently disposed to bring civilization to us. I look at Toby. "Have you ever had pizza or ice cream before?"

"Ice cream. Every time we went to the snake church. What's pizza?"

When we're inside, I put the pistol into one of the high kitchen cabinets and explain pizza to Toby in plain terms—flattened bread, cheese, meats, and vegetables. Spicy and hot. "Be careful, Toby. I don't want you to think I'm trying to poison you. We definitely need some Coke or Dr. Pepper with this."

"Cody, tell Ginny how I did with the soldier's gun."

"He did better than I did," I say.

"I wouldn't have expected less," Ginny says.

"Can I have the pistol?" Toby asks.

"When?"

"To keep."

"No, it's too dangerous," I say. "You can only shoot it when I'm with you."

I go to the spring house and bring back ice-cold bottles of soft drink. Toby is already into his first slice of pizza when I return. I wish I had a camera.

"What do you think?" Ginny asks me, turning her head from side to side.

"About what?"

"My hair, silly. Do you like it like this?"

"It looks great," I say and look at her face and hair. "Is it different?"

"Just a little. I got some new makeup too. Had a facial."

"I thought you looked great before you left."

"Thanks, but I needed a little pampering. I bought something for you too."

"What?"

"I'll show you later," she says and nods toward Toby who is not paying any attention to us and is into his second slice.

After the pizza and ice cream, Toby starts to put on his coat.

"Are you going home, Toby?" Ginny asks.

"Yes. My Pa said to be home before dark. I got a lot of chores to do. It's almost dark now. He'll be mad if I'm not there in a bit."

"You've got to come back each day so we can work on your school lessons," Ginny says when Toby gets to the front door.

He turns and smiles. "I will. I like to learn from them books."

"*Those*," I say.

"Those what?" Toby asks.

"*Those* books," I say.

"Yeah," Toby says and shakes his head. He looks back. "I wish I could live with you and Ginny all the time."

I look at Ginny and then at Toby. "That'd be nice, Toby, but parents have first rights. You have to be with your dad. There's nothing I can do about that. Right now, anyway."

AN HOUR LATER, WHEN the food is put away and the dishes are clean, Ginny brings the bag from her room. She puts a pan of water onto the stove to warm.

"Look what I bought for you." With that, she pulls a large pair of scissors and a straight razor from the bag.

"You're going to kill me?"

Then she retrieves a can of shaving cream from the same bag. "No. I'm going to cut your hair, trim your beard, and shave your neck below the beard."

"I can do that," I say.

"No. Not as well as I can," she says and lays the instruments on the table. "After I dropped out of college and had the baby, I couldn't stand doing nothing. I went to beauty school and got my license to cut hair. Later I went back to college and got my degree in journalism and marketing."

"A double major?" I ask.

"Yes. I was in business when I was at Vanderbilt. Then I met you and liked what you did in journalism. So, when I went back to the University of Kentucky, I did both. I was on my own. My dad wouldn't pay for any more school. He said if all I was going to do was riot and revolt and run with strange hippies, he wasn't going to foot the bill."

"Who were the strange hippies?"

"Oh, that's just what he accused me of. Chicago. And Nashville. I never would tell them who the father of the child was. So, he imagined it was some hippy or such like I was arrested with in Chicago."

"Me, a hippy?"

Ginny turns her head sideways. "In fact, you look more like a hippy now than you did in 1968."

"A lot more."

Ginny leans toward me and loosens the top two buttons on my shirt. She fastens an old sheet around me with a safety-pin. Then she steps back and looks at my hair from several angles.

"I like the shape of your head, Cody. We need to cut your hair to bring out those strong points."

"No one's going to see it but you and me, Ginny. And Toby. He doesn't care what I look like."

"I do though," she says and sets about molding my hair with her hands while she thinks of what will look best. "Just close your eyes and enjoy it," she says when she picks up the scissors.

I do as she says. As I always did in 1968. I just close my eyes and enjoy. Her touch is gentle and sensual. Her fingers graze my ears and run along my eyebrows when she brushes my hair back. She leans over me and I smell her perfume. Her arm skims my neck and I remember the nights in Nashville when she wrapped her arms around me and wouldn't let go.

I almost drift off with the rhythm of the snipping scissors and the sound of the water beginning to heat on the stove. Ginny's breath is like a warm wind on a beach in the morning. She lays the scissors down and brushes my hair, looks at it some more, and then picks the scissors up again.

"You're going to look like somebody," she says when she comes to the front and smoothes back my hair.

"Thanks," I say.

She's wearing jeans today, and I feel them rub against my legs when she leans near to trim my eyebrows. "It's time for your beard now," she says. "Lean your head back." With that she starts snipping around my face. I keep my eyes closed and think of the Parthenon and the Capitol steps. She's careful not to touch me too much. Just a rub of a leg here and the glance of her arm there. I know my nose is near her neck when the scent becomes stronger, but I'm afraid to open my eyes for fear I will be staring straight at her breasts.

"All that's left is the shaving," she says in a few minutes. I feel the brush going through my beard to remove the stray hairs she's trimmed. I hear her walking to the stove and then back. "Lean your head back farther," she says. "This wet towel is hot."

My head is as far back as it can go when I feel the moist, hot towel on the underside of my chin at my neck.

"I'm going to let it soak for a few minutes," she says and goes back to the table. I hear her slapping the razor against the leather strap. "I never have used a straight razor before," she says. "I think it should be easy. I used to watch the barber shave my dad."

I gulp. "They didn't teach you that at beauty school?" I ask.

"Oh, no."

Then I begin to wonder if Ginny has harbored some pent up rage at me for thirty years that she is ready to release with one swipe of the razor against my throat.

She removes the towel. I hear the shaving cream can giving up some soap. She lathers it onto my neck.

"Keep your head back," she says. She hesitates a moment. "Cody, your chair won't adjust up like a barber's chair. Do you mind if I straddle your knees so that I can get in position to shave you better?"

"If you think that's safe," I say.

"Huh? Safe? From what aspect?" she asks, and without my answering straddles my knees.

I feel her bottom on my knees and feel her lean into me. She puts her left thumb on my chin to hold my head in place and then puts the razor to my throat. I barely notice its glide. The sound of my whiskers being cut is all that I hear or feel. She is good.

"How does that feel?" she asks.

"Good, very good," I say and relax.

"A man who will let a woman at his throat with a straight razor has a clean conscience," she says.

"And believes in the woman," I add.

"The only thing that would show more faith," she says, "is to let me shave your scrotum."

Breath hisses from my open mouth. And Ginny giggles. "Just kidding, Cody."

"Thanks. I never shaved down there anyway. And I don't have that much faith."

"Yet," Ginny says.

She gets up, brings the towel back, and wipes my neck clean of the soap. Then she re-lathers me. "One more time," she says and straddles me again. She scoots a little farther up my lap.

The razor glides even smoother this go around. When she finishes, Ginny takes some soap in her hands and rubs it on my face and nose. She laughs. Then she takes the hot towel and wipes my face clean.

"Sit up," she says when she gets off. When I open my eyes, she's holding a mirror in front of me so I can see my newly shaped head of hair and beard.

I nod my head. "What do you think, Ginny?"

"You look good," she says. She sits back down on my

knees, puts her arms around my neck, and leans toward me. When our lips meet, the first thought that passes through me is that this is the first woman I've kissed like this in over twenty-six years.

Ginny must sense my slight hesitation. She leans back. "Is everything okay?" she asks. "Is this too soon for you, Cody?"

"No, no, I was just thinking . . ."

"Thinking . . . about what?" she asks and stands.

"It's been a long time," I say.

Ginny nods. "Go take a hot shower. I want to see how your hair does after you shampoo it." She motions me to the bathroom.

WHEN I RETURN IN a few minutes, I am dressed only in my bathrobe. Ginny is sitting in front of the stove barefooted and sipping at a cup of hot tea. She has changed from her jeans into a bathrobe of her own.

"Had to change," she says. "I got some of your hair on me."

I sit down. "I've never kissed another woman since I married Katy," I say.

"That's honorable. But she wasn't the first woman you ever kissed. Nor the last, I hope. I know you loved Katy dearly, Cody. To be together that long says a lot for you . . . and her. You both must have had a special love for each other."

"Yes. Her wasting away from cancer took a toll on me."

"Cancer? Is that what happened?"

"Yes. Breast cancer. Then it went to her bones. Just terrible to watch someone who was so vibrant die like that. What happened to your husband?"

"A heart attack. It was quick. But so unexpected. I don't know which is worse. To know that you're going to lose your husband or wife or not to know it and have it happen so suddenly. We didn't even have time to say our good-byes."

"Katy and I did. But it was so painful watching her.

She struggled. She didn't give up until she saw the angels coming for her. I didn't see them, but she did. Do you believe in angels?"

"Angels are God's messengers. I believe that God sometimes uses us to be his angels." Ginny studies the embers in the stove. "Why did you come to the mountain, Cody? And why did you go to Nashville? And why did you have your suitcases packed to go find me?"

Now I turn my eyes toward the fire. Ginny always had a way of getting to the heart of a matter. I look at her. "I came to the mountain to talk to God and find out why Katy had to go and what was left in life for me. I went to Nashville to remember what it was like in the spring of '68 when we were together. I had my suitcases packed to go find you because I thought that I could bring back that love that we had."

Ginny nods her head, smiles, sips her tea, but does not look at me directly.

"Did God tell you why He took Katy?"

"No."

"Did He tell you what you should do with the rest of your life?"

"No."

"Did you find a remembrance of our spring together when you went to Nashville?"

"Part of it was there and part was gone."

"If I hadn't dropped in, would you have come looking for me?"

"Yes. Eventually. Toby's problems slowed me down."

"Cody, I think God has spoken to you, but you haven't listened."

"How's that?"

"Toby, Doc Jordan, and me."

I sit still. Quiet. Toby, Doc Jordan, and Ginny. Is she saying they all are angels—messengers from God? I thought Toby was. Doc Jordan has wisdom, but he's not an angel. Ginny? I see what she's talking about. A little. Each one has brought a change to me. Is God showing me through them what I have left to do? "You've got to move on," Doc Jordan told me.

"Ginny, can we find the love we had?"

"No. That's gone. We can find something better. We're both more mature. We both have had experiences. But we do have a child together. We have a connection."

I scoot my chair closer and put my hand out to her. She takes it. I know I must move slowly or else all those feelings about whether it's right will come flooding back. Maybe she understands.

"Are you ready for that kiss?" I ask.

Ginny stands and I rise to meet her. I let my hand slide down her back and bring her close so that her lips are near mine. It doesn't have to be rushed. We aren't teenagers. When our lips meet, I close my eyes. Her hands move to the back of my neck and pull me to her. We briefly part and look each other in the eyes, then we kiss again. This time it's just Ginny. Katy doesn't cross my mind.

She brings her hands down and pushes me away a bit. "You get going in a hurry, Cody. I had forgotten. Sit back down. I have something to tell you before we go too far."

What is it? She doesn't have another boyfriend. She's not afraid of getting pregnant. A sexually transmitted disease? What is it? My mind searches for possibilities while Ginny gathers herself. She bites down on her finger. Then she turns and looks at me.

"Cody, I didn't know exactly what happened to Katy. But I've got to tell you. I've had breast cancer . . . and I've had a double mastectomy."

My tongue lies in my mouth like a dead fish. All I can see is Ginny wasting away in front of me. I don't want to bury two loves of my life. My mouth must have fallen open because Ginny gets up, walks quickly to her door, and slams it behind her. All I hear is her sobbing into her pillow when I go to the door and bang on it. She has locked it and won't answer my pleadings.

19

I t's almost daylight before I finally doze off. All night I have considered what a lout I must have appeared to Ginny. She is telling me about a terrifying time in her life and all I do is let my mouth fall open. I was concerned with me. She knew it instantly. I can't blame her for crying all night. I try to think of some way of making it up to her.

When her door opens two hours later, Ginny is dressed and carries two of her suitcases through the doorway and onto the porch without speaking a word to me. She walks over and hands me a ten dollar bill.

"I used your cell phone to call my cab from Kentucky last night. He should be here any time. This is to pay you for the call. I won't be hanging around to bother you."

She turns, walks back into her room, and carries the other suitcase out onto the porch. Again, my tongue sticks to the roof of my mouth like it's coated with peanut butter. I've got to say something. Apologize. I can't lose Ginny this way after her coming to me. She sits down on the porch and pulls her coat tightly around her.

"Ginny," I say and stand in front of her. "I'm sorry. I know I must have appeared shocked. I was."

"Yeah. You saw me as a corpse. I'm not dead, buddy. I didn't come here to say my fond farewells. I'm alive. I'm going to live. And love. Just because I lost my breasts doesn't mean that I'm not a woman. Someone will be happy to have me." With that said, she bursts into tears again.

I hear the sound of a car's tires on the road coming up the mountain. I look around and see the Yellow Cab. Ginny looks up and sees it too.

"My ride's here. Will you help me carry my bags to the road?"

"Ginny, no."

"Then, I'll carry them by myself."

"No. I mean don't go. I'm sorry. I just had flash-backs to Katy. I couldn't bear to lose you too."

"Cody, we're not going to live forever. But I have just as good a chance of outliving you as you do of outliving me."

The cabby blows his horn and opens the trunk. Ginny stands and picks up two bags. I move in front of her.

"Ginny, don't go. I want you here. I . . . love you. I do."

"Cody, you're scared and pathetic. You're lost. You're up here searching for answers, and when they run over you in a Mack truck, you don't recognize them."

She tries to move around me, but I step in front of her again. The cabby blows his horn again and begins to walk toward the cabin.

"No, don't go Ginny. I can't live without you."

"See. It's always *you*. What about me?"

"I want you to be with me."

"And that will make *me* happy?"

"We'll work on it. Put your baggage down."

Ginny looks at her suitcases and then at the cab.

"We all have baggage, Cody. We're not who we were in 1968. We're older, frailer. We're carrying the baggage of a child together. We're both carrying the baggage of breast cancer. It seems I'm handling it better than you. Can you love me without my breasts?" Ginny asks just as the cabby knocks on the screen door.

"I never did care much for your damn breasts to start with!" I shout. The cabby takes two steps backward.

Ginny looks at the cabby and then at me. We both begin to laugh and then rush into each other's arms.

She waves the cabby away. "I'm staying, George. Sorry to have you drive all the way down here." She starts to hand him three hundred dollar bills.

"This one's on me," I say and step into the cabin to get my billfold.

I hand George his money and he scratches his head. "White folks sure are a strange breed," he says and walks back up the drive.

MY TOSSING AND TURNING during the night has worked up within me a hunger for breakfast. When the cab is safely down the mountain, Ginny and I return arm in arm to the kitchen. I place her luggage back in the bedroom and join her in preparing the food.

Clouds move in low and dreary, and a misty rain follows. This will be an in-cabin day for sure. We leave the electric generator turned off and listen to the soft sounds of rain dripping from the bare trees onto the roof.

"If we had snow instead of rain, do you know what this would remind me of, Cody?"

I turn from the stove and look at her. Ginny is a romantic, but I can't think what it would be.

"Remember the movie we saw over and over because it was on at the cheap place we could afford? It was about two years old by 1968."

Then it strikes me. "Dr. Zhivago?"

"Yes. The snow could cover this cabin, and it would just be you and me. I still carry that music box that you gave me with the ballerina. When you wind it up and let it play, it's 'Lara's Theme.' "

" 'Somewhere, my love, there will be . . .' what?" I ask.

" 'There will be skies of blue.' "

"I hadn't thought of the similarities," I say. "Do you think I look like Dr. Zhivago? With my beard and long hair?"

"Much handsomer," Ginny says and moves toward me. I reach my arms out and take her.

"With the rain, we're not going to be going out today, Ginny. I doubt that Toby will come over. We'll have the whole day to get re-acquainted."

"We already have . . . to a point," she says. "But there's so much that has happened over the past thirty years, it'll take a bit to learn each other again. We've been apart longer than we were alive the first time we met."

"Yeah. I hadn't thought of it that way."

"We've both lived a whole lifetime. I know more about you because of your newspaper than you do about me."

"But I want to know more about you, Ginny," I say

and take up my breakfast from the skillet. Ginny pours milk over her cereal and we sit across from each other at the table.

"It was after my husband died that I found out I had breast cancer. It was a double whammy. My doctor and I decided quickly on the mastectomy. It was successful as far as I know. I've had good reports for the last year and a half. I needed you then, Cody," she says and looks up from her cereal.

I nod my head. Ginny wants to talk about it, and I will listen although it also takes me back to Katy's struggle with the same disease. I pray Ginny's will be a more successful result. I have determined over the night that God has given me the task of standing by Katy and Ginny during this dark time. If that's my lot, so be it. Surely, He wouldn't send me Ginny as a burden but as a blessing.

"They took them off as nicely as they could. It doesn't look all that bad," she says. "They sold me a thing to wear that makes it appear that I still have breasts. It's just a very expensive bra with built-in falsies in my view. Flesh colored and all. It makes me feel more comfortable in public. Reconstructive surgery is a possibility."

I look past her and think of what I said about her breasts when the cabby was standing at the door. "I didn't mean what I said about your breasts the way it sounded," I say. "I meant that I loved you in spite . . . without regard to them."

Ginny smiles. "Be careful. You're digging yourself into a deeper hole. You used to say they were like large plums."

"Yes."

"They got larger after we separated. Maybe it was from having the baby and all. You would've been proud."

"I loved you because you were you. Your breasts were beside the point."

"That's better."

WE SPEND THE REMAINDER of the day catching up on years of happenings. The rain grows harder. It's just warm enough to keep it from being snow. I bring in bundles of wood, and we sit around the stove. We laugh. We talk. And we cry.

In the late afternoon, we take turns reading to each other. I read Ginny some passages from *Walden* and explain my pursuit of the simple life. She nods but I know she hasn't forgotten her horse farm and the magazine. Is she willing to give up those things to live on the mountain with me?

She picks up the book that Toby had found about Buffalo Bill Cody and reads parts of it to me. Then she takes a Bible and reads me some of her favorite psalms.

"David went through a lot. He was able to put it into words. He lost a son at birth and Absalom in rebellion. That must have been bad. When I thought about him during my roughest times, I turned to his psalms for comfort."

"It was a different time. But similar things I guess. David learned how to handle it."

When we finish reading sections, we sit in silence and think. We are growing closer to where silence is not a hindrance to our togetherness but an aid. We talk and then we listen to the rain.

"You know what I want you to read to me, Cody?"

"No, what?" I ask and turn open to another section in *Walden*.

"Your love song to me. Remember?"

I close *Walden* and pick up the Bible. "The passage from the Song of Solomon?"

"Yes."

I leaf through a few pages until I find it. I bite my lip when I glance down the passage. I'm not sure I'm up to this. Then I begin.

"Behold, thou art fair, my love; behold, thou are fair; thou hast doves' eyes within thy locks: thy hair is as a flock of goats, that appear from Mount Gilead.

"Thy teeth are like a flock of sheep that are even shorn, which came up from the washing; whereof every one bears twins, and none is barren among them.

"Thy lips are like a thread of scarlet, and thy speech

is comely: thy temples are like a piece of pomegranate within thy locks.

"Thy neck is like the tower of David builded for an armoury, wherein there hang a thousand bucklers, all shields of mighty men.

"Thy two breasts . . .," I say and look up at Ginny.

"Go ahead and read."

"Thy two breasts are like two young roes that are twins, which feed among the lilies.

"Until the day break, and the shadows flee away, I will get me to the mountain of myrrh, and to the hill of frankincense.

"Thou art all fair, my love: there is no spot in thee."

I close the Bible and look over at Ginny. She is smiling, but there is a bit of moisture at the corner of her left eye.

"Do you want to see where the deer used to feed among the lilies?" she asks.

I nod my head. "I want to be with you."

Ginny stands, motions for me to stay seated, and walks to the bedroom. She comes back out with the paper bag she had brought the scissors and razor in from town.

"The other thing I bought for you, and I was going to show you last night until you acted like such a rascal, was this," she says and pulls a black, lacy gown from the bottom of the bag. "It's what I didn't want Toby to see." She holds it up to her and whirls around. There are little red roses of ribbon at various places on it. She holds it up like a veil to her face. I can see her smile through it. "What do you think?"

"You remembered I like black and red."

"Oh, yes," she says and turns one more circle as though she's dancing with the gown. Then she stops and looks at me. "Go on into the bedroom. I'm going to change. No lamps. Just the soft light from outside."

"Okay," I say and make my way toward the bedroom,

checking the front door and back door locks as I go.

Then I sit down on the side of the bed not knowing whether I should lie down, undress, partly undress, or what. I take my shoes off and slip them beneath the bed. I look out the window to where the forest is but a drippy darkness. It's a good time to sleep but I'm fully awake. My heart is pounding like it did when I had Ben Siler in my sights. But this time it's for a better reason. I'm definitely in love again. But how should I act when Ginny comes in? Should I avoid looking where her breasts were? My fear is that whatever I do, it will be wrong. Ginny is quick to recognize insincerity.

In a few minutes the door opens. Ginny stands there holding the music box that I gave her in the spring of '68. She winds up the ballerina and sits her down on the dresser. When the strains to "Lara's Theme" start tinkling away, Ginny joins the ballerina in pirouettes beside the bed, hands held up in ballet style. She is neither smiling nor frowning.

I am the audience. The nightgown billows out slightly and I feel the air on my face. I sit in rapt attention. She is a beauty. She is fluid and powerful. She is sexy but restrained. Ginny of 1968 dances with her as a twin. I see them both like in a blurred vision. This Ginny is even better.

When the music stops, she bends down, kisses me, puts her arms around my neck, and eases into my lap. I lean over and kiss her on her shoulders and up the sides of her neck. Her perfume spurs me on. I ease the straps off her shoulders and let the gown fall in a bunch around her waist. She moves closer. My hands run up and down her back from her shoulders to the small of her back while I kiss in nibbles along her collarbones. She breathes in little gasps when my fingernails etch a line along her spine. I love the touch of her skin, the sweetness of her perfume, the grip of her arms around me. I am alive, and so is she.

I love Ginny.

20

Another thing that Ginny says she needs if she is to stay here on the mountain with me, beside her weekly hair appointments and facials, is a walk-in closet that's big enough to hold her clothes. A week ago we drove to Jamestown to pick up five large boxes filled with clothes and things she had shipped from Lexington. She's right, of course. The cabin wasn't designed for long-term living.

At the building supply house, I inquired about someone who could help me add on a closet area along the back of the cabin. Now the hammers are banging away as my helper, Toby, and I build an eight-foot-by-twelve-foot addition on to the back adjacent to Ginny's bedroom.

It's actually *our* bedroom when Toby is not sleeping over and hers when he is. We both agree that it would not be proper for Toby to think that we were sleeping together when we aren't married. And that's something that neither of us has brought up at all. Ginny only mentioned it in passing one day when she said the reason that she gave our child up for adoption was that she didn't want me to feel as though I *had* to marry her.

If I had known she was pregnant, I would have insisted on "doing the right thing."

"Am I going to get a bigger closet too?" Toby asks. He looks up at me, squints his eyes against the sun coming through the unfinished roof, and leans his head to the side.

"Why would you need a larger closet?"

"I've got a lot of stuff. All the things I can't take home. Baseballs and glove, basketball, new clothes—just a lot of stuff."

I look over toward his side of the back. If he had a larger room or closet, I could also store a lot of my "stuff" out of the way.

"What are you charging me?" I ask the old carpenter who's helping.

"Ten dollar'n hour," he says through the nails he's holding in his mouth.

"How long would it take us just to frame up a section on the other side of the back porch about the size of this one?"

"I'd say right near the same time as it takes to do this'n," he says. I can't argue with his logic.

"Can you come back tomorrow on that one?"

"If'n you come and get me. I hain't got no car. DUI three times," he says and smiles.

So, I will get more building material today when I take him home and be ready for Toby's addition tomorrow.

IN A WEEK, BOTH closets are done. I'm proud of the work that Toby and I did to complete the job after the carpenter got us well into it. The outside is finished with rough wood plank siding that will weather to match the rest of the cabin. The roof is shiny sheet metal, and I finally got to use all the lead-headed nails I brought with me back in September. The inside is paneled with cedar boards that give a pungent aroma and will help in the storage of the clothes.

When we were putting the insulation in between the wall studs, I let Toby place a note he wrote in a Dr. Pepper bottle and seal it inside the wall for some future remodeler to find.

"I said, 'I hope you like the way I write. I'm Toby Siler and this is my closet where Cody let me put my stuff. We built it together.'"

"Very good. You're beginning to write and read a lot better."

"I'm proud of both of you guys," Ginny says when she looks at Toby's finished closet. "I already have all my clothes in mine."

"The addition cost more than Thoreau spent on his entire cabin," I say. "But that's inflation."

"Who's Thoreau?" Toby asks.

"Hasn't Cody read you the book about the guy who lived in a cabin by a pond up in New England?"

"No. Where's New England?"

"Shame on you, Cody. That's one of your favorite books. You should read it to him."

I nod my head. I'm a little jealous and possessive of Thoreau and *Walden*. I've been hoarding him to myself like I should be the sole interpreter of his words. But Ginny is right. I should share with Toby what is important to me. I know his father is not a proper role model in that regard.

"I will," I say. "We'll sit by the fire at the stove and read a chapter each day. They're not long. And I think you'll enjoy it, Toby. You'll grow into it and like it more later on."

TOBY DOESN'T LET ME stop with a chapter a day, and in another week we have finished the little book.

"Did he go back to the village because he didn't want to be alone anymore?" he asks.

"Well, I guess that was part of it. But he had plenty of visitors at his cabin—just like I do. And he was doing it more as an experiment and probably a little protest at how the world was becoming materialistic."

"Mater . . . what?"

"How people became more interested in things than ideas."

He stretches his legs out toward the stove where we're both sitting on the floor with our backs braced on the front of the couch.

"Oh. It's better to like people than things, isn't it, Cody?"

"Things should come down low on our list. God, family, friends, the Earth, the rivers, the mountains, ideas." I look down at him, hoping that I'm teaching him a lesson. Priorities and such.

"Cody, am I a visitor?"

"A visitor?"

"Yeah. You said Mr. Thoreau had a lot of visitors at his cabin and you've had a lot. Am I a visitor?"

"Toby, you're just like one of the family," I say and put my arm around him. He's a very sensitive boy. He caught my words, and I'm not sure I have convinced him that he is one of us. "Those devil worshipers were visitors, Toby. The kind I didn't want. You started out as a visitor, but you're like a son to me now."

He looks up at me, tears puddling at the corner of his eyes, but then his face stretches in a smile as big as a Jack-o-lantern's. "I'm glad. I'm happy when I'm here," he says and leans his head over to my chest.

THE FIRST OF FEBRUARY comes in with a heavy snow. Toby has not appeared for the past week. Ginny is greatly concerned. But I tell her that this is not unusual. Toby doesn't operate on the same schedule as we do, and sometimes he doesn't have the leeway and ability to leave his father.

"But the way you described his house, I'm afraid he might be cold or hungry. His clothes are rags. Do you think the state children's services would do anything now?"

"Ginny, it's no use. I've tried. I think it will take time. We have to be patient. He's abused, but I haven't seen anything real bad lately. I look at his face and legs and hands every chance I get. You know I'd let him stay here all the time if I could."

"Nothing lately? He can only have his mother killed one time. Cody, you're going to have to do more. That's what drove me crazy about you in '68. You were content to be an observer. You wouldn't get involved when the world needed you."

"That was my job. I was a reporter," I say and feel the old frustrations of thirty-year-old arguments boiling to the surface.

Is that really why we parted in 1968? I could never be as involved as Ginny thought I should. I would not lead protests. I would not and, of course, could not write editorials decrying the war and poverty.

I lost my graduate deferment from the draft when they were all ended. For nearly a year, there was uncertainty. I was called for my physical. And then a spectacular thing happened. On December 1, 1969, when the first draft lottery in a generation was held, my birthday—March 14—was selected as number 354. This meant the Vietcong would have to be marching down Gay Street in Knoxville and making a turn onto Main and then to Cumberland to go toward the University of Tennessee before I would be rousted out of my law school classes to carry a gun.

Ginny must see the concern etched on my face. She sits quietly and doesn't push it. We both look outside where the snow is deepening.

"You know what would be nice to have?" she asks.

"What?"

"Instead of having to walk to the spring house for the things we're keeping cold, how much trouble would it be to have a refrigerator—just a small one—sitting on the front porch? It would be cool there anyway, and you still could run the power for just a few hours each day."

I think of the things I have added to the cabin since September—insulation, a solar-powered water heater, a propane gas water heater, two beds, two walk-in closets, spotlights, and a gasoline-powered electric generator. My rustic cabin is turning into a mountain condo. My generation has just become too used to the modern niceties of life. Now, it's a refrigerator. What's next? Television?

"And you know what else would be nice for us to have on these days when we can't get out and to help Toby learn about the outside world?"

"What?"

"A television. I don't mean to have on all the time. Just a little. I miss some of the educational and talk shows, the news and such. We could just limit it to watching the news and *Crossfire* on CNN. And let Toby watch the Learning Channel and Discovery."

"They don't have cable up here," I say and sigh a breath of relief.

"Not cable. Satellite. One of those little dishes aimed at the sky. It could be attached to the side of the cabin in an out-of-the-way place."

I shake my head. "I don't know, Ginny. I came here to get away from the world. Do you think it would be good to have all that's on television available to Toby? There's a lot of filth on the airways."

She laughs. "You sound like our parents when we were growing up and going to the movies."

I lean back and smile. "Yeah, we're becoming our parents. They may have been right."

"Not me. I'm not becoming my mother."

"I tell you what. I'll go for the little refrigerator. But we'll go together and check on the satellite television. If there's a way we can block out most of that trash, we'll see about getting it. But we'll only have the refrigerator and television hooked to the power for two or three hours a day. And we'll agree to have the television on for only an hour for us and an hour of learning time for Toby when he's here, okay?"

She smiles. "Sounds great."

IN TWO DAYS THE snow has melted enough that we can drive the Jeep to Jamestown where Ginny and I buy a little refrigerator and visit the local satellite television dealer. The salesman convinces me that we can tune out any of the channels we don't want a child to be exposed to and just pay for the ones we want. They will install it the next day.

TOBY SHOWS BACK UP a day after the satellite dish is attached to the side of the cabin.

"What's that?" he points and asks.

"The official wildflower of the mountains," I say and smile.

"What?" He wrinkles up his nose. "It don't look like no flower."

"*Any*," I say. "No, I was just kidding. It's a mechanism to capture broadcast signals from satellites in space for television. We now have television, Toby. Ginny's going to help you learn by watching some programs on it."

"Wow!" he says and rushes inside where the ominous box is attached high on the living room wall. I follow him in. "Is that it?"

"Yes, dreadful thing that it is."

"I don't see anything but the reflection of the window in it."

"It's not turned on," I say. "And won't be except for an hour a day for you to learn, and an hour a day for us to get the news and watch *Crossfire*," I continue and look over at Ginny who is sitting on the couch reading.

I turn the power and set on. Toby sits enthralled on the floor with his head leaned back watching the animals on the African plains. He has seen some of these in books but not where they're moving and look real. The camera then enters a village where a traditional dance is set to the drum-beats of natives.

"There's some more of those black folks. Is that their houses?"

"*They are*," I say.

"I like their animals and music, but they need sides on those houses or they'll get cold."

"It's hot there most of the time," I say.

When the news comes on, Toby heads for home.

"What can I watch tomorrow?" he asks before he leaves the porch.

"I don't know, Toby," Ginny says, "but I'll check the schedule and see if I can find something that will go along with your studies."

Ginny and I sit together on the couch and watch the latest news and the combatants on *Crossfire*. At a break, I lean over and whisper, "Maybe this will work okay. A little television for us and a learning tool for Toby." I take the controls and flip through the channels until I find the country music video channel where Shania Twain is singing and showing her navel.

Ginny grabs the controls and flips back to CNN. "Just the news, Buster. Remember? We don't want you to be perverted by modern entertainment."

When the program is over, Ginny turns the power off to the set, walks out to the new refrigerator, and brings us each a Dr. Pepper. "Do you think it's about time, Cody?"

"Time for what?"

"Time for you to go to Nashville and meet your son—your birth son and his family."

I take a long sip. I'm excited and afraid. From the day that Ginny first told me that we had a son, I've been an ocean of emotions. One wave would break across me of joy. That one would be replaced by terror. What if he didn't like me? What if he wanted to know why we didn't get married and keep him? How would he compare me to his father that reared him, nurtured him, supported him, and brought him up to be what he is? Maybe, being a man of the cloth, he will have an understanding heart. Apparently, he accepted Ginny and was anxious to know about me.

"I guess," I say. "You know I'm a bit anxious about this."

"You'll be fine, Cody. Jerry really wants to see you. I'll call him now and tell him we'll come down tomorrow."

"No. Don't call him. He might want to talk to me. I want to talk to him in person the first time. I can't stand to meet him over the phone. We'll just drive down and pop in. Preachers must always be about their work. He'll be there. I'm sure."

"Okay, if you don't mind the possibility of a wasted trip."

"It won't be wasted. If I have you in Nashville at the Parthenon or at the Capitol, it won't be wasted," I say and smile.

"Cody, it's February. Cold. I'm athletic, but I'm not as limber as I used to be."

"Are we going to take Toby or leave him here?"

"He's welcome to go as far as I'm concerned," Ginny says. "Can you explain the relationships to him?"

"I don't know. We'll see if he wants to go."

21

I am up long before Ginny the next morning. I have thought about my new son all night. I bring the electric generator to life and then turn the television to the Weather Channel to see how things look for Nashville today. I sit back with a cup of coffee and watch the colored maps move across the screen with their lows and highs.

"It's still dark. What're you doing up so early? And why's the generator and television on?" Ginny asks when she leans around the door of the bedroom.

"I couldn't sleep any longer. I want to see Jerry and his son. I'm checking the weather for a few minutes. I don't want to get caught in a snow storm."

Ginny comes over and sits with her back against my knees. I put my hands down and rub her neck and shoulders. "You're still a little anxious, aren't you?" she asks and turns her head slightly.

"Yeah, I just don't know what to expect."

"You'll be okay. He looks a lot like you."

In a few minutes, I turn the television off, flip the switch that silences the generator, and walk outside to bring in more wood for the stove. Night is turning to day, but it's a gray dreary morning with the clouds moving low across the hills and keeping them veiled in a dark fog.

On my second trip out for wood, the sound of gunfire in the distance makes me turn my head in the direction of Toby's house. My first impression is that he's out squirrel hunting early. Then, when the sharp cracks repeat, they sound more like rifle fire than his 20-gauge shotgun. The shooting ends in a bit with two more cracking reverberations that are different from the first two series. Then all is quiet. I carry my armload of wood in and join Ginny at the table where she is already eating her cereal.

"I think Toby is out hunting early this morning. He must have one of his dad's guns. It didn't sound like a shotgun. He has such good aim, though, that he could hunt squirrels with a rifle."

"What does he do with the squirrels?"

"They're okay to eat. You can skin and cure their hides for the fur."

Ginny puts her spoon back into her cereal bowl and doesn't take another bite. "I don't believe I could eat a squirrel," she says and takes her bowl toward the sink.

"They make pretty good soup," I say. "It's been a while since I had any, but it's not bad." Ginny turns and gives me a retching expression. "I'm going to carry in some more wood, so there'll be plenty when we get back."

"Do you think we'll spend the night?" she asks.

"We'll see how it goes."

"Well, I'll pack like we are, and if we don't it'll be okay."

I walk back outside to the wood pile and pick through the stack for the best pieces to take inside. When I have an arm load, I start back in.

From out of the gray forest, I hear a rustling of feet and then see Toby standing but bent over. I blink my eyes to be sure I'm seeing what I think I'm seeing. Toby is leading a line of four goats tethered to a rope and is carrying chickens in a wire cage. When the strange procession draws nearer, I notice that he's crying again, his face is red, his eyes and nose watery, and tucked into his belt at the waist is the . . . .44 Colt revolver we found in the cave. His lips quiver when he looks up at me.

"Toby, what are you doing?" I say and throw my load of wood down to the side. "What's the meaning of this? The goats? The chickens? And what're you doing with my gun?"

He sets the caged chickens down and takes the gun from his belt. He hands it to me.

"My Pa started shooting my goats. He said they were useless. He shot some of my chickens. When I begged him not to shoot my animals, he hit me. Then . . . then . . . ," he says and falls to his knees. He turns loose of the rope holding the goats and rubs his eyes. He looks back up to where I'm standing. "Then . . . the soldier's gun shot him," he says and cries out a haunting scream that wanders down the valley and back like a ghost on a horse. "My Pa is dead and the house is burned down."

IN A HALF HOUR, I leave the sobbing child with Ginny. I have placed the caged chickens on the back porch and tied the goats to the railing there. The "soldier's gun," as Toby describes it, is still at my waist tucked inside my belt when I begin my walk to Ben Siler's place. If what Toby has told us is accurate, I will not find either Ben Siler or the house standing.

My mind is a whir of thinking as I walk the mile. I could drive, but I don't want to leave my Jeep's tire prints on his land. When the cops come—and some time they surely will come—they might become suspicious that I'm the culprit that did Ben in, especially if my Jeep has been there.

I don't know what to expect. I cannot see smoke from the burning house. If it's afire, the clouds and smoke are blending into a masking mixture. I think of Toby. What about Toby? He had the pistol. The soldier's gun shot his Pa, but it must have been at the end of Toby's arm. He had reason enough. But will the law accept that? An abused child. A father who doesn't love his son. A murderer of the child's mother. A drug dealer. The law. What will the law do? Will they take Toby from the mountain and place him in a home where he doesn't belong? It will kill him.

On my short walk, I determine that I will do what I must to protect him. Ginny didn't mention a thing that I should do. But I didn't take any action in 1968, and she recently told me that I should have been more active in taking Toby from the home of the abuser. Now I will rise up and do the necessary—even if it's wrong. I will not be just an observer.

The pistol chafes against my leg, and I take it out, holding it in my hand as I walk. When I reach the place where the drive leads off the road to the Silers, a log truck chugs up the hill. I absent-mindedly wave at the driver with the hand in which I carry the pistol. He ducks down and guns the truck's engine.

When I reach the bend in the driveway from where the house was previously visible, I now see flames licking at the charred remains. The house has burned and fallen in on itself. The tractor and big pickup truck stand to either side like guardian demons. I walk closer and smell the stench of burning flesh.

There's not much left of Ben Siler. He is not recognizable as a human being—if he ever was. It's a scorched carcass of a large animal. He is sprawled on his stomach near where the porch steps used to be. The barrel and metal parts of his rifle lie next to him.

I look around. Only the small barn where the goats and chickens lived is still standing. Two chickens lie dead there and a goat. The man finally took too much from the child who struck back.

When I mount the tractor, I know what I'm going to do. Legally it might be called obstructing justice or some such crazy term. It would be enough for me to lose my law license. The tractor starts and I lurch forward with the front-end loader scraping the ground like a grader. I begin to push all the smoldering boards into one small area where they will burn better. The steaming body twists and writhes as though it's still alive when I push it to the middle of the pile. I scrape all the burnable remains of the house over the body. Flames shoot back up when the fire finds more fuel.

I attack the corner of the little barn and knock it down. I add the boards to the fire and, from time to time, scrape the wood into a smaller area where it burns.

In the end, I take the tractor and push the pickup truck into the fire and then ease the tractor beside it and jump off into the soft ground beside the ashes. The tires of the tractor and truck begin to blaze first. Then when the fire reaches the gas tanks, a great ball of orange flame explodes and billows up toward the gray sky.

There will be no remembrance of Ben Siler. An evil man is seared from my memory. Perhaps, I have cauterized the wound.

I stand back and behold the flames. Then near where the barn was, there's a noise. I turn and see a goat thrashing in the brush. When I walk near, I see blood running from a hind leg that has been nearly blasted off. I take the pistol and put the goat out of its misery. Then I carry the goat's body to the fire and heave it into the flames.

At another mountain and in another time, Abraham told Isaac that God would provide the lamb for the burnt offering. Then when God had stopped the hand of Abraham from killing his son, he found a ram caught in the thicket that he offered instead.

I survey what I have done and realize that in a brief period of living on the mountain I have left my valley beliefs and become a hill person.

I kneel before the altar and say a short prayer for Toby . . . for Ginny . . . and for me.

22

N o face which we can give to a matter will stead us so well at last as the truth."—*Walden*.

It's been a week now since the shooting and fire. There have been no policemen or other investigators. We hope that no one will notice that Ben Siler no longer walks the paths of the Earth. Except for the clouds that hugged the mountain like a soapy hand on the day the Siler house burned, the smoke would have been seen from Jamestown to Oneida. For the cloaking palm of the clouds, I have given God thanks.

Toby can't sleep more than two hours without jumping up and running to my bed or to Ginny's. He's scared and dreams about his last moments with his father.

"Are the police going to kill me?" he asks me this morning.

"No, Toby. You were a battered child. I should have done what you did. Or the police should have taken your father away before this happened. He killed your mother."

He buries his head in his open hands where he sits on the steps. "Pa said if I told that he killed my mama the police would kill him and me. He said I helped hide her body and it made me just as much at fault."

"No. You're a child. You had no choice. Is that why you didn't tell the police?"

"Yeah. He said if they took him they would take me too and kill me or put me in a prison where bad men would beat me up."

FOR THE WEEK, THE chickens have been on the back porch, which is messy enough. But there's a rooster and six hens. Each morning beginning at four, the rooster lights on the top of the rocker and begins his crowing to waken the sun. He succeeds in waking me and Ginny too—but she sleeps in the other room. We have scattered hay, and the goats root around on the porch in it.

Today, Toby and I are building a more permanent solution for his animals. We're erecting a small three-sided barn about ten yards behind the cabin where the forest begins. The goats will sleep there, and the chickens will have a place to roost near the top. It's the first time in thirty-five years that I've been near farm animals.

We don't really need them. But they're Toby's connection to being a worthwhile boy. He raised the chickens from the time they hatched. The goats are his second generation. He has named each goat and each chicken. This explains to me even more his anger when his father went on the shooting rampage.

WHEN TOBY HAS GONE to bed, Ginny seems more pensive than before.

"What are you going to tell them when they come asking questions?"

"Who?"

"The police."

"Maybe they won't come. Maybe nobody will care that a drug dealer is gone from the mountain."

"But if they do? Are you going to turn Toby in?"

"No. Of course not. I'm his lawyer. Anything he told me is confidential and privileged."

"You told me what you did, Cody. Is that a crime?"

"I stopped a possible forest fire from spreading. His body was already burned. I just helped the process along and kept it all in one place."

"And that's what you're going to tell the police?"

"No. I'm not telling the police anything. Hill people don't talk."

"What're we going to do with Toby then?"

"Keep him here. He's better off with us than he was with his father. We'll teach him until he's up to his grade level and then put him in school."

"He's not ours. We don't have custody. We can't enter him in school without some kind of custody or guardianship. Even I know that. You're the lawyer. You should know that."

I shake my head. I had almost forgotten I am a lawyer. My Tennessee Code is still on the shelves in Toby's room. I probably need to brush up on child custody.

"You're right, Ginny. I was thinking with my heart and not my head."

IT'S TWO DAYS LATER when the deputies arrive. I recognize Deputy Crawford when he tugs at his shirt collar and jerks his head as he walks down the drive. The other deputy wasn't among the ones that joined us on the day we went to Ben Siler's house. They leave their cruiser on the road and motion to me as I'm carrying wood into the cabin.

"Mr. Rogers, how're you doing?" Crawford asks.

"Fine, Deputy. What's up?"

"That's what we were going to ask you. Someone called the office yesterday and said Ben Siler's little house had burned down. What do you know about it?"

"Come on in the cabin. Out of the cold. We'll sit and talk."

When we walk in, I look around to see where Toby is, but his door is closed. Ginny nods toward his room when the deputies aren't watching me. I introduce the deputies to Ginny.

"I didn't know you had a visitor? We won't stay long."

"It doesn't matter. Ginny's living here now."

"Oh," Crawford says and looks at his partner. "Yeah, the mountain's a lonely place. Everybody needs someone up here." They look around the cabin. "Looks like you've added a few modern touches since I was here last. I saw that satellite dish on the side out there. You get good reception?"

"Yeah, pretty good," I say.

"You watch them bullfights from Mexico?"

"No. Just a little news on CNN, the Discovery Channel, and The Learning Channel."

"Oh," Crawford says. "Anyway, did you know that Ben Siler's house burned?"

"Yes. I walked over there when I heard about it."

"Heard about it? Who from?"

I clear my throat. "That's just an expression. I heard the sound from way over here."

Crawford shakes his head. "Yeah, we were just over there. It's funny though, you know?"

"How's that?"

"The way the tractor and truck are parked side by side. And they burned too. Just rusting hulks of metal there now. That was a fine truck. Probably cost thirty thousand or so. The tractor too."

"Well, as I told you before, Ben was in the marijuana growing business. Drug dealers sometimes make enemies."

"You seen Ben since the fire?" Crawford asks.

I think about the question. "Have I seen Ben since the fire?" It's a question I can answer truthfully. I have not seen Ben since the fire, and I tell them that.

"You know where he's at?"

"Burning in Hell," I want to say, but bowing to God's grace and forgiveness, I can honestly say, "No." And I do. I look at both deputies who are staring at each other. "I gather that I'm not a suspect since you haven't given me my Miranda warnings," I say.

"No, Mr. Rogers. We don't think you would burn down Ben Siler's cabin . . . and leave him alive. You know what an animal he is. If he thought you burned him out, he'd kill you, skin you, and tack your hide to a tree." They smile at each other.

"Thanks," I say.

"What about the boy or Ben's wife? Have you seen them?"

"I told you some time ago that Ben killed his wife. What are you doing, still looking for her in Atlanta?"

"Well, we haven't really had any luck on that. No hospital down there knows anything about her."

"And they won't," I add.

"What about the boy?" Crawford asks. "You seen him?"

"Yes. Daily," I blurt out.

"You seen him since his house burned?" Crawford asks and leans forward in his seat.

"Sure. He's staying here now."

"That so? Where is he?"

Toby must have been listening at his door, for when the officer asks where he is, his door eases open and the boy comes and stands next to me.

"Hi, son. I forgot your name. What is it?" Crawford asks.

"Toby."

"I noticed that your house burned."

"Yep."

"Do you know where your dad is?"

"Sorta."

"Sorta?" Crawford says and smiles. "You know where he is or not?"

"I think so."

"Well, where is that, Toby?"

"He went to visit my mama."

23

D *ependent and neglected* are the words that jump out at me five days later when the petition is served on me concerning Toby. I politely show the officers out and then I begin to bang my fist against the door facing.

"What the hell do they mean!? Dependent and neglected. Toby is not neglected. He is dependent on us. If he was neglected, it was when he was living with Ben and being abused. It's just like the state bureaucracy to let that go and then serve us with papers because we're taking care of him."

Toby had told the officers no more than that his father was away visiting his mother. Apparently the deputies felt they were not getting the full story and reported what they knew to the department of children's services. Now they are tightening the screws on all of us by taking this petition. They would take Toby out of our home and put him with foster parents until his real parents returned or until they learned the truth.

"What can we do?" Ginny asks.

"Fight it," I say and start toward Toby's room where my Tennessee Code has gathered dust on the shelves since September. "You wanted me to be more active. Hell, I'm doing it!" I say and throw open the door. Toby is lying on the bed, his blanket clutched to him.

Ginny follows me to the door. "I'm glad, Cody. But I'm on your side. Remember that. We're working together."

I nod and scoot a chair over to the shelves and scan

the volumes for the one containing laws about juveniles.

"Are they going to take me away?" Toby asks.

"No. You're going to stay right here."

"Are they going to kill me? Or put me in prison with bad men?"

Ginny goes and sits on the edge of the bed next to him. "No, Toby. You have one of the best lawyers in the state working for you. He'll keep you right here. You're safe with us."

After a few minutes of looking over the laws about minors, I take a legal pad and begin to write.

"What does it say?" Ginny asks.

"If there are no parents, or a child is abandoned by his parents, the state can take the child into protective custody and place him with foster parents."

"Foster parents? What's that?" Toby asks.

"Nothing for you to worry about," I say and continue writing.

"What are you writing?" Ginny asks.

"A petition for me to be granted temporary custody. I'll beat them to the punch. If the judge finds that Toby's parents aren't present, he still can place him with me instead of turning him over to the state." I look up at Ginny. "Will you join in the petition with me?"

"Sure."

"We'd be well served to have a counselor or psychologist see Toby who could testify that he'd be better off with us than with foster parents who are strangers."

TWO HOURS LATER, WE'RE on the road to Jamestown with Toby to find a counselor. Ginny had taken me aside and said that she was sure Toby needed counseling anyway because of the loss of his mother and father. I agreed. Such traumas could affect him for his entire life.

FORTUNE SMILES ON US when we find an office in Jamestown with a marriage and family counselor who is in and between appointments. I leave Toby and Ginny in the reception area and go into the counselor's office alone.

"I'm Cody Rogers," I say and extend my hand.

"Sarah Fontaine," the counselor says.

I look at her. She can't be much older than my daughter. I wonder how much experience she has had, and whether she has ever seen a boy like Toby before. She is neat and dressed very businesslike in a Navy jacket and matching skirt. On the wall behind her, are her diplomas and license from the state. I will have to take my chances with her.

"I'm a lawyer, Ms. Fontaine. I'm also a very close friend with the boy out in the reception area. He's Toby Siler. I'm also *his* lawyer."

She nods, but I can see the question marks in her eyes.

"The reason I'm saying that," I continue, "is that Toby will be relating some disturbing facts to you. He may even recount actions that could be considered in some circles as criminal."

With the mention of the word *criminal*, Ms. Fontaine's brow wrinkles.

"I know that you counselors and your clients have the same rules of confidentiality and privilege as we lawyers do. Am I not correct?"

"Yes, that's true," she says and leans forward a bit more.

"Anyway, I know that unless Toby relates to you that he is about to commit some other crime or is about to put himself or someone else in imminent danger, everything he tells you will be confidential and privileged. Right?"

"Absolutely."

"I'm his lawyer, so I can tell you that Toby killed his father."

Ms. Fontaine's jaw drops slightly, but she recovers nicely by bringing a pencil to her lips.

"He was an abused child. He finally couldn't take it any longer and killed his father. Shot him with a pistol."

"And the police don't know?"

"No. That's the beauty of it. Only his lawyer and counselor know. You see, he needs counseling to deal with that. It's been very traumatic."

"Yes, I can imagine. And his mother out there wants me to see him? And work with him?" She nods toward the door and beyond to where Ginny is sitting with Toby.

"No. That's not his mother. She's a friend of mine. His mother's dead. His father killed his mother a couple of months ago."

"What!?"

"Yes. It's true. Toby saw it. That's another reason why he needs counseling."

"Oh, my. This is a rough one. So, you have guardianship?"

"No. I'm filing for custody. But that's still another thing. I thought it would be good for you to examine him and say whether or not he would be better off with me and Ginny or with foster parents who are total strangers." I sit back and wait for Sarah Fontaine to absorb this and reply. She is silent for most of a minute.

"I can't see him, Mr. Rogers," she finally says.

"Why?"

"A parent or guardian has to consent for me to see a minor."

"He has no parents or guardians. I just told you."

"I understand. But until someone is appointed, I can't do anything."

"Not even examine him to testify about his best interests?"

"Not without a court order. You should know that."

I nod. There's a lot I should know. It wasn't my area of law practice. "All of what I have told you will remain confidential, won't it?" I ask.

She reaches over to a receipt book and writes on it. "That will be twenty-five dollars, Mr. Rogers."

"What for?"

"You're my client. Everything you told me will remain confidential and privileged."

"Oh. I see. I'm your client. Great. I could always use some counseling anyway," I say and reach for my wallet. She's sharper than I first thought.

"I'd love to work with Toby once you get custody," she says and hands me the receipt.

"Did you take any notes of our conversation?" I ask.

"No. It's more confidential that way. I won't take any with Toby either when you bring him back. I wish you good luck in getting custody."

"Thanks."

THE JUDGE THAT WE appear before a week later also has jurisdiction over traffic tickets, divorce cases, probate matters, preliminary hearings in criminal cases, and civil cases under fifteen thousand dollars. He has to look at his weekly calendar each day just to know what kinds of cases he's trying that morning. Court is supposed to start at nine, but the judge, lawyers, and sheriff's deputies congregate in his office to talk about all kinds of things. I walk by and hear them discussing last night's basketball game.

I know from experience that in rural counties, this is also where the judge might get the first inkling of what awaits him that day. A court officer might say that so-and-so is back, or that Joe Jones has another DUI, or a certain would-be divorcée looks very attractive in her low-cut dress. The judge is not supposed to hear from the parties or about the case except in sworn testimony, but often something sneaks in the back door. I don't go in because I'm a party, but I stand nearby so I can be certain no one else discusses my case.

A half hour late, the court officer announces, "Hear Ye, Hear Ye, . . . draw near and you shall be heard. No smoking or drinking in the courtroom. And take off your cap, please," he says to a youth sitting on the back bench.

The school attendance officer appears with his list of truants. They step meekly toward the bench, some with parents and some without. The judge scolds a youth who leans his elbow onto the wooden elevated bench. He straightens up.

One by one, they step up and get a lecture or a warning. They all are rebelling. I can tell it by their uniform. They all want to be different, but here they are wearing the same kind of clothes—loose shirts and pants with cuffs dragging the ground. The pants are pulled so low on their hips that it appears they are assless. When they're through here, they'll go out, put their baseball caps on backwards, and laugh about how they snookered the judge.

We are the last case of the morning. It's near noon when the judge calls us up. He's not going to take a lunch break he tells us, as he wants to leave early in the afternoon for a trip out of town. He turns to the attorney for the children's protective services and asks whether she's ready and how long she anticipates the case will take. "An hour at most," she says and looks at me. I nod my agreement.

"I see that we have a petition by the state and one by Mr. Rogers. Is it okay with both sides to combine them and have one hearing?"

"Yes, Your Honor," we say simultaneously.

The children's services lawyer puts the department employee on the stand whom I had talked to when I first noticed Toby's physical abuse. She testifies in a monotone about what I told her and her whole knowledge of Toby Siler, which isn't much. She recommends that Toby be placed with department certified foster parents until Mr. or Mrs. Siler returns to claim him. I ask her no questions.

Next, Deputy Crawford reports that he found the Silers' house burned to the ground along with Ben's vehicles. He tells about me reporting to him that Toby told me Ben had killed his wife. When they inquired of Ben and Toby in person, they both reported that Mrs. Siler was in Atlanta for cancer treatments, but efforts to locate her there had proved unsuccessful.

A lot of this is hearsay, which I could object to but I don't because it doesn't matter and is accurate as to what was said.

"When you went to the site of the burned house, was there any indication that Mr. Siler died in the fire?" the judge asks Crawford.

"None that we could find. Everything was burned completely. Just ashes. It almost looked like everything was scraped together and burned," Crawford says and looks at me. I look back and don't blink.

"Has Mr. Siler been heard from by anyone?" the judge asks the deputy.

"No."

"Has anybody reported to you where he is?"

"The boy said that he'd gone to visit Mrs. Siler," Crawford answers and nods toward Toby who is sitting next to me.

I have no questions for Deputy Crawford either as I know his familiarity with the facts to be just as he said.

Next, I take the stand to tell why I should be award- ed custody of Toby along with Ginny who is holding Toby's hand as I'm sworn to tell the truth.

I go through my background, making sure the judge knows that I am a fellow member of the bar, educated, with sufficient means and ability to care for Toby. I relate our friendship of the past five months and how he had often stayed at my cabin, even before his parents *left* and his house burned. I am careful not to lie to the court, but I skirt around my knowledge of the whereabouts of Toby's parents.

When I'm through, the department's attorney stands to question me.

"How old are you, Mr. Rogers?"

"Fifty-one."

"Do you have other children?"

"Yes, two . . . or three," I stammer and look at Ginny.

The attorney smiles. She knows she has me in a spot. If I don't even remember how many children I have, how could I be a suitable parent for Toby?

"Well, is it *two* or *three*?" she asks and looks at the judge who is peering over his glasses at me.

As Thoreau and the Bible recommend, I tell the truth. "I have two by my marriage to my wife who died last year. And I just found out that I have another one that I didn't know about with Ginny here." I nod toward Ginny who drops her head at the way I answered.

The attorney has me on a hook and she won't let go. "Ginny here? Are you talking about the other petitioner here, your wife?"

"Yes . . . and no," I say after hesitating for a minute. "She is the other petitioner. But she's not my wife."

"You're living together?"

"Yes, in the same cabin, but not in the same bedroom . . . when Toby's there."

The attorney nods her head, smiles, and looks at the judge who is writing a note on his legal pad. I sound silly, just like one of those husbands caught living with someone during a divorce suit. They're always living in the same house but in separate bedrooms. I know what the judge is thinking.

"Do you have any plans to get married?"

"No," I say and look at Ginny. "Do we?" Ginny slinks a little lower in her chair while Toby looks first at her and then at me. I was doing well until I started answering questions.

"So, you're asking this court to place this ten-year-old child in a home where two people are living together who are not married to each other?"

"Yes."

"What kind of impression will that give to this young child?"

I think for a minute before I answer this time. She has asked me a wide open question that I should be able to answer. She wants me to say, "I don't know," but instead I say, "He'll see two people who love each other and who love him. He'll see two people who will teach him, care for him, clothe him, feed him, and take care of him as best we can."

This time Ginny sits back up and nods her approval.

"That's just your opinion, isn't it, Mr. Rogers?"

"No. That's what we have done, and that's what we will do."

She sees that I'm warming up to testifying now and using any question to bolster my case, so she sits down and ends her cross-examination.

"I'd like to hear from Toby Siler," the judge says when I'm seated. "He can just talk to me from where he is. He doesn't need to come up here, be sworn in, and have these lawyers ask him questions." He smiles and leans forward.

"You want to tell me what you want to do, Toby?"

"I want to live with Cody and Ginny," he says without hesitation.

"Why's that?"

"They're the only people I know. I want to stay in the mountains. I don't want to go to jail or to a fos . . . fos . . . foster home," he says and wipes the back of his hand across his eyes.

"You have any other relatives besides your parents?"

"No."

"No uncles, aunts, brothers, or sisters?"

"No."

"The officer said you told him your mother was in Atlanta getting cancer treatments and that your father went to visit her. Is that what you told him?"

Toby lowers his head, but nods it up and down.

"Do you know where in Atlanta they are?"

Toby shuffles in his seat, rocks back and forth, and then answers. "They're not in Atlanta. My Pa told me to tell the police that. My Pa killed my mama. And when my Pa started shooting my chickens and goats, the soldier told me to use his pistol and shoot my Pa. He's dead, and I burned the house down."

The judge holds up his hand. "Don't say any more, Toby. You're not under oath, I didn't give you any Miranda warnings, and I didn't even ask you what happened to your parents. So, please don't say anything else." The judge shakes his head, looks down at his pad, and writes a few notes.

When he raises his head, he looks at me. "Mr. Rogers, I'm going to give you temporary custody and guardianship for thirty days or until further order of this court." Then he looks at Deputy Crawford. "I want you to investigate the disappearance of the Silers and report back to me in thirty days." And finally he glances down at the state's attorney. "You may supervise this custody arrangement and check on the circumstances from time to time. Court is adjourned."

24

T he next day, the last day of February, Ginny and I are sitting near the front window of the cabin when a line of law enforcement vehicles climbs the mountain road and eases past our place in the direction of the Silers. A tractor with a backhoe is pulled along in the middle of the procession.

"There were five marked patrol cars, an unmarked car, and the tractor," Ginny says. "What are they doing?"

"I expect they're going to spend the day looking and digging around at the Silers. Now that they have word from Toby that his mother actually was killed, they can probably dig up the area where her remains are."

"That'll help to prove he was right?"

"Sure. Then they'll start poking around the ashes to see if they can find any remains of Ben Siler."

"And that won't be good?" Ginny asks.

"They won't find much. But with Toby confessing, it won't take much for them to arrest him under a juvenile petition."

"But his dad was abusive. They shouldn't arrest Toby."

"The law's funny. It says we should let the police protect us and only take action when our lives are threatened. They may not consider Ben's killing goats and chickens sufficient to excuse Toby's shooting him."

"But it wasn't about goats and chickens. He was physically, emotionally, and mentally abused."

"You and I know that. They don't."

LATER IN THE MORNING we go with Toby to Jamestown for counseling with Sarah Fontaine. She sees us as a family unit for the first hour, we break for lunch, and then she sees Toby alone for another hour. She listens more than she talks. She takes a lot of history on a white board about all of our families—families of origin, she calls them. While we're present, she doesn't mention the death of either of Toby's parents, but that is something I suspect she brings up with him alone.

I expect a report after her last session with Toby, but, instead, Ms. Fontaine says we need to see her twice a week between now and the next court hearing. I mentally calculate my monthly one thousand dollar budget and know that this expense is going to destroy it.

While Toby was in the session alone, I read some in *Walden*. Thoreau didn't have to pay for counseling, but he did say:

"However mean your life is, meet it and live it; do not shun it and call it hard times. It is not so bad as you are. It looks poorest when you are richest."

I look beside me and I have Ginny and Toby. I glance in the mirror and I have my health. I am rich, so I resolve not to resent this necessary expense for Toby's sake—and all of ours.

WHEN WE'RE BACK AT the cabin, Ginny goes to the wall calendar and marks the days and times that we are to go back for counseling. Toby tags after her.

"This is my birthday," he says when he sees her write on today's date on the calendar.

"It is? Are you sure?" Ginny asks.

"Yes. My mama taught me the months and seasons. She told me I was born the last day of winter."

"Winter's not over until along toward the end of March," I say.

"She said winter was December, January, and February. Spring was March, April, and May. No matter what the calendar said. She told me I was born late at night on the last day of February—of winter—and when she woke up the next morning with me in her arms, I was the sunshine of spring that she always wanted. I'm eleven years old today."

Ginny and I are both silent. I'm sure we're thinking something similar. Toby has some good memories of his mother. All wasn't dark. He—at least at birth—was the light of her life. And she told him. Wonderful. I almost cry but bite my lip. Tears streak down Ginny's cheeks.

Toby looks at both of us. "What's wrong? Did I say something bad?"

"No, Toby. You said something great," Ginny says and hugs him to her. "We've got to go out and celebrate your birthday with cake and ice cream and . . . and I don't know what."

ON THE SPUR OF the moment while we're in Jamestown enjoying ice cream and cake for Toby's birthday, I blurt out to Ginny, "Let's adopt Toby. We have the custody papers. Let's go to a lawyer's office while we're here and start the ball rolling. What do you say? And, Toby, would you like that?"

"Adopt? What does that mean?" he asks.

"You'd be our son. Our boy. Officially. Legally. I'd be your new dad, and Ginny would be your new mom. Is that okay with you?"

He doesn't say anything but instead reaches over and hugs Ginny and then leans across the table to me. "Mom and Dad? Is that what I'd call you?"

"Yes," I say. "Ginny, is it okay with you? We'll go right now."

"I'd love to be Toby's mother," she says and smoothes down the hair on his head.

IT IS AT THE third law office on the square surrounding the courthouse that we finally find a lawyer who is willing to talk to us without having an appointment.

"Adoption?" she says when we're sitting comfortably

in our chairs in front of her desk.

"Yes, I have official custody through the Juvenile Court, and Ginny and I want to start the adoption. I know it'll take some time to complete.

The lawyer, Brenda Sexton, scans the court order while I continue telling her that both of Toby's parents are deceased and he has no other near kin.

She takes a note pad and begins to get our vital information. Names, addresses, birthdates of Ginny and me.

"Let me see Toby's birth certificate," she says.

I look at Ginny and then at Toby. "I don't have one," I say.

"Well, we'll need one so that we can change it to reflect your names as his new parents. I know someone in the state vital statistics office. Give me his birth parents' full names and his birthdate and I'll call while you're here."

Toby struggles with what his mother's name was but finally says it was Emily Marie. He knows his birthday is February 28.

Ms. Sexton chats with us while she is on hold with the state office running a computer check for the certificate. In five minutes, she turns her attention back to the phone.

"Is that so? Nothing for either parent or for the child?" She hangs up and looks at us. "They can't find a record of his birth. Do you have a Social Security number?"

Again, Ginny and I look blankly at each other before admitting that we don't.

"Well, maybe the school records will show that," Ms. Sexton says.

"He was home schooled," I say.

"It doesn't matter," she says while dialing another number. "The school office will still have a record. I know somebody there who can cut the red tape too." She talks to someone at the schools' office, waits a few minutes on hold again, and then listens to the word from her friend. "Is that so? No Social Security, no birth certificate. Born on the mountain and attended by a mid-wife according to your records?"

When she is off the phone, she turns back to us.

"This is not insurmountable. We know his birthdate. If you can get an affidavit from two people who knew his parents when he was born and know when he was born, we can file for a birth certificate and then apply for a Social Security number. Can you do that?"

This time I look at the floor and search my memory for two people who might have known Ben and Emily Siler. "I don't know of anybody. They were reclusive. Never came off the mountain except to buy groceries and such."

"We went to snake church every year," Toby says. "There's a man there who has my name in his Bible. I see it every year. It has my name and birthday."

"Snake church?" Ms. Sexton asks.

I smile. "Up near Newport. They sold snakes to the snake handling folk up there. Toby's good at catching rattle snakes. You don't need any do you?"

She wraps her arms around her and shivers at the thought. "No. But you need to make a trip up there. I'll prepare the affidavits for them to sign. We need two people. And get a copy of that entry in the Bible. It'll be corroborating evidence."

"Good. We can drive up there tomorrow or the next day and try to find them."

Ms. Sexton turns back to taking other information for the adoption petition. "Now when were you and Ginny married?"

"What?" I ask.

"I need the marriage date for the petition."

"We're not married. We just want to adopt him together."

She drops her pen, leans back, and heaves a great sigh. "You can't do that. You can adopt him by yourself—either one of you—but you can't adopt him together unless you're married."

"That seems odd," I say.

"It's our anti-homosexual provision," Ms. Sexton says. "The law prevents two people who aren't married from adopting. And in Tennessee two people can't get married if they're of the same gender. That's why the provision is there—although no one will admit it."

I turn to Ginny. "Will you marry me?"

Ginny doesn't say a word but gets up and walks out of the room.

My eyes follow her.

"You want me just to draw it up in your name?" Ms. Sexton asks. "I don't believe Ginny felt you were being very romantic in your proposal."

"No. Draw it up in both our names. William Cody Rogers and Viginia Lynn Rogers. Leave the marriage date blank. Before we sign it, we'll be married, and we'll fill it in then."

Ms. Sexton smiles. "Good luck. I think you have a little work to do. Let me know as soon as you have a date."

GINNY'S SILENCE ON THE drive back to the cabin makes my mood dark too. I try to stay up-beat for Toby's sake on this day of celebration of his birthday. I stop and let him pick out his choice of a new carving knife as a gift. We also buy a half-dozen more baseballs. Ginny wavers from her resolute silence only to help Toby pick out a new jacket.

"I know it wasn't the right place and time to ask you to marry me," I tell Ginny when we're sitting near the stove a little later in the afternoon. "But I did mean it. I want you to marry me. And I want to marry you."

She sips at her tea and peers through the window like she's a thousand miles away. But when she speaks, I know it's not miles but years that is the distance between us.

"Cody, it's the same as it was in 1968 when I discovered I was pregnant. I could have called you and told you. You would have felt a need to marry me. I know you. You do have a sense of responsibility.

"But I didn't want our marriage—if there was to be one—to be one of necessity. I didn't ever want any thought in your mind that you *had* to marry me to give our child a father. Now, here we are a lifetime later, and it's the same. I don't want you . . . or me . . . to ever think that we had to get married for our child's sake. There has to be more than that. And if we start off on that footing, I don't know what will happen if rough times come along."

I don't say anything. Instead I get up and go into Toby's room where he is resting on his bed, rubbing his new knife with an oil cloth.

"Toby, will you be okay if Ginny and I are gone for a while? We should be back before morning. But it'll probably be real late."

"Sure, Dad. You and Mom go anywhere you want. If I could take care of myself when I was ten, I can when I'm eleven."

I GRAB MY COAT and Ginny's. From the bookshelves, I take one of my journals and stuff it in my coat pocket. Back in the living room, I pick Ginny up from her chair and carry her to the Jeep.

"Where're we going?" she asks when I pull out of the driveway and head down the mountain.

"Nashville," I say. "Toby knows we're going to be gone late. He'll be fine. You and I have to work on this. We're going back and start all over."

THE CAPITOL IS CLOSED when we arrive, but Ginny and I walk up the steps anyway. We go to the north side to the steps beside the tomb of architect William Strickland and sit down where once we lay and made love. It's too cold for that today and too many people nearby.

We stare to the north and see the changes from 1968. Where once there were seedy motels and a warehouse district, the state has made a Bicentennial Mall. There are walks, a river history of the state, and an amphitheater.

"It's different," I say.

"It's better," Ginny says.

A young couple walks near us, holding hands and giggling.

"That's the way we were then," Ginny says.

"No, we were better," I say.

AT THE PARTHENON, THERE'S hardly anyone present. It's totally dark now, and the spotlights make the sandstone-colored temple appear like an eerie relic from a thousand years ago. We walk around the east and north sides until Ginny points at a now-leafless tree.

"That was my favorite," she says and takes my hand. She leads me over to its base where we sit down with our backs against the trunk and our eyes facing the Parthenon. "Do you remember all the good times we had here?"

"Yes," I say. I pull the journal of April 1968 from my pocket and read to Ginny. "Two trees tonight . . . three trees . . . one tree . . . two trees."

"What were you talking about?" she asks.

I explain my code, and she laughs. "Now, it would always be only one tree? Right?"

"Well, there might be some two-tree nights left in me."

Ginny puts her arms around me and we kiss. Her nose is cold and the wind is biting at her ears where I put my hands.

"Ginny, I want to marry you because I love you. Do you think our children will understand and accept it?"

"Mine will. And Jerry will. He'd be the happiest one to know that his birth parents are getting married after all these years."

"It's only been six months since Katy died, but I think my children would understand too."

"And will you love me forever?" she asks.

"I do and I will," I say and kiss her again.

I look at my watch. "It's past midnight. It's the first of March—the first day of spring according to Toby. So, in the spring of this year when we're remembering the spring of '68, I want to ask you again, will you marry me?"

"Yes."

25

T oby receives the news with great enthusiasm the next morning when we tell him that we are going to be married.

"I told you that you should marry her the first day she was here, Dad," he says. He hugs Ginny and then me. He likes to use "Dad" and "Mom" whenever he can.

Ginny begins on the cell phone in the living room and then moves out to the Jeep when the battery runs down and plugs it into the cigarette lighter receptacle. She talks first to her daughter and then to her son. I sit beside her at first and eavesdrop. All seems well with the ones receiving the news.

She tells her children first because I'm still searching for the right words for mine. The fear I have is that they will think I have forgotten their mother so soon. It's not that at all. Katy will always be very special to me. Two children, twenty-six years together, and a lifetime of happiness, joy, pain, and suffering. You can't have the good without the bad.

It's time now. Time for me to move on to a new page in my life. Time to have a new wife, other children, and a different measure of joy, pain, and suffering. I don't know what lies ahead, but whatever it is and however long it may be, I want to share it with Ginny. Now, if I can just relate this in so many words to Sallie and Johnny.

When Ginny finishes, she hands the phone to me and holds my hand while I dial up my children. Neither one is home, so I leave a message that I will call them tonight with important news—not bad news—just important. I don't want them to worry.

Then Ginny looks at me and says it's time for us to call the child we have together—Jerry—in Nashville.

I didn't want to meet him first by phone, but I give in. Ginny finds him at his church office. She talks to him and tells him that she has found his birth father. I'm sitting next to her, she says, and I would like to talk to him and tell him some important news.

I take the phone while Ginny leans her head on my shoulder. "It'll be okay," she says.

"Jerry, this is Cody Rogers. I'm sorry I'm meeting you first by phone. I want to see you in person . . . if you want to see me."

"I sure do," he says with an earnestness I can feel through the phone. "When can I see you? I want you to meet my wife and see my son . . . who'd be your birth grandson."

"Well . . .," I say and look at Ginny. We have already talked about this and she has helped me with the words. "Well, I want to invite you up to my cabin near the Big South Fork. We're between Nashville and Knoxville."

"I know it well," he says. "We go up there to hike and ride horses. It's one of the few decent wilderness-type areas left around here. I love the Big South Fork."

I put my hand over the phone and whisper to Ginny, "He's been to this area before. He likes the Big South Fork."

"When can we come up?" he asks.

"Jerry, we have something special planned in less than three weeks on the twenty-first of March—the first full day of spring. We'd like you to be here for it."

"What's that?"

"Ginny and I—your birth mother and father—are going to get married that day. And we'd like for you to perform the ceremony."

I hear a scream on the other end of the connection and Jerry's phone drop to the floor. "I think he approves," I tell Ginny.

"It's about time!" he shouts when he picks his phone

back up. "I'd love to."

"And we'd like your wife and son to be in the wedding party too. We're just going to have family and maybe a couple of friends. Right here behind the cabin—between the cabin and spring house."

I hand the phone back to Ginny who fills Jerry in on more of the details. I'm relieved that so far the family is taking it really well and everyone is enthusiastic about the prospects. Of course, Ginny has been a widow for two years. That's an appropriate time. I will have been a widower just seven months at the time of the wedding.

IN THE EARLY AFTERNOON the three of us get into the Jeep and head out toward Newport with the affidavit forms that our lawyer, Brenda Sexton, has prepared. We still have to have some proof of Toby's birth place and time in order to pursue the adoption. Brenda now knows the marriage date for filling in on the adoption petition.

We will sign it and file it on the afternoon of our marriage, and in six months from then—which coincidentally marks my first anniversary on the mountain—the adoption can be final. When we walk back into court on the twenty-eighth, Ginny and I will be married, no longer "living in sin," and have a filed adoption to show the judge. Toby's future should be safe with us.

Toby's face is glued to the window. He is fascinated with the scenery that has become his annual sojourn to his Mecca. He is on the way to the only holy place that he has known—the snake church. He's our guide. I know how to get to Newport that sits on the flanks of the northern boundaries of the Great Smokies and Cherokee National Forest, but I have no idea where the church is that the Silers went to on their snake-selling ventures.

"Look at that gold ball on that tower," Toby says when we drive near the Sunsphere in Knoxville on our trip east.

"It's not a ball," I say. "It's a building. Built for the 1982 World's Fair. Before you were born."

"Oh."

Within an hour, we exit I-40 at Newport and begin to make some discreet inquiries as to where we might find a snake-handling preacher. Everyone I ask looks at me as though I'm some Yankee tourist in Bermuda shorts with a camera hanging around my neck.

Yet, Toby points and tells us to drive on. Turn here, turn there, over this hill, around this curve until we're out of Newport and heading into hill country. His eyes widen when he sees something he recognizes, and he jabs his finger at the windshield. "It's not much farther," he says after an hour of steadily declining roads—from four-lane, to two-lane, to paved, and then to paved, but narrow and rutted.

"We're getting closer," he says. "Brown is the preacher's name. Pastor Brown. He has a nice wife and a boy who's a few years older than me. They all have scars on their arms. Snake bites. They let the snakes bite them. I've never been bitten," he says and shows us his bare forearms.

Ginny pulls the sleeves of her sweater down more over her wrists and wraps her arms snugly to her sides.

"There it is!" Toby shouts when he sees a concrete block building squatting between two sloping hills to our right. I pull into a drive that takes us a hundred yards off the road until we reach the point where I can read the hand-lettered sign on the front of the church. It doesn't say anything about snakes or the times that the congregation meets.

There are no other houses or buildings in sight. I'm about ready to pull back out when Toby says, "They live here. Around back."

I ease the Jeep slowly toward the rear, staying on the gravel parking area, not wanting to startle anyone who deals with snakes and poison. An old pick-up truck is parked almost touching the rear of the building, and I can see a door. Smoke comes from a flue-pipe that makes a right angle after leaving the roof.

"They're home," Toby says and climbs between Ginny and me to get out. I open the door and let Toby go knock. In a minute the door cracks open, and then spreads wider when the woman sees Toby. She is a heavy middle-aged woman with long hair that falls to her waist in tangled bunches. She wears a loose-fitting dress that nearly touches the ground. It does well in hiding any shape she might have that would prove her female.

She smiles broadly, takes Toby in her arms, and hefts him up and over her head.

"She's strong," Ginny says. "Don't get in a fight with her, Cody. She could knock you down and sit on you."

Toby motions for Ginny and me to come over. As we're getting out, a man—Pastor Brown, perhaps—comes to the doorway.

We're invited in to where the aroma of beans and pork fat simmering hangs heavily in the air. Pastor and Mrs. Brown, though, are very hospitable and offer us food and drink of hill country variety.

Now knowing the rules of the mountains, I partake of a bowl of pinto beans, fatback, sliced onions, and cornbread. Toby digs in too. Ginny acts like she's eating but stirs it around more than anything.

"Where's your father and mother?" Pastor Brown asks Toby.

"They're dead," I butt in. "It's a long story that's better left unsaid at the time," I say and nod toward Toby. "We're adopting Toby, but we need to prove his birth. Toby thought that you might have a record. We brought affidavits for you to sign saying when you first knew him and how?"

"Yeah, we put all the children in my Bible," Mrs. Brown says and reaches behind her to a wooden stand where the big Bible is at the top. "They brought him up here when he was just a week old," she says while flipping the pages. "His mother was so proud of him. I thought he was too young to travel. But his father . . . did you know his father?"

I nod my head.

"Well, his father was kinda peculiar. Didn't seem to care for much. I don't really think he was a true believer. Wanted to sell us the snakes is all." She finds the page with Toby's name and birthdate.

I look and it is the day, month, and year that Toby said it was. While we're talking, I take the affidavits from

my pocket, fill in the names and dates, read them to the
Browns, and have them sign them. I bring out my notary
seal and make an impression on both papers. I go to the
Jeep and retrieve my camera to take a picture of the page in
the Bible for corroborating evidence.

When supper is done, the Browns invite us to a back
room to see their snakes. He has a collection of six and has
names for each.

"Are you a believer, Mr. Rogers?" he asks me. "Mark
16:18, 'They shall take up serpents; and if they drink any
deadly thing, it shall not hurt them.' "

" 'I believe; help thou mine unbelief,' " I respond.
"Mark 9: 24."

Pastor Brown first stares and then nods in approval.
"Very good. Mark Chapter Nine comes before Mark Chapter
Sixteen. You're moving in the right direction."

When we're out to the Jeep and ready to head for the
cabin, Toby takes out his overnight bag, and from within it
withdraws a burlap sack and hands it to Pastor Brown.

"Two gooduns," he says.

The preacher looks in, smiles, and nods in agreement.
"They are. Thank you, Toby. How much do I owe you?"

"Nothing. It's a gift."

Pastor Brown invites us to come back to a service
later in the spring. We say something about how we would
consider it, knowing all along that neither Ginny nor I want
to be near snakes that are being handed from believer to believer.

"You don't have anymore snakes back there, do you,
Toby?" Ginny asks when the Jeep finally reaches the road.

"No. Two's all I could find on short notice. It's still
cold."

THE MONOTONY OF THE broad highway has me
daydreaming about my future married life until my cell
phone rings. It's Sallie.

"No, it wasn't an emergency," I say. "I'm on the road
between Newport and Knoxville. I'll explain later."

Ginny leans over and puts a hand on my knee while

I listen to my daughter.

"Well, what I was calling about was to tell you that . . . that I am . . . am going to get . . . get married." The words come from my mouth like cold syrup from a bottle. I listen for a reaction and hear Sallie yelling the news to her husband.

"It's that woman who called Johnny, isn't it?"

"Yes. Ginny's her name. We were . . . were friends before I ever met your mother."

"That's great, Dad. Johnny and I hoped you would find someone to pull you out of your depression. Where did you find her?"

"She found me, actually. It's a long story which I will tell you a bit later. But there's much more news too. Do you think Johnny will take it as well as you?"

"Oh, yeah. He was hoping she would look you up when she called him. Remember us asking you at Thanksgiving and Christmas if you had had any visitors? We were afraid that she gave up on the idea. We're both excited. When's the wedding?"

LEAVES ON THE TREES are no larger than squirrels' ears when the first day of spring—our wedding day—arrives. The mountains are beginning to reawaken to the sun's warmer rays, but full-fleshed spring is still a month away. Leaf buds look like the fuzzy knobs of young deer antlers. They give the forest a glowing red tint that brightens the gray deadness of winter with the hope of spring.

I look out from the front porch and see all our male children and sons-in-law gathered along the drive. This is going to be a large family—Ginny's son and daughter and their spouses, Sallie and Johnny with their spouses, Toby, and Jerry with his wife and son.

Ginny's still in the bedroom with her daughter, Sallie, and Jerry's wife, putting the final adjustments and touches to the wedding gown, veil, and flowers. I and all the boys and men are dressed in tuxes. Toby grabs the collar from time to time where it rubs against his neck.

There are only two non-family members present—Doc Jordan and a harpist who was hired by Sallie and Ginny's daughter to do the music.

This is going to be a memorable day. I can feel it in my bones. A wedding and the merging of three families. Jerry's boy is three years old. Jerry told him that since he already had a Granddad and a Grandpa, he could call me Gramps Cody. There are never too many grandparents.

When I hear the door to the bedroom open, I turn and see Jerry's wife and Sallie coming out.

"It's time," Sallie says.

"Where's Ginny?" I ask.

"You can't see her until she marches down the steps and down the carpet to where you'll be standing."

"Oh," I say and go out the screen door with them. Jerry and Doc Jordan are standing near Jerry's car talking in sign language. "They're talking about me," I whisper to Sallie.

"Don't be paranoid, Dad," she says and takes my hand. "You get in place with all the groomsmen. All the bride's attendants will be on that side." She points to where the rolled-out red carpet ends near an arch of flowers.

I go stand in my place. Johnny stands next to me, Doc Jordan next, Ginny's daughter's husband, and then Toby. Jacob, my new grandson, stands just behind me bearing the rings. Jerry brings his Bible and positions himself in front of the flowers. The sun's morning rays glisten off his red hair and beard creating a halo effect. His smile is genuine. He is marrying his birth mother and father.

Ginny's daughter joins Sallie and Jerry's wife on the other side of the carpet. We all turn when the harpist plucks the first strains of the wedding march and watch Ginny come down the steps on the arm of her son. She is as radiant and white as mountain dogwood blooms. Her attendants are clothed in the shade of redbud blossoms, giving the wedding the color we wanted—spring in the hills.

THE CEREMONY IS SHORT as weddings go. When the "I do's" are said, I lift Ginny's veil, bend near her, and—

before I kiss her—whisper, "This is just like the spring of '68."

"Better," she whispers back, and we seal it with a kiss.

The children have a luncheon spread on a table on the front porch with the wedding cake nearby. It's simple. We had told them that we didn't want any fuss. We just wanted the whole family here for a good start to our life together.

Johnny and his wife volunteer to take Toby with them to Crossville for the night so that the newlyweds can have our first night alone. It's okay with us. We have an early afternoon appointment with Brenda Sexton to sign the adoption papers, and then we'll return to the cabin for our first night of marriage.

WITHIN A COUPLE OF hours everyone is gone, leaving us with more food and cake than we can possibly eat in a week. We change and drive to Jamestown to do our first legal act as a married couple—the signing of the adoption papers.

"This is great!" Brenda says when we tell her about the wedding. "All your children are happy with the situation?"

"Yes," I say.

"And they know you're adopting Toby?"

"Yes," Ginny says.

"You've done a great job raising them," Brenda says.

We both nod our agreement while looking at the adoption petition.

"Six months is the waiting period, right?" I ask.

"Yes, six more months. You need to continue the counseling with Toby, and they'll do a home study for a report to the court. Everything else should be routine unless Mr. or Mrs. Siler show up."

"They won't," I say. We both sign the papers and head back to the cabin.

PARKED ALONGSIDE THE ROAD at our driveway

are two county sheriff cruisers when we arrive back at the cabin. Deputy Crawford and three others are talking as we approach.

I lean out and ask them, "Are you here to see Toby?"

"No, we need to talk with you," Crawford says.

"Come on down and have some wedding cake," I say and motion them toward the cabin.

Ginny slices them each a piece of cake and we walk into the cabin where the stove's fire makes it warmer.

"You been digging around up at the Silers?" I ask.

Crawford nods and swallows a bite of cake. "Yeah. You remember the judge told me to investigate some more and report back."

"You find anything?" I ask.

"Yes. I'm afraid we did," Crawford says, puts his plate of cake down, and withdraws a card from his pocket. "I've got to read you your rights, Mr. Rogers, before I can ask you any questions."

"My Miranda warnings? You want to talk to Toby, don't you? Not me."

"I'm sorry, Mr. Rogers. It's you I need to ask. You know you have the right to remain silent, the right to have a lawyer, and if you can't afford—"

"Yeah, yeah, yeah," I say. "Let me sign the paper. I know my rights. I don't have anything to hide." Crawford hands me a card, and I sign it.

"We have a search warrant, Mr. Rogers. For a .44 caliber pistol, shells, and a pair of boots. You want to give those to us voluntarily, or do we need to look around for them?"

My hands start to tremble. They're serious. I'm the target of the investigation. I blink and look at Ginny. She is turning paler by the second.

"Well?" Crawford asks and hands me the search warrant.

It's official. Signed by a judge. Identifies the articles they want. "I'll get them," I say and start toward the cabinet where the gun is. I think before I open the door and look back toward the deputies. "You better come here and reach it yourself. I don't want you to think I'm about to shoot you when I pull it out of there."

Crawford takes the pistol by holding it with a pencil through the finger guard where the trigger is. I retrieve the only two pairs of boots I own and set them down at their feet. Crawford picks both pairs up and looks at the soles.

"This is the ones we want," he says and hands the boots to one of the other deputies.

After he takes the box of cartridges from the shelf, we all sit back down. Crawford takes another bite of cake.

"You want to tell us why you did it?" he asks.

"Did what?" I ask.

"Killed Ben Siler."

"I didn't," I say.

"I'm sorry, Mr. Rogers and Mrs. Rogers, to spoil your wedding day, but we have a warrant for your arrest, Mr. Rogers, for the murder of Ben Siler. We have to take you in."

I am so weak that I can't stand. My trembling becomes noticeable. Ginny takes my hand which must feel like an icicle.

"Can't I just drive in myself and make a bond?"

"No," he says. "We have to cuff you on this serious a charge."

The next sound I hear is that of the handcuffs coming from the belt of one of the deputies, and then the muffled cries of Ginny.

They stand me up, cuff my hands behind my back, and frisk me. Then it's out the door and down the steps toward a cruiser. Ginny follows along, dabbing a handkerchief at her eyes.

26

From tux to jail jump-suit orange within twelve hours is hard for me to comprehend. Harder is going from groom to inmate. And even more difficult is the change from the freedom of the mountains to the confinement of this little cell I sit in without the trappings of human dignity that I'm used to having.

They took my shoes, keys, money, and all personal items when they checked me into the Fentress County Jail. I was issued the orange clothing, a change of underwear, and a pair of flip-flop type sandals. They thought they stripped me of who I was and made me into a jailbird.

But I know who I am. I am William Cody Rogers. That is not just my name. It's who I am. My heritage is of the valley. They will try me as though I'm a mountain man.

After I lunch on a bologna sandwich, hash brown potatoes, applesauce, and a cookie, two deputies come to take me to court for the bond hearing. They act like I'm dangerous and a threat to escape. Leg manacles and handcuffs are mandatory. I shuffle along in short steps searching for Ginny. I know she won't desert me.

Just as I arrive at the courthouse, Ginny pulls up in the Jeep as though she's driven it all her life. She comes and walks behind me.

"Where've you been?" I turn and ask.

"I've got your bail money."

"How much?"

"Enough."

The deputies push me on into the courthouse and to the courtroom where five other men and a woman line the front bench, all dressed in the same type orange suits. They remove the handcuffs but leave the leg shackles.

The others are there to receive their sentences on misdemeanors and drunken driving charges. I'm the only one charged with a felony. They all eye me when word spreads that I killed Ben Siler. One leans over and whispers, "Way to go, dude. He was one bad character. You should get a medal."

I nod. That's not what they have in mind, I'm sure.

When they get to my case, I stand and walk to the front of the judge's bench. He's the same one who heard our custody petition.

"Mr. Rogers, do you have an attorney?"

"Not yet, Your Honor."

"Do you want to wait until you do?"

"Not for the bond hearing, Your Honor. I want to get one set and get out of jail as soon as I can."

"Okay. Have a seat." He looks at Stan Goddard, the assistant D. A., who's handling the case. "What do you say, General?"

"Your Honor, this is a first degree murder case. We have strong evidence on this one. Pre-meditated, accompanied by destruction of evidence and a coverup. This could be a death penalty case. We ask that there be no bond. But if you do set one, it should be a minimum of a half million. Mr. Rogers is a lawyer of considerable wealth and nothing less would be a deterrent to him leaving the jurisdiction."

The judge reviews the charge and other papers that have been provided him by the prosecutor.

"You always say you have a strong case, General Goddard. I see here that the defendant has no prior arrests or convictions. Is that right?"

"Yes," General Goddard answers.

"And where did you arrest him?"

"At his cabin."

"And is that next door to where the victim lived?"

"Yes."

"He didn't flee during a whole month and a half? What makes you think he would run now?"

"Because we've caught up with him. His game of blaming the murder on a child has come undone."

"Well, let's not get into evidence or your theory of the case. I just don't think Mr. Rogers is a threat to flee or a threat to any citizen in the community. I'm going to set his bond at ten thousand dollars. Anything further?"

"But, Your Honor, this is a first degree murder case. That's the lowest bond I've ever heard of," General Goddard says.

"No, it's not. Make it five thousand dollars," the judge says, bangs his gavel, and walks off the bench.

Ginny comes up behind where I'm sitting, opens a bag, and begins peeling off hundred dollar bills. "Where do we give them the money?" she asks.

"The clerk's office next door," I say. "Where did you get that?"

"I've driven to Lexington and back while you've been taking it easy in jail," she says. "I brought a hundred thousand just in case."

A DAY LATER, ALL our children know that I've been charged with murder. They know I didn't do it and rally around me in a family circle of support. I'm just thankful that none of them saw me in jail. What a humiliating condition—a common criminal locked up in jail where roaches fight over bread crumbs.

"We have to get you a lawyer," Ginny says after all the children, except Toby, are on their way home again. "Your preliminary hearing is next week"

"The day before our next custody hearing with Toby," I say and sit down hard on the chair near the stove.

"Do you think they will take Toby away?" she asks.

"If I'm accused of the murder of his father, I'd say the chances are pretty good. I'm surprised they haven't asked for an earlier hearing on the custody."

"Who do you think for your lawyer?"

"I'm a lawyer. I don't need another one. I know what I did and what I didn't do."

"Yeah, and look where it's gotten you."

Ginny insists. After making a call to a lawyer friend, I ask Ginny to go to Knoxville with Toby to make a retainer fee payment of fifteen thousand dollars. I'm glad the lawyer is a friend. I don't know what he would charge otherwise.

"I've got to make one more trip to the mountain," I say before she pulls out of the driveway. "I'll be back in the morning. God has to tell me why this is happening. I'm going to insist."

"Cody, wait until I get back. I'll go with you."

"No, I have to talk to Him alone. It's the third time. He'll tell me something this time. I'm sure. Toby knows where it is in case I'm not back by mid-morning."

BY THE TIME THE sun is down, I'm high on the rocky bluff looking over the edge again at the Big South Fork flowing with a bit more force after an early spring rain. I fell twice crossing this time. But I had my clothes in a plastic bag and was able to walk off the chill on the way up.

I lie back and think of all that's happened to me since last August. I still carry my copy of *Walden* along with a tattered New Testament and Psalms. Since Toby shot his father, I seem not to have had time to read either very much. Things have changed so precipitously. When I thought the bad was wiped out and I was on my way to happiness, I was hit with a sledge hammer in the stomach.

Until the light fades to where my eyes will not focus, I read the psalms of David, the Sermon on the Mount, and the chapter in *Walden* on higher laws. Then I lay the books aside and pray silently for Ginny, Toby, and all of our new family. I want to be with them if I can. I ask God to make that possible.

Then I talk out loud to Him in the stillness of the deep darkness and ask Him to answer. Again, all I hear in reply is a faint echo of my words off the canyon walls below. I sleep.

When morning comes and I see the edge of the sun rising over the eastern ridge, I begin to talk to God again. I'm desperate now, and my soft pleading gives way to shouts. "Why, why is this happening to me? I've tried to do Your will! Why are You doing this to me?" I turn over and bang my head against the log until tears flow.

Then there's a voice. Very faint at first. I keep my eyes closed and listen. I recognize the words. It's from one of the Psalms. The words are repeated three times and become clearer and louder with each repetition.

"Be still, and know that I am God—*Be still and know that I am God*—**Be still and know that I am God: I will be exalted among the heathen, I will be exalted in the Earth.** The Lord of hosts is with us; the God of Jacob is our refuge." The last syllables come to me as soft as a whisper from the tongue of an angel.

I finally turn when the voice hovers over me, expecting to be blinded by the presence of the Lord.

Instead, standing side by side are Ginny and Toby. "It's time to go home," Ginny whispers in the same voice.

ON THE DAY OF the preliminary hearing, my mind wanders back to Ginny's voice on the mountain. She wasn't telling me that she was God. She wanted me to know that God *was* in charge, and He would do things in His own time and His own way. "Accept it and go on," she told me on our walk home. Toby volunteered to get on the stand and admit that he shot his father as he had told the judge earlier from his chair. No, I will not let him do it.

My lawyer recommends that I not testify. He says it rarely works out, especially at the preliminary hearing. They will have enough to bind it over to the grand jury and take me to a full jury trial. "Don't let them know your side of the story at this early stage," he counsels.

The first witness is the woman from the child protective services who recounts my complaint to her about Ben Siler.

"Did Mr. Rogers appear angry?" the assistant attorney general asks her.

"Yes. Very angry with Ben Siler."

Next, they put on the hardware store clerk where I bought the high-powered rifle.

"And after Mr. Rogers purchased the rifle, did he

purchase a deer hunting license?"

"No, just the rifle and bullets."

"Did you ever see him again?"

"Yes."

"And what was the occasion?"

"He came in with an antique .44 caliber revolver and bought some bullets for it."

"Did you see the pistol?"

"Yes."

"Do you recognize this?" General Goddard asks and pulls the Navy Colt from an evidence bag. He hands it to the clerk to examine.

"Yes, I'd say that's it, or one just like it."

"Do you remember the make of ammunition that he bought?"

"Yes, I even loaded some into the gun to show him that it fit."

Goddard goes on to ask the clerk to identify the remaining shells that they seized at the cabin.

Then, a man dressed in jeans and a plaid shirt takes the stand. I don't recognize him or his name.

"And what do you do for a living, Mr. Duncan?" Goddard asks.

"I'm a truck driver. Mainly drive log trucks up near the Big South Fork where they're cutting timber."

"And were you so engaged on February Sixth of this year?"

"No, I'm not engaged. Divorced. Never will marry again," he says and draws laughter from everyone in the courtroom except from Goddard and me.

"No, I mean were you working as a truck driver on February Sixth?"

"Oh, yes, I was."

"Did you see anything strange that day?"

"Yes. I was pulling up that little mountain road off of St. Helen's when I saw that man—" he says and points to me. "He was near a little driveway that leads off to my left. He pointed a big pistol at me. He looked real crazed and—"

"Objection, Your Honor," my lawyer says, "I hardly

feel that a truck driver is capable of giving a psychiatric opinion."

"Sustained," the judge says. "Just keep to what you saw, heard, or observed with your senses, Mr. Duncan."

"Anyway, I just ducked and floorboarded my truck on down the road. When I came back about an hour later, I looked down that driveway. I was going real slow to be sure he wasn't there and gonna shoot me. You know how some of them environmentalists are."

"Objection," my lawyer says again.

"Sustained. Just keep to the facts, Mr. Duncan," the judge admonishes.

"Did you see Mr. Rogers?"

"No."

"Did you see anything?"

"Saw some smoke over the little ridge. But I was too far away to see any fire. I just drove on. It was cloudy. I told my boss, and he reported it to the ranger station."

Motive, weapon, opportunity, and presence. Goddard is tying up a neat little package of circumstantial evidence to convince the judge that I should stand trial for Ben Siler's death. He's almost convinced me that I shot Ben Siler.

"I'm Vance Moody of the Tennessee Bureau of Investigation," the next witness says.

He opens a briefcase and withdraws a large slab which is covered with black plastic. When he unwraps it, I see what appears to be a brown cast of some kind.

"Is that an impression that you made near the remains of the house of Ben Siler?" Goddard asks.

"No. This is the actual ground that was baked by the fire near where the truck and tractor burned," Moody says and turns it over to where the judge and I can see the impression of a boot sole.

Goddard hands Moody one of my boots from another bag and Moody places it onto the brick-hard clay. It fits exactly.

"Did you find anything else at the scene?"

"Yes. We found three bullets from a .44 caliber weapon. Two were near what we identified as human remains, and one was near goat remains."

"Some distance apart?"

"About ten feet."

"Did you only find remains of one body?"

"No. Two. About fifty yards from the house fire, we dug up burned remains of another body—we believe human. Tests are being conducted now. There were teeth and bone fragments enough to use for DNA testing."

When Deputy Crawford takes the stand, I feel like I may have an ally. He ate wedding cake with Ginny and me. I think he believes I'm innocent.

"Where did you get this pistol?" Goddard asks and once again holds up the .44 revolver.

"From the cabinet of Mr. Rogers."

"And this boot?"

"Mr. Rogers had it in his closet."

"How many bullets were in the pistol when you received it?"

"Three had been fired and there were three live cartridges."

"Now, Deputy Crawford, have you ever been with Mr. Rogers when he's been near Ben Siler?"

Crawford tugs at his collar and his head jerks while he's thinking. "Yes, about the middle of November, a bunch of us deputies went to Ben Siler's house because Mr. Rogers had made a complaint that he had seen marijuana growing there. He went with us. And you did too."

"Did you find any marijuana?"

"No."

"Did you ask Ben Siler and his boy about where Mrs. Siler was?"

"Yes."

"What did they say?"

"Objection, Your Honor. That's hearsay. Mr. Siler is not here."

"Because your client killed him," Goddard says.

"Hold it. That's enough of that. Objection sustained," the judge says.

"On that day, did Mr. Rogers act like there might be

violence between him and Mr. Siler in the future? Did he say anything?"

Crawford scratches, tugs at his collar, and jerks his head before answering. "Well, I do remember him saying something like, 'If'n I die under mysterious circumstances, you better know it's murder.'"

Goddard looks at me and then back at the deputy. "He didn't die, though, did he?"

"No."

"Was that day the last time you saw Ben Siler alive?"

"Yes."

"Did he die under mysterious circumstances?"

"Yes."

AFTER A HALF HOUR break, I insist to my lawyer that I'm going to take the stand and tell the truth. I destroyed evidence, but I didn't kill Ben Siler.

But when I start to walk up to be sworn in, the judge holds up his hand.

"Wait a minute, Mr. Rogers, I believe your lawyer has a motion."

I look back to my high-paid lawyer who is just getting to his feet with a blank look on his face.

"You have a motion to dismiss, don't you?" the judge asks.

"Well, yes, I move to dismiss for lack of evidence because . . ."

"There's no proof that Ben Siler is dead," the judge finishes my lawyer's sentence and begins to write on the warrant. "You never identified the bone fragments or the teeth as being those of Ben Siler, Mr. Goddard. You don't have to have a body, but when you do have body parts we need your best efforts to know who they belong to. There's no statute of limitations on murder. You can still take this to the grand jury when you identify the remains as those of Ben Siler, but until you do, I see no need of holding Mr. Rogers. Case dismissed."

27

I left the woods for as good a reason as I went there. Perhaps it seemed to me that I had several more lives to live, and could not spare any more time for that one."—Walden.

In and around the valley country of Lexington, Kentucky, the leaves are once again turning their gold and red of autumn. The grass still glistens in the early morning dew, and the horses snort and frolic on Ginny's farm.

We left the cabin six weeks ago on the day that Toby's adoption was final. It marked one year for me on the mountain. Just half as long as Thoreau spent at Walden Pond. But it was enough. The experiences of that year I will carry as a gift and as a burden for the rest of my life.

There is no statute of limitations on murder—or cancer. Ginny and I travel under the darkness of similar clouds. But we look beyond to the sunlight and live for each day. Neither of us knows when a deputy will come for me and say they have identified the remains of Ben Siler or when a doctor might say that he has identified another location of cancer in her.

During the six months we stayed at the cabin after the preliminary hearing, I was not indicted. Ginny has had two years of no recurrence. The more time we both put behind us without bad news, the better we feel. They came with a court order and took blood samples of Toby for DNA comparisons with the remains they found at and near his house. So far, there's been no word.

Ginny is a woman of immeasurable wealth—of spirit and optimism. I don't know how much money she has. We have never talked about it. I was amazed when she brought the hundred thousand dollars to my bond hearing. I work now at the farm and write for her horse magazine. I like it because I'm near Ginny and Toby.

Toby has increased his barnyard menagerie. He brought his goats and chickens from the mountain to the horse farm. Now he's also one of the best horseback riders around.

When they tested him for school placement, he only scored at the fifth grade level. Ginny and I were satisfied that he had made such progress in so short a time. The school authorities allowed us to enroll him in the sixth grade with the assurance that we would give him extra attention so that he would pass. On the athletic field, he amazes his young friends with what he can do with a baseball. He's still in counseling because much of this world is new to him and much of the old still clutches at him. His adjustment has been remarkable.

When Katy died, I thought I knew who I was and how the world was supposed to work. I went to the mountain to get answers to my questions. Instead, I received questions for which I had to work out my own answers. The year changed me more than any other. I have a larger family and a new understanding of mountain and valley people. All have their own values. The judge who dismissed the case could just as easily have sent it to a jury trial.

The soldier's pistol lies gathering dust in the sheriff's evidence vault. It freed the soldier of his captivity and Toby of his shackles of abuse. Perhaps it will be used in another hundred years when it's needed again.

When we left the cabin, we removed the satellite television, the electric generator and spotlights, the propane water heater, and disconnected the water outside. I took my law books and *National Geographic* collection. And my prized possessions—the journals of the spring of 1968 rest safely in my study here.

The cabin is now back to it's rustic appearance that my father and grandfather would recognize. We will go back. I don't know how often. I deeded forty-five acres to the Big South Fork and only kept the five acres of land and timber around the cabin. It is willed to Toby. Of all our children, he is the one who will appreciate it the most if he can go there without being tortured by the remembrance of his father. He'll have to be the judge of that after I'm gone.

My other wealth I had already given to my two children by Katy. Jerry said he received the greatest gift of all. He knows that he was conceived by two people who loved each other in the spring of '68. Now he knows they also love him. He's a good man of the cloth.

A letter from my lawyer is in my pocket. When I open and read it, my hand begins to tremble. He has received a letter from Assistant Attorney General Goddard. They have linked, through DNA testing, Toby and the remains found where we thought his mother was buried. However, the results from the other remains show that they do not belong to Toby's father.

I lay the letter aside. I'm sure in my own mind that it was Ben Siler's body that I scraped into the fire. It explains though—but doesn't justify—some of Ben Siler's actions toward Toby and his mother. He wasn't Toby's father.

Ginny comes and sits beside me on the bench near the fence where the horses are on the other side.

"Good news?" she asks.

"It looks like I'm not going to be indicted. They can't identify it as Ben's body."

"Good. You didn't kill him. You shouldn't have to stand trial. Besides, you're under another sentence."

"What's that?"

"You have to spend the rest of your life with your love of spring and now fall."

"And winter too, I hope."

"I am your love for as long as we both shall live," she says and kisses me.

I take the ragged copy of *Walden* from my pocket, open it, and read aloud to Ginny.

"I did not wish to take a cabin passage, but rather to go before the mast and on the deck of the world, for there I could see the moonlight amid the mountains."

About the author

Chris Cawood is a native Tennessean, graduate of the University of Tennessee College of Law, and former member of the State Legislature. He is a board member of the Tennessee Mountain Writers and attends their annual April conference in Oak Ridge, Tennessee, where he sometimes helps with teaching the basics of fiction writing.

When he is not writing, Chris practices law in Kingston, Tennessee, and explores the Tennessee, Ohio, and Mississippi Rivers by pontoon boat with his best friend Jerry Seale.

Order other books by Chris Cawood

For autographed copies of any of the following books, send $12 (includes postage) to Magnolia Hill Press, P. O. Box 124, Kingston, Tn. 37763.

The Spring of '68, 216 pages hardback.

Carp, 310 pages softcover, an adventure-mystery set in Tennessee, Louisiana, and Kentucky.

1998: The Year of the Beast, 310 pages softcover, a political thriller set in Louisiana, Washington D. C., and Kentucky.

Tennessee's Coal Creek War, 264 pages softcover, an historical novel of the 1890s in East Tennessee.

Phone Orders: 1-800-946-1967
Visa or Mastercard

You can read the first twenty pages of any book by visiting the publisher's homepage at:
HTTP://user.icx.net/~booktalk

Name:_____

ADDRESS:_____

_____

Books wanted:_____

At $12 each for a total of:_____

Autographed to:_____

Visa☐ or MC☐ Number:_____ Exp:__

Mail to: MHP, P.O. Box 124, Kingston, Tn. 37763